READERS PRAISE

THE ANTAGONIST

"*The Antagonist* has you on edge the second you open to the first page... Dinova skillfully builds suspense and tension, one layer at a time. And as a reader you feel the weight of every layer... You feel the unease of the secret you cannot name coupled with the terror of being watched... *The Antagonist* is a compelling psychological thriller that provides a stark exploration of trauma, including the depths of loss and injustice."

— *Danielle*

"Emily Dinova did it again! This book had me on the edge of my seat... The unpredictable twists and turns had me questioning everything I know, and I loved it! No character alliance is safe and the antagonist could be anywhere!... Can't recommend this book more!"

— *Lorely*

"...mid-way through, the readers are given a gut-punch in a twist narrative shift where the story is told from another perspective and in reverse... While some pages may be a difficult read, the author tackles hard subject matter with careful grace and tact... it leaves one asking, how well do we really know any of the people around us?"

— *Taryn*

"I could not put it down…It was truly brilliant! Trust me, you will want to rea d this novel several times and explore what is truly known about ourselves and others."

— *Debbie*

"…a thrilling and emotionally charged novel that brings to life a complex web of characters and relationsips. It explores themes of conflict, resilience, and self-discovery with subtleness and sensitivity… Dinova's ability to blend emotional depth with a compelling story makes *The Antagonist* a standout read that will resonate with anyone who appreciates rich, character-driven fiction."

— *Tracey*

"…a well-written, slow burn-type psychological thriller. This novel took me through a rollercoaster of emotions as the words sucked me into the pages, and shocked me in many ways as more and more was revealed… an intense read, but a good one…"

— *Rebecca*

"If the road to hell is paved with good intentions, how do you find your way back home?"

— *Alex*

THE ANTAGONIST

Copyright ©2024 Emily Dinova. All rights reserved.

No part of this book may be reproduced in any manner whatsoever without written permission except in the case of brief quotations embodied in critical articles and reviews. For information, contact: henrygraypub2022@gmail.com

Publisher's Cataloging-in-Publication Data:

Names: Dinova, Emily, 1989—
Title: The antagonist / Emily Dinova.
Description: Granada Hills, CA : Henry Gray Publishing, 2024.
Identifiers: LCCN 2024903284 | ISBN 9781960415158 (hardback) | ISBN 9781960415141 (pbk.) | ISBN 97860415165 (ebook)
Subjects: LCSH: Family secrets — Fiction. | Man-woman relationships —Fiction. | Marriage —Fiction. | Sex crimes — Fiction. | Revenge — Fiction. | BISAC: FICTION / Thrillers / Psychological. FICTION / Crime. FICTION / Family Life / Marriage & Divorce.
Classification: LCC PS3604.156 2024 | DDC 813 D56—dc23
LC record available at https://lccn.loc.gov/2024903284

Library of Congress Control Number: 2024903284

Cover Design by Patrick Aievoli, © 2024 Patrick Aievoli. All Rights Reserved.

Made in the United States of America.

Published by Henry Gray Publishing, P.O. Box 33832, Granada Hills, California 91394.

All names, characters, places, events, locales, and incidents in this work are fictitious creations from the author's imagination or used in a fictitious manner. No character in this book is a reflection of a particular person, event, or place. The opinions expressed are those of the characters and should not be confused with the author's.

For more information or to join our mailing list, visit HenryGrayPublishing.com

THE ANTAGONIST

Emily Dinova

Granada Hills, CA
"Select books for selective readers"

Prologue

Late Autumn 2017

THE ANTAGONIST

The fresh and radiant glow of dawn descended on Parrish Street and Dave Collins knew in that moment, the one between blue hour and brilliance, that it was the most beautiful sight he could and would ever recall seeing. For that day was the start of something uncontrollable, unstoppable—a thread had been pulled, the tug of a string was unraveling and derailing his carefully planned life—it was only a matter of time before he was condemned by all those he once thought to trust.

And for what, what had he done to deal himself this hand?

This was the alarming thought that sounded in Dave's mind as he walked along the silent street that morning, knowing deep in his guts that today would be the end. He braced himself as he was met with the spectacular blaze of fury that gleamed with hope and light…he was plagued with the terrifying notion that this might be his last sunrise.

Dave Collins was wrong.

He would live to see many more sunrises.

And every morning from this morning on, he would beg for death.

Part I

Black Olives and Paralegal Pleas

Early Autumn 2017

THE ANTAGONIST

I

The morning routine was the same as it had been for the last five years. Unaltered, blissful—just as Dave knew it would be. He awoke early as he always did and went about preparing a scrumptious breakfast. Dave truly believed that it was the most important meal of the day, the fuel the body would need to consume to keep up with the energy of everyday life.

Regardless of that life being the same every day, there was no denying it was a strenuous one. Filled with chaos and noise and even a little bit of madness. But that was completely acceptable to Dave, being the average—and one could argue slightly boring—person he was. This was perhaps why Dave chose to surround himself with those who existed and thrived in temperamental, unpredictable states.

This morning's meal would be French toast with raspberries, one of Georgette's favorites—his beautiful and currently slumbering wife. Unlike himself, Georgie was perfectly happy with sleeping her mornings away. She was unbothered and unconcerned with things as trivial as sunrises. She told him a million times she preferred sunsets anyway. Having been the daughter of an oil billionaire her entire life, Georgie was not actually concerned with much. She lived the life of an artist without any of the talents to accompany it, though she was kind and caring and spent most of her time and money doing for others. But the one thing she absolutely demanded was sleep. And a Bloody Mary. As soon as Dave finished with his breakfast preparations, he would concoct Georgie's preferred wake up call with Gorgonzola stuffed olives and an extra shot of vodka. He had no idea how she stomached the stuff first thing in the morning, but like Dave, Georgette Collins also believed in breakfast, it just happened to be a liquid one.

The TV clicked on in the living room and Dave was alerted to the other, and much less enjoyable presence that lived in their 'small 'mansion. Samantha, or Sam, as she demanded Dave call her, was as sixteen and angst-filled as they came. She usually only had time to snarl in Dave's direction—especially if he attempted to engage her in conversation before she had her coffee. Always black with too much sugar. But Dave made sure it was prepared long before she descended from the third floor.

To be fair, they had come a long way in terms of a relationship since he married her mother five years earlier. Dave was hoping Samantha would continue to soften towards him as time wore on—he made sure never to tell her what to do, or come between her and Georgie. He did not try to replace her father who had been described to him as a vile maniac, but did offer to step in if she needed help. She'd gone from telling him she hated him every night to now mumbling "yeah later," before stomping off to bed.

Dave's patience was boundless, all he had to do was put himself in her shoes and imagine how crap life had been before her mother had fled and saved them both from the abuse. He couldn't assume that just because Georgette was happy now that Sam was too. So he was careful not to cause any further dissonance. Both of these women were hurt, and they were healing. He would do anything for them, as Dave took family matters quite seriously.

"...Beauty in death, they say there's something romantic about putting someone in the ground..."

Dave was barely listening to whatever morbid program Samantha had stuck on as he made his way across the freshly polished marble floors, keeping time with the schedule. Up the stairs, to the left, down the corridor and through the third door on the right, a silver tray with Georgie's cigarettes and morning Bloody balanced precariously on his steady palm.

Dave flung the shades wide, giving him the spectacular view over their immense backyard that ended a few hundred feet away at the edge of a dense forest. The high ceilings of their chamber were illuminated with sun as Georgie groaned in protest and rolled onto her stomach, head buried under the pillow even while wearing an eye mask. She always complained she could still see through the damn thing.

"Good Morning, my love," Dave cooed as he went about picking up after her.

His wife had the horrible habit of always stripping bare and falling into bed, leaving her clothes and accessories in a trail across the floors.

"Already?" she whined. "Oh please, honey, another hour at least, I didn't get to bed until almost 4."

Dave smiled as he listened to the soft honey twang of her voice. Originally from Oklahoma, her accent was still the least bit detectable, though she left home at eighteen and had spent the last thirty-eight years gallivanting around the globe.

"What were you doing up so late?" he asked with amusement, "I didn't even hear you come to bed."

She huffed and propped herself up against the pillows, slowly peeling back her eye mask to reveal a grumpy green glare.

"I was working on the charity gala if you must know. I have meetings all week at the shelter and I'm still trying to make sure Margo doesn't get sent back to that piece of shit husband of hers, he's been sniffing around the home for the last few weeks."

Dave frowned in thought. "Worst case scenario, she could always stay here for sometime."

Georgette gave him a brilliant smile as she leaned over and snatched the cocktail he'd left on the bedside table. She took a long, slow sip, clearly savoring.

"And that's precisely why I married you."

THE ANTAGONIST

Dave raised an eyebrow. "My bartending skills? Or offering our home to abused women?"

"Mm. I'll let you decide." She reached her arms out for Dave, who was more than willing to comply and allow his lips to fall against her own.

Although Georgie was 16 years older she looked just as good, if not better than Dave. Both worked out regularly, allowing them to maintain their physiques.

It was still unbelievable to him, even five years later, the circumstances that had brought them together.

Their story was one for the books.

Dave rubbed Georgie's feet as she lit her first cigarette—she blew back the smoke and Dave marveled at the way the wisps took form. His wife breathed a deep sigh before looking down at him with absolute adoration.

Dave glowed back, enjoying the praise and love she bestowed on him—his devotion to her so achingly endless.

"Is Sam up yet?" Georgie asked as she tousled her short blonde hair. The light bouncing off her curls reminded Dave of an ethereal creature.

"Yes, in the kitchen, having her coffee just the way she likes it: in peace."

Georgie's lips lifted into her trademark smirk, "So considerate of you, as always."

"I don't like to stir the pot. I'm happy to stay out of her way if it makes her feel more comfortable."

"Is she being a little bitch to you?" Georgie glowered as she started to rise from the bed. "We'll have a chat about it right now."

Dave hid his smile at her eagerness to come to his defense. He playfully moved in front of her, blocking her with a warm embrace.

"Honey, it's fine. I'm not here to pressure her. Or force her to like me. She tolerates me and that's perfectly okay. I have no right to ask her for more."

Georgette's features softened as she reached out to stroke his freshly shaven cheek—a look of awe crested her eyes.

"How did I get so lucky?"

"I'm the lucky one."

And Dave meant that. He was very fortunate and very lucky, not just because his wife's outrageous wealth allowed them to live a very comfortable life, but because he genuinely loved this woman, and even Samantha, for all her faults, he knew deep down was a good person.

He could have lounged in Georgie's presence for the rest of the day but there was work to be done. With a last kiss and the promise of a delicious meal that evening, Dave took himself back downstairs to prepare for the inevitable confrontation.

2

Dave entered the kitchen to find Samantha, as he knew he would, perched on the top of the counter, her eyes buried in her phone as she sipped from the steaming and cracked mug that read: *Goest and Fucketh Thy Self.*

"Coffee's not bad, you finally got the sugar right."

"Good morning Sam, would you like a little breakfast?" Dave asked with a calm and neutral tone. Any sort of emotion he showed to Samantha, she was most likely to exploit it, or explode. He preferred to avoid this all together.

Dave was an excellent listener, a great studier of humans. He made sure to always observe before attempting to establish the correct way to deal with, how could he put it nicely, strong personalities. They surrounded him.

"Nah, I have to get going."

Dave looked up in surprise. Samantha was a wonderful student but she absolutely hated school. Usually he would be out in the car for twenty minutes while she and Georgette screamed bloody murder at one another. They fought about boys, or clothes or periods or existential dread—these confrontations were always filled with tears and raging hormones. And like a sudden and violent storm, it was over as quickly as it began. They would hug and kiss goodbye, laughing and joking their tears away, everything completely fine as Georgie waved her daughter off.

With a sullen glare, Samantha would drop into his passenger seat and roll her eyes out of habit all while blasting screaming metal music on her headphones. Dave loved rock music; it didn't bother him in the slightest, which at one time had been Samantha's goal. No, the only thing that disappointed Dave was that he wasn't able to talk to her, get to know her better. He never really planned on having kids, but he was more than happy to fill the role of stepfather in any way he could. He knew it meant a lot to his wife and Samantha was bright, filled with potential. If Dave could contribute to making sure she stayed on the right path, he was more than up for the job.

He would drop her off at the curb, like he did every morning—tell her to have a great day. Then she would half wave and disappear into the throngs of moody teenagers.

It was their morning routine. But now it seemed she was changing it up.

"Great, let me just grab my jacket," Dave said, as he crossed the kitchen with haste.

She jumped down off the counter, snatching up her backpack and one of Georgie's spare cigarettes. Dave frowned but didn't comment as they headed out the door.

"You have a test or something?" He asked casually, as he held open the car door for her. She yanked it shut in response.

3

It amazed Dave that he could absorb so many emotions, reactions and spontaneous behavior all before 9 a.m.

His office was no different. Schworst & Stone was the only law firm in the small town of Repo Ridge, a quaint and quite removed settlement named after some puritanical pastor who laid claim to the valley and set down roots in the mid-seventeenth century. Dave was sad that although the town had grown since then, the small-mindedness of some of its citizens had not. Repo was a place much like any other, with its progressive youth, devout churchgoers, a façade of happy couples, small business owners, a few bars and so on. It had its poor, its wealthy and everything in-between.

Dave didn't dislike his job, but he didn't feel any sort of passion for it either. It was just that, a job—a job that many laughed at when Dave informed them of his position. Some assumed that it was a joke, especially those who knew about the tremendous wealth of his wife. But Dave couldn't care less. He really didn't bother himself with the opinions of outsiders. His job was his own and his family accepted his decision. Georgie understood more than anyone, she knew what it felt like to have so much money you didn't have to work. She knew how boring it could be and if Dave found it necessary to keep the job he had long before she waltzed into his life that was completely understandable, even admirable.

Dave took his duties as secretary very seriously. Being the organized person he was, he enjoyed structure and regularly occurring tasks. He also possessed excellent communication skills that made him an enjoyable asset to the office. People liked to chat with him, be around him and found him extremely helpful. He always went above and beyond for the lawyers and their clients, creating and maintaining a peaceful environment while putting out fires when necessary. The only person who seemed to despise Dave for existing was one of the partners, Schworst, or as Dave privately referred to him. "The Worst."

It was exhausting yet not surprising to Dave that the alpha male of the firm would target him. Where Dave exuded calmness and a trusting manner, Kyle Schworst was the antithesis of this—he excelled at causing severe anxiety in anyone within ten feet of his temper. When he wasn't screaming about something not going his way, he would parade around the office, looking down his nose at everyone—a pompous jackass with the arrogance and immaturity of a fourteen-year-old king.

And today, like every morning Dave walked in the door, Schworst had something to say,

"Hey Davey, nice sweater. I need those subpoenas by noon. Think you can handle that in-between answering the phone? I know you like to have your 'girlie-girl time' with the ladies first."

Dave always smiled blandly in response, not giving rise to this childish behavior. Kyle's jealousy was always showing. None of the women in the firm wanted to go near him. The thing they all found the least repulsive about him was his huge gut and sweaty red face. But they would stop by Dave's desk and make small talk and that was enough for Schworst to seethe with envy. It was ridiculous. So instead he tried to insinuate that maybe Dave wasn't into women, even speculate on the reasons for his marriage. This couldn't be more opposite than how Dave actually felt. He loved women. He admired them. He enjoyed their company and their conversation over that of his own sex and for obvious reasons. Dave was a sensitive soul; having quite a few exceptional women in his life made him very grateful for their care. But the women at the office were friends, colleagues. It baffled Dave that Schworst couldn't understand that if he just treated them with respect and kindness they would respond with the same. The lack of self-awareness that some functioning adults exuded was unreal to him.

Besides, everyone knew he was married and very much in love. Everyone except the new paralegal who started two weeks ago—her name was Desiree and she was extremely attractive. She'd been hired by the other partner, Stone, who was getting up there in age and frequenting the offices less and less—in turn giving Schworst additional power.

Desiree was not only a 'damn fine piece of ass,' as Schworst described her, she was also highly intelligent and a ruthless opportunist. Dave watched her interactions, keeping his distance and dreading the moment she would turn her gaze on him, someone in a subservient position to her own. Dave worked in a law firm for 15 years—he knew a predator when he saw one. The one thing he did enjoy about Desiree was her absolute refusal to be bullied or hit on by any and all of the men that threw themselves at her, especially Schworst, who she flat out humiliated in front of his clients three days earlier. Dave secretly enjoyed it, why not? Desiree apparently had Stone to protect her—Dave wondered what the story was there. But he didn't ask, he didn't talk about her at all and continued to keep his distance.

The days usually passed quickly for Dave as he kept himself immersed in his environment. But the moment five o'clock hit, he was packed up and stepping out the door. Sometimes, if Schworst was feeling particularly vindictive, he would call Dave back in for some menial task just to satisfactorily gulp up more power. Dave would complete whatever job was demanded of him without complaint, for all he had to do was consider how sad it must be—to be as lonely and insecure as Kyle Schworst.

THE ANTAGONIST

4

It took Dave fifteen minutes to reach the next stop on his daily journey: The Devil's Eye. It sounded a lot more sinister than it was, though from the outside the place definitely looked the part. It was the only dive bar in town—a place quiet enough for Dave to have an hour of solitude before heading back into the chaos.

A couple of atheists owned the establishment, Shawn and his girlfriend Mara—they were nice enough, a little rough around the edges, but always courteous to Dave and once in a while even threw in a free drink. Dave liked them because they didn't crowd their customers, it was a place he felt free to sip his Peroni in peace. Every time he set foot through the door, Dave felt as if he'd escaped to some other reality. The Devil's Eye was dimly lit and often smoky from the cigarettes employees puffed away on in the back room. Dave always sat at the smallest corner table in the joint, away from the bar, and waited for the waitress Ruth to come around and bring him his regular brew. It was practically empty today. There was usually a lone bartender washing glasses but he didn't see the guy anywhere in sight.

Dave let his mind drift as he slowly savored the one alcoholic beverage he allowed himself per day. He found vice to be more enjoyable if it wasn't overly indulged. Therefore it could be much more pleasurable and greatly appreciated. He wasn't one to consume anything lavishly or in excess. Life was about balance. Dave attempted to remind those around him of that very thing. He prided himself on being a good example for the rest of the family and hoped that his healthy habits would at some point rub off.

THE ANTAGONIST

5

Dave was a shopper. He had an eye for good quality. He enjoyed frequenting independent grocery stores as opposed to going out of town and giving his hard earned money to chains and corporations. This allowed him to support local businesses and keep their community thriving. He was insistent on doing his part.

He'd stock up on fresh vegetables and organic meats and return home to prepare a meal for his family, a large one.

With Dave's parents and sister living just down the street, it was often that they all ate together. This was both a blessing and a curse. He loved his parents quite a lot but June and August were a handful. Harmony, his sister, wasn't much better. Dave always played the peacekeeper between his overbearing parents and his eccentric twin. But when Georgie and Samantha were thrown into the mix, the dynamic completely changed. Over the years they'd all learned to co-exist; well, they could now get through a meal without someone bursting into tears, throwing a glass, storming out or demanding emancipation.

Tonight's dinner was Scottish salmon with fresh dill and garlic, a side of couscous and some brilliantly green asparagus and peas. Dave loved the time he spent in the kitchen. It allowed him to create—a thing he was not predisposed to doing. It wasn't until he met Georgette that his palate and cooking skills significantly improved.

Throughout his youth, Dave's parents fed their children what everyone else did: white bread, milk, plenty of canned goods and whatever meat happened to be on sale that week.

THE ANTAGONIST

He grew up with very little, as June and August dedicated most of their time to the church instead of steadily working and providing for their twins.

Still, there was always a meal—even if it wasn't hot, it was never taken for granted.

Growing up in Repo Ridge and living there his entire life allowed Dave to appreciate his recently found wealth in ways that he could not imagine. Georgette, being the free spirit that she was, had absolutely no issue with moving to Repo to be close to Dave's somewhat needy family. In fact, she was thrilled for a new project—to buy a new house and redesign and decorate to her heart's desire. Not only that, but she went above and beyond and bought a beautiful home just down the road for his parents. There was even a guesthouse for his sister to live in, when she wasn't in the hospital.

Dave couldn't believe how generous Georgette was as he insisted that it was entirely too much. But she wouldn't be deterred. She said it would be wonderful, perfect to be so close to the people who'd raised the love of her life. In Georgie's eyes, they deserved all the wealth and happiness in the world. Being raised by nannies and ignored by her egomaniac father for all of her life, she wanted as much family surrounding her as possible.

His parents quickly accepted their new daughter-in-law's offer and made themselves comfortable, too comfortable. And over the years things had become strained at times. His parents and Georgie did not always see eye-to-eye, mainly on things such as morality and eternal souls. His parents had been under the preconceived notion that because Georgie was Southern that meant she was a devout Christian, conservative and morally sound. His glorious wife was none of these things. She was a raging liberal atheist with a heart of gold and had more good will and charity in her heart than every church in the county combined together. But morally... she drank quite a bit, smoked often, was very outspoken and swore like a sailor when she sensed injustice. She never shirked from a well-researched and firmly opinionated belief. She went head-to-head with his parents more times than he could count. No one could debate quite like his wife, not even Schworst. Georgie always had the final say.

6

Dinner that evening was served precisely at seven-thirty on the dot. That was the agreed-on time that worked for all parties involved. Eating together was a tradition that allowed for everyone to recount their days, fill the family in on upcoming events, vacations, new projects or even the weather. Dave knew Samantha hated these dinners more than everyone else put together, but his twin wasn't too far behind her.

Harmony was a sullen woman, just as she had been as a child. She often complained to Dave about how he had been given all the good genes. Harmony always played with her food. She ate like a bird and probably weighed as little as one. Dave watched as she picked at one single pea despondently, her hair hanging limply around her face.

She'd spent most of her life indoors, and occasionally locked behind them. But self-isolation was natural for his sister. She was sensitive to even the most basic emotions with a neurotic nature that convinced his parents that she was inescapably possessed. Dave stood up for her over the years, attempted to educate his parents on the importance of mental health and the possible conditions that Harmony showed signs of exhibiting. They were reluctant for her to go to therapy. June continued to insist that what her daughter really needed was to speak with God. Georgette intervened at this and insisted that she would personally cover the cost of Harmony's medical bills. His parents eased up after that, but only a little.

Dave sat enjoying his salmon as he listened to Georgette rattle away about her day of rescuing women and children before turning her attention to her daughter. Samantha was surprisingly animated this evening. She was smirking quite a bit too. Dave knew what a smile like that meant—he'd seen the exact same one playing around Desiree's mouth at work yesterday after she successfully subdued an upset client. It was victory.

"How did that test go, babes?" Georgette asked as she refilled Sam's wine glass.

Drinking was a regular thing in their home. Georgie insisted that if Samantha were allowed to drink now, she would be infinitely more well-adjusted for when she went off to college.

"Aced it," Sam gloated as she twirled the wine glass around, grinning at the disapproving, though silent, mouths of June and August.

His parents made it very clear to him on several occasions that they worried about such a disturbed child. Dave promised them she was mature for her age—Sam gave them no reason to worry about her behavior. Dave couldn't help but feel as if his stepdaughter might do well with a bit more structure, but he wasn't about to challenge his wife's ability to raise a daughter that she'd taken care of long before him.

Georgette beamed with pride. "Course you did, my love. You and those big beautiful brains of yours!"

June cleared her throat, unmistakably needing to express herself posthaste. Dave's mother was unable to stop talking unless she was asleep or in church. Even during the latter, she would still sing, recite and pray.

"Work was extremely busy today," she began with her ever-present sweet yet softly patronizing tone.

Georgette raised her eyebrows and exchanged a look of mock surprise with Harmony, who snorted into her water glass. Georgie was the only one who could make his sister laugh and coax her out of her shell. Dave loved her a little bit more for that.

Emily Dinova

June droned on about her "job." Doing the Lord's work—as she put it. August sat beside her, nodding at everything she said as he shoveled food into his mouth at an alarming rate, moaning and groaning with every bite.

His father was a large and sedentary man, only one rib eye away from needing a new stent. Dave attempted to cook healthy meals every night—especially when his parents were over. But he couldn't control what they did when he wasn't around. It was naïve for Dave to consider that his sister might show an interest in his parent's health—that relationship, he feared, was passing the point of being repaired. If only his parents could listen to Harmony, try to understand her, instead of shoving their religion down her throat and choking her with it.

Georgette privately referred to his mother's place of employment as a "Jesus Pop-up Shop." But every day, whether rain or snow or the heat of the baking sun, June stood by her little booth in the center of downtown with her religious pamphlets. Offering guidance and an ear to all who needed protection and love, all but her own daughter—at least that's how Harmony saw it.

"Dave," Dave's attention turned back to his wife, who'd just cut across his mother's monologue, "What have you got going on this weekend, darling?"

Before Dave could respond, June jumped at the question. "He's coming to ten a.m. Mass with August and I, aren't you? Of course, all of you are invited to attend, as well." June reiterated this little speech at least once a week. It was usually on Pizza Fridays.

June and August attended church daily, but Dave usually joined them on either Saturday or Sunday, out of respect. He himself was not particularly religious. It was probably because it was all he and his sister ever heard about growing up. God was life, and in a way, his parents overdosed their children on the subject, in some ways abandoned them for their beloved savior. Harmony used to say as a child how jealous she was of Him.

Dave just preferred not to think about it altogether. If God was real, great, and if he wasn't, that was fine too. There was nothing Dave could do to control that. He only controlled his own actions, which allowed him to live a guilt-free and happy life. He didn't need church, but it made his parents happy and so he complied. Relationships were all about balance, the give and take. If those requirements shifted out of fairness, that was when things could deteriorate.

No one else at the table would set foot in a church, even if they were being held at knifepoint.

"I was thinking about painting this weekend," Harmony piped up.

"That's wonderful, Har!" Georgie looked genuinely excited at this news.

"My therapist says it's good for calming the mind. Focusing."

June made a face at this. Georgie frowned but leaned forward, encouragingly,

"Is this the same one you've been seeing regularly?"

Harmony nodded. "For six weeks now, twice a week. She's absolutely wonderful. I feel like I'm actually starting to—"

"—David what did you say you were doing this weekend?" June asked loudly.

Harmony's face went red as she slowly receded back into herself. Before Georgette could say whatever was likely to ruin the rest of the meal, Dave cut in.

"Harmony, please, finish what you were saying," he encouraged, frowning at his mother, who looked anything but contrite.

His sister shook her head vigorously with denial and returned to her pea, now stabbing it with resentment. He heard his wife huff impatiently beside him.

"To answer your question, yes, Mom, I'm coming to Mass with you. Like I always do."

Emily Dinova

"Like he always does," Georgette reiterated, glaring daggers at the pleased and plump smile smacked across her mother-in-law's selfish face.

Dave sighed to himself. He tried to please everyone, he really did. It was one hour out of his weekend that he didn't mind giving up. Sam was usually out with her friends on the weekends, or cooped up on the third floor writing music and banging away on her instruments. There wasn't one she couldn't pick up and not master.

And Georgie worked all of Saturday and most of Sunday. The only time she really took for herself was an hour here or there for 'tennis,' which she'd been trying to pluck up the courage to start. She never played any sport, never even went to school but had private tutors instead. His wife spoke five languages fluently but was absolutely terrified of learning a team game. Dave encouraged her to live outside of her comfort zone. He suggested tennis, a sport with minimal contact. One he enjoyed in his youth. Georgie bought the clothes, the racket, joined a country club—yet still had not scheduled her first lesson. Instead, she went and watched other people play, while enjoying a cocktail. Dave knew she'd get there eventually.

THE ANTAGONIST

7

And like the good son he was, Dave sat calmly and patiently through Saturday morning Mass, nodding and gesturing and doing what was expected of him, all while dreaming he was still asleep in his wife's arms.

A quick breakfast of eggs and sausage at the local diner allowed ample enough time for his parents to reiterate the entire sermon they'd just sat through. Dave smiled and occasionally added his thoughts, staying as neutral and general as possible.

After breakfast wrapped up and Dave drove his parents back to their home, his mother took the time to encourage him to consider Georgie, Sam and Harmony's eternal souls—she instructed him to push them towards the light. Dave always said he would do what he could, which was absolutely nothing.

His chest felt light after waving them off and finally having a bit of the solitude he was craving. With the rest of his afternoon and evening completely free, Dave would either return home to dive into a good book, or go for a long run. At least once every two weeks he would clean the entire house, top to bottom—all 10,000 square feet. Georgie begged him to let her hire a cleaning service but Dave refused. He relished the activity; if he was to enjoy such an illustrious home, it was only fair that he be the one to maintain it.

He loved spending a whole day in the gardens, planting and pruning. It was calming and beautiful work. Being out in nature always put Dave's mind at ease. Away from his family, he could hear his own thoughts and allow himself to come up with ways to continually improve their quality of life. Not that it could get much better. But Dave was a strong believer in always pushing oneself to strive for more.

The one person, more than all others, that he was constantly trying to help improve was his best friend, Robb. Dave usually saw him once a weekend. And today, Dave decided that's what he'd do in lieu of returning home.

Robb and Dave had been best friends since they were kids and in a lot of ways Robb was still that teenage boy who never wanted to grow up. A few years ago, after Dave loaned him a bit of money, Robb purchased the burger joint they used to frequent as kids and turned it into the only pizza place in town. It was a success, and though Dave refused to take credit, Georgie insisted that Robb would have never been able to pull it off without her husband's help and guidance.

Robb was a good guy—he just didn't take life seriously at all. He had no interest in getting married or having kids, no aspirations of growing his business—he basically let the kids who worked there run it for him. Robb's favorite pastimes were smoking weed and playing video games. This didn't bother Dave in the slightest—he was more than willing to stand by his friend no matter what his life choices were. They were basically brothers in Dave's eyes—he the responsible one and Robb the one who needed looking out for. They'd been through some hard times together. In the end, no relationship was perfect, but loyalty was there. And for that, Dave put aside all other flaws that Robb might exude—as long as he wasn't harming anyone, Dave felt justified in leaving his friend to his devices.

Normally Dave wasn't one to enjoy nostalgia and reminiscing. He always preferred to be moving forward. And sometimes, when Robb smoked some extra intense marijuana, he tended to always dive back into the past. And the past for Robb hadn't exactly been an easy one. He rarely opened up about his parents and the broken home he came from. But he immensely enjoyed reminding Dave of all the trouble they'd gotten into as kids. Dave would laugh and smile along, while feeling sorry for his friend, and wondering how he could help more.

Being that it was Saturday afternoon, he found Robb at Repo Pizza, popping pizzas into the wood fire oven Dave helped him build. Robb made great pizza. Dave ordered six personal pies every Friday night, considering no one in his family enjoyed the same toppings. Sam was vegan, Georgie allergic to gluten. June hated anything spicy and was the only one who could stomach a Hawaiian pizza. August always needed bacon and pepperoni. Harmony ate hers with no sauce and no cheese. And Dave just liked a regular cheese pizza.

Robb greeted him with a shout of joy, a backwards hat thrown over his shoulder length hair, giving him the appearance of a forty-year-old teen.

"What's up, bro? Good to see you, man!"

It was always the same with Robb—he acted like a dog that hadn't seen his owner in years. They'd hung out just last weekend.

But Robb's enthusiasm was contagious. Dave embraced him in a quick hug as Robb patted him roughly on the back, slapping flour all over him.

"Oh come on," Dave sighed, dusting himself off.

Robb laughed.

"You look like you could use some powder," he joked, shoving his hands back into the bag of flour and turning to knead the dough. The place was basically empty giving them time to catch up before the evening rush.

"How's the fam? Keeping you busy?"

Dave smiled in response. Robb always told him he was a superhero when it came to staying sane amongst the madness in which he lived.

"It's all good, you know, I just take it one day at a time."

"And Georgie? She's good?"

Robb was sort of fascinated with Dave's wife. He couldn't really blame him—most people were.

"She's busy, but great."

"Good. That's real good, man."

THE ANTAGONIST

"Sorry I didn't get back to your text, things have been a little insane. But what about you, how's your week been?"

"No worries brother, no worries. It's been rad. I got some new bud, just bought my first futon so I'm psyched for that. Pizza's been busy, I can't complain. I hired a couple new kids to help out, so, yeah." He shrugged his shoulders as if to say, 'that's it!'

"Really happy to hear. The place looks great." Dave gave it a sweeping glance—there was a couple at one of the corner tables—the guy was consumed with his slice and the girl was drinking a Coke. She looked like she was about Sam's age. The way she was sucking on her straw gave Dave the impression that as soon as her boyfriend finished his pizza, she was going to regain his attention.

Dave spied a bored-looking waiter standing out front, smoking a vape and repeatedly swiping his finger across the screen of his cellphone, over and over again.

"Is it still just you back here making the pies?" Dave questioned. It had been at least a month since he last visited here. Usually they hung out at Robb's apartment or Dave's house.

"Yeah, but it's been picking up, mostly on Friday and Saturday night—I'm literally half out of my mind!"

"Have you thought about hiring someone to help out on weekend nights?"

"Nah, man. That's a great idea! You're always so full of them."

"Put out an ad, it will free you up a bit. Hey, if business is good then you can afford it, right?"

"Hell yeah, man. Thanks. I really appreciate it."

"Anytime."

"So what's new with you?" Robb asked as he slid the pizza he'd rolled out and seasoned into the oven. "You haven't stopped by here in forever. All okay?"

As much as Robb was immature, he was extremely attuned to other's emotions. He had street smarts like no one that Dave had ever known.

"Ah, it's nothing. I just didn't want to be with myself today. If that makes any sense?"

"Totally," Robb confirmed, eyeing his friend carefully.

"I know it sounds absolutely ridiculous, especially after how we grew up…but I still can't get used to being in that big house all alone. It…" Dave trailed off, not exactly sure what he was trying to convey.

Robb was nodding vigorously. "I get it, bro. Seriously. I don't know how you do it. It freaks me out being there at night, to be honest. Especially when it's just us two."

"It freaks you out?" Dave laughed despite himself. "I didn't mean it like that. It's not haunted, you know."

"Nah, I know. But being by yourself, especially at night… that's when the demons come out, and the more space you got, the more room they have to play."

"Sure," Dave agreed, understanding Robb's metaphor better than he probably did himself.

They chatted for another hour about the inconsequential before Dave returned home and spent the rest of his weekend with his wife in the beautiful world they created.

8

That was Dave's life.

Weeks passed and all stayed the same. The same constant chaos, the same reiterated conversations, yet the same happiness and appreciation for his life that Dave had come to know and love, also persisted. Yes, it was all the same but he was thankful for it.

The good, the bad and the ugly, it was his and he was content.

Friday, October 6th, 2017

THE ANTAGONIST

I

He gasped for air as his conscious mind surfaced, his eyes snapping open and the frantic racing of his heart leaving sweat beading down the sides of his face. He threw back the covers, swung his legs over the side and dropped his head in between them. He was lightheaded. Felt chilled, shaken by whatever nightmare had been plaguing him.

Dave never remembered his dreams, but this one was terrifying. So much so, that it was already fading from his grasp, his mind scurrying to protect itself. All he could recall now in the quiet reality of the dark morning was screams of agony as he listened to the uneven spurts of breath falling from his trembling mouth. He could hear the rain hammering relentlessly against the glass windows just beyond.

Dave shook his head, forcing the thoughts from his mind as he carefully turned towards Georgette. He'd not awoken her. He wiped the back of his hand over his forehead and forced himself to his feet.

As he went about brushing his teeth, Dave risked a glance out the windows. A thick fog had moved down over the valley as it was known to do this time of year. The damp leaves were just beginning to coat the autumn ground. Usually the trees' foliage was stunning even on the gloomiest of mornings. But today, a film seemed to drape over the entire landscape, setting it in a perpetual state of muted dismay.

Thunder rolled ominously across the sky as Dave made his way downstairs to commence breakfast. He headed into the kitchen just thinking how he might make some blueberry and yogurt smoothies, when he spotted something out of place.

It was shimmering on the metallic gleam of the refrigerator—a sticky note.

Dave frowned.

No one ever left a sticky note, or any kind of note on anything in this house. He reached for it quickly, scanning it with his tired eyes.

The words were written in black sharpie. He wrinkled his nose at the pungent smell. He hated the intense aroma of permanent markers. It said—

"You're special!"

— accompanied by a sloppy smiley face.

Dave stared blankly at the message.

His first thought was that this might be some prank of Samantha's. He opened the fridge door carefully, just in case she left some surprise waiting for him. But nothing was out of the ordinary.

Dave looked back to the note. It wasn't in Georgette's handwriting, but perhaps she'd had a few too many gins. Work was rather stressful for her at the moment, so he made her a homemade peach cobbler last night while attempting to wait up for her. Of course this note was just her showing her gratitude and not wanting to wake him.

Dave smiled, putting the note into his pocket before resuming his raid of the refrigerator.

"Good Morning." Dave nearly jumped out of his skin as he spun around.

It was Samantha. And she was once again smirking. "What's for breakfast?"

"You're up unusually early," Dave commented. He could feel his heart—for the second time this morning—skipping several beats. The residual of the nightmare was clearly still affecting him. *I haven't had one that bad since I was a kid*, he thought involuntarily.

Emily Dinova

"I have things to do, Dave," Samantha explained in a bored tone, tossing her long purple hair over her thin shoulder.

Dave motioned to the blueberries and dairy-free yogurt in question before Sam nodded in approval. She was chatty this morning as he went about making breakfast. She took a few minutes to mock his parent's beliefs before explaining the global benefits of veganism. Dave took it all in, listening and honestly shocked at her candidness.

This was the most Samantha had spoken to him in the five years he knew her.

It was as if she was keeping a secret she wanted to brag about, yet did not want to share—with him of all people. He watched her as she ate breakfast, that same smile playing about her lips as she told him she finally realized who he reminded her of.

"Who?" Dave questioned, despite himself. It was likely he was falling right into one of her traps.

"That guy who played Bilbo Baggins in The Hobbit."

"The actor, or the character?"

"I dunno," she cocked her head, studying him as she slurped up her smoothie. "I can't decide."

Dave nodded with a sigh. There were much worse comparisons she could have made.

"Ready when you are."

THE ANTAGONIST

2

They headed out into the misty morning. Dave breathed in the chilly air, relishing the feeling of being cleansed. The conversation helped distract him, but still he could not shake the slight feeling of uneasiness that continued to creep into his bones. Maybe it was because he was prioritizing Sam's request to leave extra early over Georgie's breakfast. He cooked for her all week though, she wouldn't mind, he was being ridiculous. It was just the change in schedule that was throwing him off—that was all.

He turned to look at Samantha as she dropped into the passenger seat. It was never the case that they exited the house at the same time.

"Aren't you going to say goodbye to your mom?" Dave questioned with a frown as he started up the car.

"Like I said. I have things to do." Quite out of the ordinary.

"Alright," he confirmed as he put the car in drive.

Samantha was definitely up to something. For one, she didn't even put her headphones on. She was content to sift through the radio until she found something she liked: Metallica, *The Day That Never Comes.*

Perfect. Dave loved this song, grew up to it in fact.

Push you cross that line
Just stay down this time
Hide in yourself
Crawl in yourself
You'll have your time.

Dave was grinning as she turned it up. Sam scowled back at him then yelled over the music.

God I'll make them pay.
"Guess what?"
Take it back one day.
"What?" Dave yelled back.
I'll end this day.
"You have to guess!"
I'll splatter color on this grave.

Dave had a slight inkling of what would cause a teenage girl to act the way Samantha was acting, even one who pretended to be as emotionless as his stepdaughter. He did, after all, grow up with a sister. Blushing cheeks, perpetual smirk, interest in school, a dirty secret…

"You have a boyfriend?"
Waiting for the one,
the day that never comes.

Samantha's mocking smile slipped from her face as she slammed the music off and turned towards him, seething with rage.

"You absolute shit! How did you know?!"

Dave smiled. "I'm a lot older than you. I know things."

"He knows things!" she cackled back. "Don't tell mom or I'll shave off your eyebrows in your sleep," she threatened.

"I was just thinking they needed a good trim." He chanced a glance and was thrilled to see she was fighting against amusement.

"I'm serious. Not a word."

"Scout's honor."

"Whatever that means." She rolled her eyes and flipped her hair, turning her face towards the window and once again ignoring his existence.

All was silent except for the steady swiping of the windshield wipers and the patter of the rain before it was washed away. Dave navigated a little slower than usual across the slick streets. He was just slowing down in front of the school when Samantha spoke again.

"I'll tell her on my own time. So don't be a narc."

Dave couldn't help himself. "I won't but Sam, please just tell me you are being safe."

She looked at him with absolute revulsion as she flung the door open wide.

"Ew, don't ever try to have a sex talk with me ever again or I will GUT you."

She slammed the door with fury and took off across the front lawn shielding herself with her book bag from the now driving rain.

Dave sighed to himself, "Have a great day."

He turned the music back on but Metallica was already finished and replaced with an irritating commercial. Dave shut it off and hoped the strange feeling of edginess left him by the time he reached the firm.

THE ANTAGONIST

3

Dave pulled into the parking lot two minutes behind schedule. A tree had come down overnight, blocking the closest route from Samantha's school to his office. As he splashed through the puddles, he felt the urgency of being tardy slowly close in on him. He did not want to give Schworst an opportunity to jump on his back—Dave was not in the headspace to deal with that sort of confrontation this morning.

He smiled weakly and nodded to a few of his coworkers as he made his way swiftly to his desk. He shrugged out of his jacket and cast a quick look towards the main office. It was still dark—the glass windows reflected emptily back at him. Schworst had probably been drinking hard last night and that meant he wouldn't be showing his face until at least noon. As much as this made for a nice peaceful morning, when Schworst did finally surface accompanied by a hangover, he was explosive with rage towards anyone who even looked in his direction. Dave dreaded these occurrences, not because he couldn't take the unfounded humiliation, but because of how pathetic his boss revealed himself to be when he chose to demean someone the rest of the office respected. He shrugged it off and took a deep breath.

The moment Dave sat down he felt some of the tension leave his body. Here, he was away from the house and his family. Here he could focus, complete his tasks, and find his inner balance once again.

THE ANTAGONIST

He worked steadily through the morning, as precisely and efficiently as he could. He completed double what he would have in a normal day. Dave felt such vigor, a burst of adrenaline that allowed him to attack the work in a way that would leave no place in his mind for bad energy.

He didn't look up until he heard the front doors slamming open at half-past two. In stormed Kyle Schworst looking haggard and enraged. *Confront the beast before it confronts you!* The thought immediately jumped into Dave's mind as he swept up all the motions, subpoenas, contracts and messages and sprung from his desk. He strode purposely towards Schworst, ready to meet him head on.

"Good Afternoon, Sir," Dave began in a clipped though polite tone. "I think you'll find everything you need here for the next three days or so."

Schworst stared at him through wide, bleary eyes before ripping the stack of papers out of his hands with a snarl and storming off towards his office.

Dave felt a surge of satisfaction, maybe something would go right today after all.

The rest of the afternoon was busy. Dave spent most of the time on the phone. But whenever he stopped for a moment to take a breath, he felt eyes on him. He wasn't sure who it was since he'd not looked up from his work since Schworst came in. He didn't have to wait too long to find out.

At ten to five a set of long, sharp, crimson fingernails rapped against the top of his desk—directly on top of the contract he was currently reading. Dave glanced up to be confronted with a set of startlingly blue eyes and a pair of pouty red lips to match the nails.

"Hi there," her voice was smooth like honey.

Dave cleared his throat, feeling as if he swallowed sandpaper.

"Can I help you?" he asked politely.

She leaned closer over the desk, allowing him an ample view of her very generous cleavage.

"Actually yes," she purred, sliding her toned thigh onto the side of his desk so she could perch above him. Dave did not miss the line of her garters before they slipped back beneath her tight pencil skirt as she shifted her hips seductively.

He raised his eyebrows at her and waited. Her smile deepened with interest before she continued. "I was wondering how I've been here for two weeks and have still not been introduced to you."

"I didn't want to crowd you, um—" Dave pretended as if he did not know her name.

"Desiree," she whispered smoothly, extending her hand towards him. "Desiree DeLongo."

"Pleasure," Dave assured her with a tight smile and quick shake, before turning back to his work.

"You're Dave, right?" she continued, clearly unbothered by his dismissal of her.

"That's right," he frowned in concentration, focusing on the words in front of him.

"Well, *David*," she drawled, "How is it that every man in this firm has tried to fuck me except you?"

If Dave had been drinking his coffee, he would have spit it everywhere. He glanced around terrified that one of his co-workers might overhear this suddenly lewd conversation.

He accidentally locked eyes with Schworst, who was watching the two of them through his office windows with pure malevolence. Desiree followed his sight line and gave Kyle a mocking little wave before turning back to her prey.

"So? Why is that?" she prompted him.

Dave realized he was going to have to be strong with her, it was obvious to him that Desiree very rarely heard the word no.

"I'm married. Happily married," he included, leaving no room for her to push forward.

Instead she let out a big yawn.

"Well if you ever get bored of that..." She slid a card out from under her sleeve like a magician and dropped it on his desk.

THE ANTAGONIST

"Nice to meet you," he said, his tone suggesting he was done playing her game.

"Pleasure was all mine, David. I hope it continues to be."

For some reason her voice made Dave feel an increase of the dread he thought dissipated—it returned to him now in full force. Desiree sauntered away, swinging her alluring hips, he was sure, for his distinct pleasure. But Dave felt no pleasure, and with good reason.

He began to pack up his things, the desperate need for fresh air overtaking him when Schworst bellowed his name. With a deep breath, Dave turned and headed into his boss's office. Schworst was smiling, which was never a good sign. It only took Dave three seconds to identify his glee. All of the paperwork Dave had given him only a few hours before was now covered in what looked like a half-eaten Sloppy Joe.

"Spilled my lunch," Schworst explained, looking anything but sorry. "Guess you'll have to stay late tonight Davey—redo all of this crap." He gestured to the pile of ruined papers.

With a nod of his head, Dave grabbed his ruined work off the desk and turned back out into the office. The feeling of injustice made his chest tight with the words he longed to say to his boss. He sent a quick text to Georgette as the office emptied, letting her know he would be late. As he sat back down at his desk, Desiree strolled by and sent him a sly wink as she left. With a firm frown, Dave tossed her card into the trash and got down to it.

4

He didn't leave the firm until almost 8:30. He'd not completed everything, but refused to rush through the work and make mistakes. That would only give Kyle more fuel for tomorrow. But at least he'd gotten some alone time.

It wasn't until he arrived at the grocery store that he realized it was Friday—he heard one of the cashiers telling a shopper to have a great weekend.

Pizza Friday.

With a growl of frustration, Dave returned the few items he'd picked up and headed back out into the wind and rain. The weather had only proceeded to get worse, and now in the dark, Dave was especially careful. There were not a plentiful amount of streetlights in Repo Ridge, especially in their neighborhood, where the houses were stretched out by some distance, spaced with long copses of trees or empty fields easily swallowed up by the gloomy night.

Dave opted to listen to some classical music on his ride home. He couldn't help but feel his day had been, there was no other way to put it, bad. Like a slightly lingering cold, or seasonal allergies that persisted no matter what you did. A cough that just wouldn't disappear. That was how his brain felt. No matter how hard he tried to think of the positive, something was keeping all his good emotions under lock and key. He just needed a decent night's sleep and to stay the hell away from Desiree DeLongo. No doubt she was more trouble than he needed, both personally and professionally.

THE ANTAGONIST

Dave shook the rain out of his hair and proceeded to remove his shoes as Georgette came bounding into the foyer in one of her many silk kimonos. She had a Pimm's cocktail in one hand and a glorious smile on her face. She threw herself into his arms, kissing him soundly.

Dave tasted the alcohol on her tongue and was reminded that he had to forgo his one drink at The Devil's Eye tonight because of his psychotic boss. Dave frowned again as Georgie pulled back and looked into his eyes. Her smile vanished to be replaced with concern as she reached up to stroke his cheek.

"What's the matter, my love?"

"Oh just a long, miserable day."

She immediately began fussing over him. "Nothing a stiff drink and some pizza won't fix! Everyone is here and I put in the order already so that's one less thing you have to worry about! Now come on, I'll get you a drink."

She kissed him again and then gently led him by the hand towards the kitchen where the rest of the family was congregating. They never ate dinner in the formal dining room on Fridays, but preferred to spread out around the massive kitchen with its long counter top and window booths.

"You never work so late! I was afraid you started having an affair," she joked as Dave felt his heart skip another beat. When he didn't laugh, she turned around to look at him.

"Darling, what is it?" His wife stopped and gave him her full attention.

Dave let out a great sigh. "This new paralegal, put me in a bad spot with my boss, that's all. I don't trust her."

"You can't trust any lawyers, dear."

Dave smiled. "I'm sorry, I'll cheer up."

"You don't have to do anything you don't want to do. You know that's the house rule."

"I love you, Georgie," he sighed and relaxed a little into her arms.

"I know."

Emily Dinova

The doorbell rang a half an hour later.

"I'll get it!" June insisted, as she bustled out of the kitchen where Dave now sat with a Pimm's cocktail in hand—apparently Georgie made an entire pitcher—though he had absolutely no interest in drinking it.

He wanted a beer.

Samantha was sipping on her own fruity delight; her face looked flushed. She was immersed in a large textbook that Dave could not see the cover of.

"Big test?" he asked casually as he watched his father flirt shamelessly with Georgie—as he always did the second June was out of earshot.

"The biggest," Sam replied, not looking up.

"Here we are!" June trilled, much like a kindergarten teacher addressing her class. "What a nice delivery boy, I gave him $20, was that enough?" she asked, despite knowing it was more than enough. She set the personal pies down on the counter with a loud thwack.

"So sanctimonious," Dave heard his sister mutter under her breath.

"Just ignore her," he whispered back, startling Harmony, who looked as if she just noticed he were present.

"I try, but hell, living with them is a nightmare. At least you've got your own place."

"So do you," Dave insisted as everyone moved forward, crowding around the counter and grabbing each specific order. "The guesthouse is all yours."

"It's not like this," he could hear the passive-aggressiveness creeping into her voice.

"Go eat, Harmony, and then we can talk about your living situation. I might have a few ideas."

Her face brightened as she gave her brother a small smile. "What would I do without you?" she wondered as she wandered off towards the rest.

THE ANTAGONIST

Dave honestly didn't know. But he hoped she would never have to find out.

Once everyone was settled and eating, Dave got up and grabbed the last pizza box, marked with a D., as Robb made sure to do for their large and fussy family.

He opened it with relish, realizing he'd not eaten the entire day—his hunger suddenly rushing full force to the surface.

Dave stared down in disappointment.

Confusion.

Black Olives?

Dave never once ordered a pizza with black olives. He hated them. Couldn't stand the taste, the texture, everything about them turned him off.

"Georg?" he asked after a moment, "Did you order me olive?"

She looked up from her own cauliflower crust that she was immensely enjoying.

"No darling, regular cheese as always. Did they mess it up?"

Dave confirmed with a nod. "Yeah, funny enough, it's the only pizza topping I can't stand."

"Oh my God, just pick them off!" Sam complained.

"Don't you use the Lord's name in vain, young missy." June's eyes were flashing with fury. She kept silent about most of the things Samantha said and did—Dave assumed it was out of fear—but speaking God's name was not one of them.

"Why do you think it is, June," Samantha began, a light blush creeping up her face, which was a telling sign she was quickly becoming combative, "that God needs so much money? If he's so all-powerful and all-knowing, then why the hell does he need so much cash?" Sam had been watching old George Carlin reruns for sure.

"Great question, honey." Georgette interrupted.

"To do for others, you poor, ignorant girl," June spoke with slow sympathy, as if instructing a small child.

Georgette fired up at this. "Sam is the farthest thing from ignorant, June. She's highly educated, cultured, well-travelled."

"Spoiled." August added with a sharp nod of his head.

"Oh, very spoiled. Ungrateful some would even suggest," June continued on in her sweetest, unctuous voice.

Sam yawned in their faces and returned to her textbook. She clearly decided the conversation was no longer worth her time.

"How was your day, Mom?" Dave asked, knowing this would center June back on herself, and away from antagonizing his wife and stepdaughter.

"Oh, it was just lovely, Davey. Thank you for asking. The church is currently trying to expand, so we've been tasked with recruiting at least 2 to 5 new members a week. I think I might have gotten three just today!"

"Isn't it *always* trying to expand? I mean, hello? Colonialism, anyone?" Georgie commented, raising her eyebrows at Harmony who burst into giggles. It was becoming their routine.

Throughout the evening June and Georgette continued to have words. But Dave's attention went back to his pizza as he drowned the voices out around him. He picked off each olive, careful not to miss even the smallest bit as he tossed them onto the top of the box. He felt consumed by the task. It seemed more arduous than all the extra work he had to complete today.

"You used to like black olives."

Harmony had snuck up on him.

"What? No I didn't."

"Yes, you did. When we were kids. Remember, June would put them in meatloaf."

"That's precisely why I can't stand them, Har."

She smiled at that. "And that pie you used to sometimes get from the old pizza place the next town over, remember? That had olives on it."

"Nope, that was Robb."

"Oh."

THE ANTAGONIST

His pizza was once again plain cheese, but Dave could still see the little indents the olives had made. He took a bite.

Harmony looked at him hopefully. "How is it?"

Dave chewed, nodding his head, it was fine—he could eat it. He wasn't picky and he wasn't going to make a fuss. But he could still taste the metallic essence coating his tongue with each bite. He couldn't get rid of it, and after only one slice he felt his stomach begin to roll in protest.

He was no longer hungry. The distaste of the olives soiled his palate, like pretty much everything else had today. He picked up the cocktail instead, pulled the stupid little umbrella out of it, and took a large gulp, as he attempted to wash away the flavor of something he could not, for the life of him, stomach.

Dinner came to a premature and abrupt end as tempers flew across the kitchen, escalating as June took underhanded shots at Georgie's moral compass, insinuating the women she helped at the shelter were there because they'd ignored God. And when Samantha finally yelled FUCK GOD at the top of her lungs, Dave knew it was time to intervene. His parents walked backwards out the front door, crossing themselves while Samantha stood there, arms and legs spread wide, reciting Latin in her best demonic voice.

It would have all been so comical, if Dave could have watched them through a television screen and not in real time.

He fell into bed that night with the hope that tomorrow would be infinitely better. However, the rain continued to drive, the wind rattling the branches against the windows, and before Dave could do much to empty and calm his mind, he slipped into an uneasy and fitful sleep.

Saturday, October 7th

THE ANTAGONIST

I

Morning dawned with the same spiteful and raging force as the previous one. The fog was so thick it pressed incessantly against each window of the mansion, leaving the grounds outside obscured and filled with dark shadows.

Dave rang his parents as he went about making toast for breakfast. His stomach was still feeling off from last night's dinner and he was in no mood for anything too heavy or elaborate.

When he explained to his mother that he wasn't feeling one hundred percent, she told him not to worry, and that he could come to church with them tomorrow instead. Dave was thankful for the reprieve, he felt what he really needed was a day to himself. To get over whatever malady seemed to be plaguing him. He felt so bone tired that he was sure he must be coming down with the flu—he checked his temperature to be sure, but it was normal even if his body felt tense and tight. Dave mulled about the house—he browsed the library, watered the plants in the conservatory, he even took a spin around the ballroom. Georgette would be leaving for work soon and the distant sound of drums clashing led him to believe Sam would be cooped upstairs for the remainder of the weekend working on her music.

By noon, Dave was itching to get out of the house. He couldn't put his finger on it, but a combination of paranoia and claustrophobia was starting to lean on him. He considered going outside, but the wind was so wild he wasn't willing to risk getting hit with a falling branch.

THE ANTAGONIST

"Screw it," he murmured to himself as he paced once more along the upstairs hallway, looking for something to occupy his time. He turned suddenly and headed back down the stairs with a rush of inspiration.

2

The Devil's Eye was completely empty. Dave allowed his pupils to adjust to the dim lighting as he shrugged off the chilly mist he brought in with him.

He was breaking his schedule. Dave wasn't the type of man to drink this early in the day, even if it was a weekend. But considering he missed his drink last night because of unforeseen circumstances, he didn't feel too guilty about making up for lost time. This was the only place he felt comfortable going today to be able to be alone and think.

It was then that Dave noticed the inexplicable. It was so ridiculous, too fitting, that he actually laughed out loud. After how yesterday had gone, he was unsurprised to find himself facing another obstacle—a man already sitting at his table—the only other customer in the entire place.

Dave approached him carefully, feeling suddenly that this must be some sort of sign. He was not a superstitious man by any means, but after living with Georgette for five years, he'd learned to appreciate an odd circumstance when experiencing one. Perhaps he was supposed to meet this man.

"Mind if I join you?" he asked.

The man looked up through heavily bagged eyes. His gaze was watery yet intense, his skin sallow and cracked. He must have been in his seventies, or just lived a particularly hard life. Dave was a regular, and yet he had never seen him in here before.

The man nodded, gesturing to the seat across from him as he straightened up, much like an ancient sea creature awakening from a long undisturbed slumber.

THE ANTAGONIST

Dave had no idea why he was engaging with this man. On a regular day, he would have sat at another table, or slouched up to the bar. He never really conversed with anyone there, only Ruth to put in his order and an occasional 'hello' to whatever bartender was working. Something seemed to be pulling him towards this peculiar man. Dave was curious.

"I'm Dave," he began.

"Name's J," the stranger croaked out in a voice that sounded as if it hadn't been used for centuries.

"Just J?"

"Yup."

"What are you drinking, J?" Dave asked as he looked around for Ruth.

"I can't afford to drink. Came in for a bit of warmth, that's all."

"Well then, pick your poison and we'll both get warmed up."

Dave knew instantly he'd done the right thing. This man was alone, with probably no family—he certainly looked very poor if not completely homeless. The least Dave could do was buy him a drink. Why else would he come into a bar for comfort?

"Really?" J asked eagerly. "You'd do that for me?"

"Of course," Dave motioned for Ruth just as she came through the backdoor in a cloud of cigarette smoke. "What'll it be?"

J cocked his head to the side and scratched his jaw, deep in contemplation.

"Whiskey. Neat. Double if you don't mind."

Dave put in their orders with Ruth while he enquired about Shawn and Mara. Ruth explained Mara's mother died and the two were out of town for the funeral. Ruth was running the place until they got back.

"Not that it's been particularly busy, but Stan quit last week, so I'm trying out a new bartender," she complained as she headed over to the bar to fill the order. "Who, by the looks of it, " she frowned as she grabbed a note taped to a half empty vodka bottle, "took off early! Typical, am I right? If you know anyone send 'em over, yeah?"

"Will do," Dave replied.

Dave and his drinking partner sat in silence while Ruth quickly put the order together and returned to the table.

She looked down at the drinks and opened her mouth to say something, but was cut off by a buzzer coming from the back of the establishment.

"Oh damn, I forgot we were getting a delivery today. Ugh, if you need anything else, just help yourself, hun. I trust you."

And she was gone. Dave turned back to J and lifted his glass. "Cheers."

"To your good health." J sucked the drink down in one shot.

Dave took a sip of his beer, enjoying it even more than he would have yesterday. A sense of calm descended over him as he sat there, contemplating this man. But before Dave could settle on any one question to ask him, J interrupted his thoughts with a query of his own.

"Are you a tired man, Dave?" Before Dave could reply, he continued on, "I'm a tired man, and I know what one looks like. Staring at you right now, for me…it's like a reflection."

Dave's expression must have shown doubt and surprise because J laughed boisterously.

"You're handsome no doubt, hope you never look like this old bag. What I mean is your eyes. I can see the same worry that I had when I was your age."

"Worry? What am I worried about?" Dave asked with a little skepticism in his tone. This man didn't know anything about him.

"You're overworked."

Dave contemplated this. He worked the same as any average citizen. He shook his head in disagreement. "I have a regular nine-to-five."

But J was shaking his head. "I don't mean overworked as in your job. Overworked in life. Always the rock, the backbone, the person to take everyone else's burdens and place them on your own shoulders until you finally crumble beneath the weight."

THE ANTAGONIST

Any solid defense that Dave had ready to answer with was blown to pieces as J finished his little sermon. Dave stared numbly at the stranger, wanting to understand how he could possibly know all of that by just looking in his eyes. J smiled with a bit of triumph.

"I'm a lot older than you, kid. I know things."

Dave started at the man's words. They were practically the same ones he spoke to Samantha yesterday morning.

"You're too nice, Dave, I can tell," J went on as he got to his feet and limped over to the bar to refill his drink. "You hold things in, don't you? When you're done fixing everyone else's problems, is there anyone there to fix yours?"

"I don't have problems, not real ones anyway," Dave insisted. "I'm happy, I can handle everything life throws at me. I am utterly grateful for it and I take nothing for granted. If my family feels content and safe, then I can sacrifice a little bit of my sanity in return."

J nodded as he returned to the table, settling himself back down. "If you say so."

"And you?" Dave asked after several minutes of quiet thought. "Are you overworked?"

"I'm practically dead! Overworked to death!" J jeered with morbid humor. "God, if I have to make one more decision, I think I'll just end it all."

"That seems drastic."

"Does it?"

"Where will you go after this?" Dave asked before he could stop himself. He could hear his wife in his ear, instructing him to help.

"Back from where I came, I suppose."

"Do you need money? A place to stay?"—thinking he could at least help this man to a shelter.

J looked angry for the first time, "I don't need help."

Dave frowned at him as he threw back the last sip of his beer and got to his feet.

66

Emily Dinova

"Well, if you change your mind, just let Ruth know and she will give me a call, alright?"

J nodded and closed his eyes, looking ready to return to his previously petrified state. Dave threw down some extra money on the table and hurried out.

He emerged feeling both disorientated and confused, as if he just traveled down some odd rabbit hole. Hours must have passed since he'd gone into the bar, for any light the day possessed was now extinguished.

Dave could taste the fog on his tongue, feel it pressing against every inch of his exposed skin. Knowing that the house would still be empty, he decided to head across town to Repo Pizza, hoping to get himself a slice and pass a few hours away hanging out with Robb in the back.

But before he could even put his car in drive, he felt a thrill of dread race down his spine. A split second later, his cellphone rang. It was Harmony and she was crying and gasping for air like she did every time she had a panic attack. With a sigh and a longing look back in the direction of the bar, Dave instead drove to his parents, and spent several hours holding his twin in his arms until she finally gave way to sleep.

Sunday, October 8th

THE ANTAGONIST

I

It was safe to say Dave did not enjoy Mass the next morning. Although he only had one drink at The Devil's Eye he awoke bleary-eyed and with a slight headache, which only seemed to get progressively worse as the bright morning light shot through the stained glass windows of the packed church, blinding him with furious righteousness. The smell of flowers was also getting to him—the place was so stuffy, so stagnant, he could feel himself nodding off once or twice. But each time, Dave was jolted back into reality by a sharp pinch in his thigh and a withering look of disappointment from his mother.

June lectured him throughout breakfast and the entire ride back to their house.

"Davey, if you aren't feeling well you really shouldn't have come to church. Mommy wouldn't have been mad at you," she cooed before her voice became brisk and emotional. "But falling asleep while the Lord is watching, such blatant disrespect. Can you imagine what our brothers and sisters must all think of us?"

Dave wanted to say he really didn't care one hoot what anyone thought of him, but he knew it would only incite further recrimination. His head was pounding by the time he said goodbye to them.

He sent a quick text and then pulled out of the driveway, heading west towards the less affluent side of town.

THE ANTAGONIST

2

Robb opened his apartment door in a bathrobe and one slipper. Hickeys littered his neck and he smelled like a liquor-soaked brothel.

Dave raised his eyebrows as he took his in his friend's disheveled appearance. Robb grinned in response.

"Had yourself a night, did you?" Dave asked as he cautiously picked his way through discarded lingerie scattered across the living room floor.

"Oh man, I wish I could remember it all!" Robb sighed as he dropped down onto the futon and resumed smoking the lit joint he'd been enjoying before Dave's intrusion. He offered a hit to Dave like he always did, and Dave declined like he always did.

"Just making sure man, you never know!"

"Actually, if you have any Advil that would be perfect."

"Always brother, always. When you live a lifestyle like mine, you gotta stay stocked!" he jumped up with the agility of someone much younger than himself.

Dave listened as he rustled around in the small kitchen, thinking about the fact that Robb and Georgette shared many similar habits. Starting with their inability to pick up after themselves. The thought made Dave smile and then frown, those strange old man's words returning to him: *When you're done fixing everyone else's problems, is there anyone there to fix yours?*

Dave was still frowning when Robb returned with a glass of water and some pills.

THE ANTAGONIST

"These are Advil, right?" Dave asked knowing Robb liked to mix and match all sorts of drugs back in the day. "They aren't going to make me hallucinate or fall into a coma?"

Robb chuckled, "Man come on! I rarely do that shit anymore. Have a little faith!"

Dave smirked, popping the pills and taking a long drink of water.

"What'd you get into last night, bro?" Robb asked, his eyes brimming with curiosity. "I haven't seen you like this since we were 25."

"Nothing at all, actually. I think I'm getting sick maybe."

Robb shook his head. "You work too much, man."

"So everyone seems to be telling me," Dave said more to himself. Thinking again of J. *Overworked.*

"Everyone?" Robb inquired, a keen interest rising in his eyes.

Dave shrugged, "That's an exaggeration."

"You need to blow off some steam. A release. Why don't you two take a vacation or something? It's not like you can't afford it."

Dave detected the slightest hint of jealousy in Robb's tone, though he knew it was not malicious. "It's not that, we've just got too much going on at the moment. We will though, once Samantha is out of the house and Harmony is more settled."

"Man, I know you like to stay optimistic, but you have to consider that those things might not happen. Ever."

"Why do you say that?"

Robb shrugged, taking another deep drag. Dave stared as the red ember burned brightly in his direction. "Life. Things change. One day it's this way, the next day it's something else. You know?"

Dave nodded. Having grown up in a somewhat unstable environment with lots of change and very little structure, Dave thrived on his scheduled and detail-oriented life. He had no desire to return to the unpredictability of the past.

Emily Dinova

A sudden thought presented itself at the forefront of Dave's mind.

"Hey, I forgot to ask you," he began, looking at Robb for signs of foolery. "Were you working on Friday night?"

Robb's wrinkle-free skin creased in deep thought. "Yeah, but only until about 7:30… A few people called for the ad you told me to put out. I got a new pizza maker!" He gave a big thumbs-up.

"That's great, I'm happy to hear."

"Yeah. I think it's gonna work out. It's only part-time anyway so it's kinda perfect," he trailed off. "But why do you ask?"

"Georgie put in our order on Friday night, I got stuck at work late," Dave began.

"Was there something wrong with it?"

He hesitated, "No, she probably just made a mistake. Or was it you, pulling a prank?"

"A prank? What kind of prank?" A mischievous grin grew on Robb's face as he rubbed his hands together in anticipation of a good story.

"Everyone's orders were right except mine. My pizza had black olives on it."

Robb stared at him eagerly. When Dave didn't continue, his face fell in confusion. "Black olives? That's the prank?"

"Robb, you know I hate black olives. I can't stand the taste of them."

"I didn't know that!" Robb exclaimed.

"Yes, you did!" Dave insisted, hearing a bit of desperation in his tone. "Come on, Harmony said the same thing to me!"

Robb looked at him very seriously, with a hint of worry resting deep in his eyes, "Dave, man, I swear. I did not know you hated olives."

"Black olives, specifically."

"Gotta be a coincidence. I have a few new waiters running the orders. One of them could have easily mixed it up. It was packed as hell when I left—"

THE ANTAGONIST

"Yeah, no, of course," Dave conceded, not understanding why he was being so adamant about this whole thing.

"Or like you said, Georgie—"

"Yeah, yeah. I know."

Robb continued to watch his friend through the haze of smoke. Dave had the distinct impression that Robb was picking up on his energy, yet not able to place the source. Much like Dave himself. The silence made him feel antsy, he felt stupid now for even mentioning the damn olives. He forced his thoughts down as he smiled reassuringly at his best friend, knowing the one way he could get Robb's mind off of his slightly strange behavior.

"Got any new video games?"

3

After a quick trip to the grocery store, Dave returned home to prepare a scrumptious Sunday dinner: pot roast, garlic mashed potatoes and a variety of roasted vegetables, all covered in his homemade gravy. He hoped the animosity from Friday night's dinner had been washed away with the seemingly neverending rain that persisted since.

Dave's headache dwindled to a small twinge as he finished his preparations. By the time dusk had fallen, he was feeling much more relaxed. The enjoyment of cooking a meal allowed him to rationalize all of the small, though illogical, hiccups that seemed to mark the last few days. Dave had to consider that he was blowing things out of proportion, that he might very well be overworked and that some small part of his brain was beginning to fray around the edges. He was worn down. Maybe Robb was right—he and Georgie should try to get away, even if it was for just a few days. He would mention the possibility of it to her tonight. He had more than enough vacation days saved up at work. It might be the perfect time.

Dave's improved mood was short-lived. He entered the dining room twenty minutes later to find his family unusually subdued. Dave felt a jolt of guilt, seeing as he was the one responsible for bringing them all together. But Dave was capable. He could right this. Mustering all of the mental patience he possessed, he went about serving dinner as if absolutely nothing was wrong. Slowly but surely, he was able to pull them each from their cocoons of loathing. The food helped. No one in his family ever wanted to talk if they were hungry.

Soon conversation began to flow normally and Dave felt proud, but a little drained. Maybe he always felt this way, he just never stopped to consider what it might mean. By giving away his energy, their moods improved while his continued to fall.

"So guess what everyone?" Samantha interrupted, practically jumping out of her chair.

Dave raised his eyebrows. Surely she wasn't about to spill her secret boyfriend news to the whole family.

"What is it, darling?" Georgette asked with interest.

"I passed my permit test! I start Driver's Ed this week!"

Georgette screamed with glee, causing June to cover her ears and scowl.

August's eyes were glued to Georgie's breasts as she jumped up and down in her seat, kissing her daughter.

"We're so proud of you!! So exciting!" Georgette beamed.

"When I get my license, I'm going to take Dave's car," Samantha informed them, sneaking a glance down the table at him.

"You are?" Dave questioned.

She smirked. "Yep."

"I also happen to have some exciting news," June added, making a show of dramatically rubbing her ears.

Harmony huffed in irritation, probably from already hearing this news on the short drive over.

"The church is hosting a new members party next Sunday, a week from today to be exact. And I was hoping, praying even, that the entire family would agree to attend."

"Will there be alcohol?" Sam questioned.

June stiffened, repressing the need to reproach, "What do you think, Samantha?"

"Blood of Christ and all that?" Samantha trilled with rising excitement at the expectation of an argument. But before June could reply, Dave cut across them.

"Georgie works every Sunday, and Sam—"

"Is old enough to make her own decisions," his stepdaughter snapped back.

"Yes," Dave agreed, "What Harmony wants to do is up to her—"

"I have therapy," Harmony interjected with a tone of finality.

"You always have Him. You just chose to ignore Him when He's right there in front of you," June lectured back.

Harmony slammed her fork and knife against the table, "Church is not therapy!"

"It is for those of us who believe," June patronized.

"Mother, please. Can we not do this right now?" Dave clipped out. "Really. Can you just let her be?"

The table went silent. Dave rarely got heated with his mother, but the expression of pain on his sister's face was greatly upsetting.

"Now," Georgie continued, as if nothing transpired, "You were saying, Harmony, you're attending therapy on Sundays?"

"Well, my in-person appointments are Saturdays but on Sundays we do a call. I always feel the most vulnerable after a session so she likes to check in on me."

"Your therapist sounds like she's on top of things."

"She's such a great listener. I never feel judged by her," she tossed an insolent glare towards her parents. "She's teaching me a new method to control panic attacks."

"Is it working?" Dave asked, knowing how exhausting her fits could be. But even after last night's episode, Harmony recovered much quicker than the norm. She usually became catatonic after a panic attack, the effects sometimes lingered for days. That didn't seem to be the case this evening.

"They don't last for as long now, they aren't as…intense," she smiled at Dave, thanking him with his eyes for sitting up with her half the night.

Georgie reached over and grabbed Dave's hand, caressing it lovingly. She knew Dave spent endless hours of his life attempting to put his sister back together. Perhaps she was finally helping herself. "That's wonderful news, darling. Truly."

"And you, Georgie," August suddenly piped up, still fixating his somewhat lecherous stare on her breasts. "What's happening in your world?"

His wife was used to his father and knew how to play him like a fiddle. In the beginning Dave had been mortified at his father's behavior towards his wife. But Georgie took it all in stride. In recent years she even encouraged it. When Dave questioned her motives, she explained that it seemed to be one of the only ways she could enrage June. And Georgie believed that a little rage was good for the psyche. To remain in a constant state of passive-aggressive oppression was unacceptable in her eyes.

"I actually have a bit of news myself!" Georgie replied with a wink at August. Dave chanced a glance at his mother who was clenching and unclenching her fists rather violently.

Dave turned his full attention to his glorious wife. Anytime she spoke, the whole room lit up.

"I have officially committed to my first ever tennis lesson!"

Samantha shrieked with joy, just as her mother had done for her. The two were once again hugging and kissing each other. Dave smiled—they were two peas in a crazy pod.

"I knew you could do it, Mom!"

"Thanks, honey," Georgie was breathless with excitement. "To be honest, I was about to give the whole thing up, I just couldn't seem to pluck up the courage."

Harmony leaned forward, listening eagerly for a solution to such a dilemma. "How did you do it?"

Georgie smiled mysteriously. "I got a little push from a friendly stranger."

This did not surprise Dave in the slightest. His wife made friends with just about everyone. If someone was within a five-foot radius of her, it was most likely she would know their entire backstory within the first 15 minutes of conversation. People loved to open up to her, she was compassionate and empathetic. It was one of the things that made Dave so proud to be with her.

"Ew mom, stop talking to random creeps," Sam frowned at her mother as if she were a small child in need of teaching a basic lesson to. "Some rapist will abduct you one of these days and we will never see you again. Right, Dave? I mean you aren't going to go save her, are you?"

"I would go to the ends of the Earth for your mother, Sam."

Georgette bestowed him with a generously extended kiss as his mother humph-ed in disapproval and Sam made a face.

"Gross."

For once the two were in agreement.

Monday—Thursday,
October 9th—12th

THE ANTAGONIST

I

Dave awoke Monday morning with a clear head. It was as if the weekend dissipated into nothing more than a bad dream. Physically, he felt great, better than usual. When he glanced to the bedside table, he realized why. He'd slept almost twelve hours. If he got up now, he might even have time for a quick run before heading into work. The tension that his body had been seemingly riddled with disappeared as well. He felt, once again, perfectly normal.

The house was in chaos for most of the week, but that was completely fine with Dave. He felt protected, as if a bubble of calm enveloped him and everything that was happening around him could not get close. He could see them, hear them—even engage with his loved ones, yet he did not feel affected in the same way. He was preserving his energy, allowing himself to slip into a sort of defense mechanism. Dave figured that the family could run without him just fine—this was just an experiment to see if he was as overworked as others said. No one seemed to notice the lack of opinion or advice he normally gave out so freely. Everyone continued on just the same. Dave felt slightly perplexed, perhaps he wasn't as important to his relatives as he'd originally conceived.

Work was the same as always, though Desiree did not attempt to engage him again, which he was eternally grateful for. Dave allowed the outside world to fall away and continued to stay focused on each task.

The major alteration of his schedule was that he now found himself with a nightly drinking partner. Each and every evening when he stopped at The Devil's Eye, he now found his normally empty table occupied by J. Dave was surprised but not shocked to see the man returned. With Shawn and Mara gone, apparently Ruth was unconcerned with her semi-permanent guest.

And each night, Dave now had two drinks, instead of one. It wasn't so much about the need to imbibe, as it was to have extra time for his thoughts. Thoughts he'd begun to voice out loud to his odd companion. J was full of anecdotes; he had one for every situation. He was like a perpetual and endless book full of fables. Lessons in morality, that seemed to be what he liked most—other than asking Dave a wandering stream of questions that truly made him think. It was so rare that anyone ever inquired about his wishes or fears. Or truly wanted to understand the things that he felt. Maybe because this person was an outsider, Dave felt more comfortable opening up about his life.

"How does it feel," J asked him casually over his whiskey on Thursday night, "to think about yourself for once?"

Dave mulled the question over. "Freeing…but it's also isolating, in a way."

J nodded with comprehension, "You free yourself from your family, but once you do…what are you left with?"

"Myself."

Friday, October 13th

THE ANTAGONIST

I

His bubble burst shortly after breakfast that morning. Dave was just flipping the omelet he made for himself when Georgie came bounding into the kitchen, a big smile on her face.

"Good Morning, my love!" she danced around the counter island, making her own drink. She'd not questioned why he stopped bringing her Bloody Mary to her on schedule every morning. But that was Georgie, she just seemed to adapt to any situation.

Samantha was already up and sipping her coffee, which she added her own sugar to when Dave hadn't. Not even accompanied by one little snarky comment.

Dave marveled at their ability to go with the flow. He felt almost the tiniest pinch of envy over their nonchalant demeanors.

"Great news, we are getting a huge donation to the shelter from an anonymous benefactor. Think of the resources we are going to be able to obtain for these women and children."

"That's excellent, Mom!"

Dave nodded in agreement. "Fantastic!"

Georgie beamed before kissing them both and floating with her drink to the hallway. "I have to shower, can't be late for this board meeting!" She popped her head back in quickly, "Oh, and Dave, darling?"

Dave looked to his grinning wife. "All those little love notes you've been leaving me are too cute! Don't think they go unnoticed. I've been finding them everywhere, you scoundrel!" She blew one last kiss and disappeared up the stairs.

"You've been writing her love notes? What are you, thirteen?" Sam jeered at him.

Dave stood rooted in place, frozen.

Love notes? Dave had never written a love note a day in his life. It was simply not in his nature—didn't his wife realize that? If Dave had something to say, he spoke it directly. And he certainly didn't go around hiding things. How odd. He raised his eyebrows at Samantha with a heavy dose of skepticism.

"Are you messing with me Sam?"

"No more than usual," was her reply.

2

They were just turning onto the main road when Samantha opened her book bag and pulled out a stack of burned CDs.

Dave did a double take as she went sorting through them, looking for something specific.

"A little old school, no?" Dave asked, as he glanced at the handwritten covers.

"Yeah, you are," she agreed before popping one out and shoving it into his car's CD player.

Dave recognized the track immediately. It was Nirvana, *About A Girl*. Dave hadn't heard this song in at least twenty years.

"Where did you get those?" he asked Sam after a few moments.

She turned the volume up louder, "A friend."

Dave nodded. The boyfriend perhaps? He wasn't about to ask. It wasn't any of his business and he was sure she wouldn't tell him the truth anyway.

"You know soon you won't have to drive me anymore. Won't that be great?"

"I like our mornings together."

"Yeah, right."

"I do, Sam, really."

She rolled her eyes and increased the volume even more. As Dave listened to the lyrics, his chest began to tighten. He took a few discreet, deep breaths—feeling the sudden pounding of his heart come to life.

"I wish someone would write about me. Isn't that romantic?" she asked him as the song finished.

Dave nodded, not really listening. He was trying too hard to control the overwhelming wave of panic that was battering him without mercy.

They both reached for the dial at the same time, their fingers brushing. Sam jumped back. She hated to be touched by anyone other than her mother. Dave was expecting her to freak out but instead she turned and looked at him. "Your fingers are like ice," she frowned, "and they're shaking."

"Can you please turn it off, Sam?"

"I thought you liked this kind of music?"

"I do. I just need a minute. Now. Please." Something in his tone must have alerted her to the climbing levels of his uneasiness. She shut it off after only a moment of hesitation.

"Do you need me to drive?" she asked suddenly, "You aren't going to pass out and crash us into a tree, right?"

"No. I'm fine," Dave assured her, feeling a drop of sweat slide down his back. "Just a little lightheaded, that's all."

"You killed those chickens for nothing," she muttered with mutiny in her voice, referring to breakfast. Dave had lost his appetite only minutes after he finished cooking the omelet and shoved it into the refrigerator for later.

In that moment, he tried to focus on the road and nothing else as they drove in complete silence with only Samantha's occasional huff and anxious stare in his direction. It was with immense relief that they pulled up in front of the school just minutes later. Sam moved to get out but Dave stopped her.

"Don't you want your CD?"

She shrugged, looking back at him. "You hold onto it. I have all these," she lifted up her bag to show him. "Get better." And then she was gone.

Dave sat in the car not moving for twenty minutes, just breathing and allowing his heart to return to normal. He never had anxiety attacks—those were reserved for the rest of the family. It was his empty stomach, his sugar was probably too low and the beat of the music pushed his adrenaline into full force. With a shaky but deep breath, Dave pulled out and headed for the firm.

3

Dave stopped dead upon reaching his desk that morning. Sitting in his chair was none other than Desiree DeLongo, and she was smirking larger than ever.

"Ten minutes late, David. What could have possibly held you up?" she asked in a low melodious tone.

"Dave is fine," he corrected her as he shrugged off his jacket and looked at her expectantly.

"Dave just sounds so…intimate to me."

"It's what everyone calls me. Can you kindly move so that I might begin my day?" he asked, his normal patience wearing thin.

Desiree ran her hands over the desk, caressing the wood in a suggestive way. "Well then I suppose I'll have to stick with David. I'm not like everyone else. I stand out," she mocked as she got to her feet and made sure to brush her curves up against Dave as she moved out from behind the desk.

Dave bit the inside of his mouth to keep from pushing her away from him and quickly took his chair. She bent down and lifted a medium sized cardboard box into her hands, sliding it across to him.

"This came for you this morning. I made sure it got to your desk, unscathed."

"Thank you."

"I figure, a favor for a favor."

"And what is it I can do for you, Miss DeLongo?"

"Desiree is just fine, or Desi if you prefer. What's in the box?"

THE ANTAGONIST

Dave ordered extra office supplies last week. He was surprised at how quickly they came. Desiree waited with a hint of impatience, shifting her hips from side to side as Dave opened what he assumed would be extra staples, paper clips and letterheads.

He paused in confusion as he pried open the box to find at least a hundred, sparkling butterfly clips—they were absolutely covered in glitter. Dave stared down at them for a moment then chuckled, handing the package back over to Desiree who looked quickly inside with interest.

"Butterfly clips? I used to wear these when I was in high school!" she smirked as she pulled one out of the box and held it up to her long dark hair. "What do you think David? Do you want me now?"

Dave slapped the top of the box, startling her as he looked down at the address label. It was made out to him, in black sharpie. His eyes shifted upward—no return address.

"I didn't order these," he said to no one in particular.

"Your name is on them," she pushed, "Surely someone thought you should have some accessories." Desiree dropped the box back onto his desk.

"Keep them," he offered.

"I don't want *them*, David," she implied sweetly, turning her sexual prowess up a notch.

"Fine," Dave roughly handled the box, dropping it beneath his desk with a loud thwack. He'd bring them home and give them to Sam or Harmony.

"Now getting back to that favor…" Desiree trailed off, eyeing him with growing interest.

Dave folded his arms and sat back in his chair, finally giving her his full attention. If that's what it took to make her disappear, Dave was willing to try anything. His reaction pleased her very much, he could tell.

"I'm new to town, I was hoping you'd consider showing me around. So far I've spent most of my time at the gym."

Dave continued to stare at her, not giving an inch. She wasn't deterred. She continued to flaunt her lovely figure as she leaned over and picked up his cellphone. He watched as she very clearly entered her number into it and hit save. "Maybe a nice dinner, somewhere cozy, romantic… and discreet?" she lowered her voice on the last word and rose an eyebrow, attempting to communicate that if Dave was worried about exposure, she would be more than willing to keep things under wraps. She slid the phone back across the desk towards him, a challenge in her gaze.

Dave watched her for a few more moments before heaving a sigh—this poor girl. What had happened to her in her life that was causing her to throw herself at him in this way? She was easily twenty years younger than Dave. Was it because he was unavailable? Was that the draw?

"Look," he began, with compassion and understanding rising inside of him. "You are a very beautiful woman, and any man would be lucky to be with you. I'm just…not like that. I love my wife, the last thing I want to do is hurt her in any way." He paused, uncomfortable with the emboldened look that entered her eyes. "I hope you understand," he finished apologetically.

She nodded once and turned on her heel, disappearing into her office. Dave considered that to be a win on paper… but if so, then why did he feel as if he'd only made her desire to conquer him even greater?

Dave almost hit delete on the newly saved contact, but decided against it at the last moment. If Desiree somehow got a hold of his private number, he wanted to know exactly who was messaging him. He felt a weary stabbing sensation that suggested that shortly after this woman's appearance in his life, things had become odd. He would keep an eye on her, just in case.

THE ANTAGONIST

4

The bar of The Devil's Eye was packed that evening, and smokier than usual. A few patrons nodded at Dave as he passed to his regular table. There was a new bartender working but they seemed to be lost amongst the dim lights and opaque haze.

Ruth was running around like a mad woman and barely had time to slam drinks down with a quick greeting, before scurrying off to catch up with the next order. J was already there waiting for him, which was an immediate comfort to Dave. He wanted to vent. He wanted to talk about all the BS of the day, and he wanted his new acquaintance to assure him he'd done the right thing, especially in regards to how he handled Desiree.

Dave ordered their second round just after he finished explaining to J who Desiree was and the odd little occurrences since her arrival.

"It's suspicious," J agreed as he took a deep sip of his regular whiskey. He scratched his scraggly beard. A tick that Dave noticed the man did when he was in particularly deep thought. "So you think she might be stalking you?"

Dave shook his head, taking an equally large sip of his Peroni. "I have absolutely no idea if that's the case, but she insinuates that she knows more than she lets on. She's always smirking, it drives me nuts."

"Because you want her?"

Dave looked at the man with revulsion. "Haven't you been listening? I want nothing to do with her. She's toxic."

THE ANTAGONIST

"You aren't the smallest bit interested in knowing what it might feel like to be inside of her?" J whispered, leaning forward with a knowing look in his eye.

Dave sat back, "I'm not."

"Well if you've given her no ideas about fucking, then you got a bigger problem than I think you're aware of, kid."

"Meaning?"

"Meaning," J emphasized, "she's not interested in you. She's only interested in conquering you. Possessing you."

"I know that."

"So what are you gonna do about it?"

"I was thinking you could tell me?" Dave hedged with a hopeful look in his eye.

J laughed in response. "All I can tell you—is that the more you ignore a woman like that, the harder she'll push back. It's a slight, you see? You're taking shots at her pride, rejecting her only fuels her need to break you."

Dave rubbed his face with agitation before letting out a great sigh. He looked down at his drink. It was empty again.

"I knew a girl like that once…"J trailed off, a far away look coming into his eyes.

Dave ordered a third round.

5

Everyone was waiting for him when he came into the kitchen an hour later with the box of butterfly clips under his arm.

"Where have you been?" Sam asked with the bite of accusation in her tone.

Dave chanced a glance at his parents, who were looking equally interested in an answer. Georgie and Harmony, however, were standing over a messy blender that looked as if it were covered in frozen margarita.

"Dave!" his wife exclaimed, a high blush rising across her chest and up her cheeks. Dave knew that look. Only copious amount of tequila could make Georgie saunter towards him the way she was doing now. She dropped herself into a low bend once she reached his arms, like a professional salsa dancer, before bringing her face up to his. She smelled of limes and sugar. "Darling, is the pizza almost here? I think if I have another before then, I'm toast!"

Dave smiled patiently, feeling some usefulness come back to him. Maybe his family did need him, at least Georgie.

"You didn't order?" he questioned as Sam brought her mother a glass of water.

Georgie shook her head, "I didn't hear from you, so I thought you must have taken care of it," her mood shifted suddenly, tears forming in her eyes, "I didn't want to mess it up again," she admittedly pitifully.

Dave felt his heart ache. "My love, you didn't mess anything up. You never do. You're perfect," he insisted, caressing her face.

Sam nodded along, agreeing with Dave. She only did this when the two of them would have to pull Georgie out of an occasional bout of depression. These lows coincided with drinking too much. It was as if she would revert back to the days of her abusive marriage—apologizing for everything and taking the blame for minor inconveniences that were not her fault. It was then that Dave and Samantha would band together, for the greater good.

"I am?" Georgie asked.

"Positive."

She was once again beaming. Dave left her in Samantha's capable care and headed back across the kitchen to the phone. He deposited the box of clips in front of Harmony.

"Here, sis," he offered, watching her face light up with glee as she tore open the box with exuberance.

"Oh wow! Where did you get these? I haven't seen them in years...not that I was ever allowed to wear them," she sounded so much like the embittered child he remembered from their youth.

"They're all yours," Dave forced a smile as she began placing them in her hair. He felt immense relief to be getting the glittery nuisances off his hands. He hadn't even realized how heavy they felt on top of his arms until he deposited them. He watched Harmony for a few moments as she threaded the clips through her thin hair—they twinkled in his direction, flirtatiously fluttering.

On his right, he heard his mother mutter something about Georgie's obvious downfall with addiction. He ignored it, thinking it was rich seeing as June the 'Jesus Junkie' basically shot religion into her veins on an hourly basis. Dave dialed the number for Repo Pizza.

He carefully put in their order. The teenager on the other end of the line sounded slightly stoned so Dave had him repeat the order back twice—also considering how complicated his family was. Once he was satisfied that everything was correct, he hung up. He left his family to their devices and went to take a much- needed shower before dinner.

Forty minutes later, the doorbell rang and Dave made sure he was the one to get it. A lanky teen girl with a buzz cut and at least twenty piercings was standing there impatiently smacking her gum. She handed the pizza over without a hello.

"60 bucks."

Dave smiled and gave her a nice tip. Her expression didn't change as she pocketed the money, put her headphones back in and went back to her car. Dave watched her pull out, feeling the hot and heavy weight of the pizza on his hands.

Robb must have not been working considering none of the pizzas were labeled, which was fine—no one order was ever the same anyway, except for his.

Dave's family surrounded him the minute he reentered the kitchen. They converged around the pizza, each complaining in their own way about how extraordinarily starving they were.

This caused Dave a sudden jolt of irritation. As if he were the only person capable of ordering pizza. Instead of appreciating the fact that Dave always did this simple task so they never had to even think about it, they instead chose to complain, as if it were his fault they weren't fed on time. Could none of them pick up the phone and dial? He sure knew they could tell, nay demand from people, what they wanted with no problem whatsoever.

His little experiment wasn't turning out how he'd seen it going.

Dave retreated to his own corner, trying to enjoy the moans of delight circulating around the kitchen as everyone dug in. He watched Georgie, eyes closed, as she devoured her pizza like a drunken college student. He conceded with a smile at their sudden silence. Dave pushed his slightly injured feelings away and opened his own pizza box.

The sight that met him had his stomach plummeting through the ground, his heart ricocheting up into this throat and causing him a temporary moment of lost breath. His short gasp halted the muted conversation in his peripheral, bringing all eyes to rest on him. A slight spell of dizziness grabbed him before he forced himself back into the present. There was a moment of silence and then,

"Well?" Samantha demanded in an annoyed tone. "What is it now, Dave?"

Dave couldn't answer. He was too fixated on the message below.

His pizza was covered in black olives. Not even placed as if they were cooked with the actual pizza. No, it looked as if a literal can had been poured on top, juice and all. On the inside of the box was a word, written in black sharpie just like the sticky note Dave found last week. The same sloppy smiley face accompanied the word: HI!

Dave started to laugh as he turned the pizza around to show them.

"You guys are hilarious, you know that?"

They continued to stare at him with varying looks of confusion.

"Alright. Who was it? Sam? Does one of your friends work at Repo Pizza now? Har? Or was this a joint effort?" he asked, pointedly looking at his wife.

"Dear," his mother finally answered, "what are you talking about?"

He stared at her in disbelief. "I told you all last Friday that I hate black olives, now this week, as you can see, someone's decided to keep the joke running."

"I didn't know you didn't like olives," August began.

Dave felt the urge to suddenly scream. He snapped the pizza box closed instead and turned to look at his wife.

"Come on, the jig is up. I recognize the smiley face. You drew the same one on the sticky note you left on the refrigerator last week."

Georgie frowned at him. Even through her tipsy gaze he could see she had no idea what he was talking about.

"Since when don't you like olives, Davey?" his mother questioned.

"Apparently forever," Harmony chimed in, "I still remember you eating olive pizza, Dave—"

He tossed the pizza box onto the counter and strode from the room, his cellphone in hand. He tried Robb, but it went straight to voicemail. Dave's irritation consumed him. He wasn't sure what was bothering him more, the fact that no one would fess up to their little trick, or that his own flesh and blood knew nothing about him. They were so selfish sometimes, how could they not know something so simple? One of the very few things he actually disliked? For God's sake he should at least be able to count on his twin! Dave knew he was being irrational, after all, it was just pizza—just a stupid prank.

He took several deep breaths, forcing himself to calm down. He could easily return to the kitchen and let it go, pull something from the freezer and heat it up. But his hunger was replaced by a much stronger and inexplicable feeling: fear. He trudged instead up the stairs to the cool quiet of his empty bedchamber. He thought briefly of Desiree, wondering if she was somehow involved. Those were Dave's last thoughts before slipping off the cliffs of oblivion and into the deep.

Saturday, October 14th

THE ANTAGONIST

I

For the first time in many, many years, Dave slept in. He ignored the ringing phone that was surely his mother calling to find out if he would be attending church. He pretended to sleep through Georgie kissing him goodbye before she left for the shelter. He thought he heard Samantha call for him at some point too, but the summons went unanswered.

It wasn't until well after noon that Dave heard a faint knocking on the bedroom door. Six short knuckle-raps—which could only be one person.

Dave opened an eye and lifted his head out from under the covers. Harmony was standing in the doorway, looking slightly timid and feeling her own intrusion. Though as soon as Dave beckoned her forward with a hand, she did not hesitate. She took a running start and leapt onto the bed, jostling Dave and bringing him fully awake as she slammed a pillow down on his head.

"Hell, Harmony!"

She shrieked with glee, beating him repeatedly until he finally grabbed her by the wrists, easily restraining her.

"What are you doing?" he asked, slightly breathless as he took her in.

"Playing," she smirked.

Dave shook his head in confusion. Harmony pulled away from his grasp with a huff before falling back onto Georgie's side of the bed.

"My therapist," she began with a slight air of superiority, "says that it's important to play."

"What's that supposed to mean?"

"Well, think about it. Children play all the time, and they are a hell of a lot happier than us."

Dave briefly pictured Robb in his one slipper with that shit-eating grin on his face. "I suppose," he commented, waiting for her to continue.

"Doctor H. says it's all about not losing that childlike part of yourself—the ability to just feel and enjoy something because you like it. The second you let go of that, part of you dies, she says, because regardless of what you do, other people will judge you. So do what makes you happy. I think that's what we do as adults, we worry too much about what other people think."

"I don't."

"Well Dave, I guess that makes you better than the rest of us."

He threw her an exasperated look as he got to his feet and went in search of a robe.

"Are you not feeling well?" she called after him.

"Fine," he responded, wondering what he was going to do with his day. More than anything, Dave just wanted to go back to sleep, but his sister was going to make that impossible.

"Are you sure? I mean, not to sound like a know-it-all, but I can tell when you aren't right." Dave took a deep breath as he looked in the bathroom mirror. "Remember, that whole twin thing?" her voice was too loud.

"Harmony, I promise you I'm fine," he insisted, gritting his teeth as he washed cool water over his face.

"Are you happy?" she pressed.

"Yes." He shrugged into his robe.

"Fulfilled?"

Dave returned to the bedroom, raking a comb through his messy hair.

"Mm-hm."

Harmony lifted herself up on her knees as she crawled to the edge of the bed to get a better look at him, "Anything you want to talk about? How are you feeling?"

"I appreciate your concern but I really don't want to be psychoanalyzed at the moment."

She became defensive almost immediately, sitting back on her heels and giving him a defiant glare, "That's not what I'm doing, you jerk! I just want to know what's up! I feel left out. Georgie is the only one who includes me in this family."

He turned to stare at her with disbelief. "How can you say that? I am there whenever you need me. I listen," he said as he tossed aside the robe in exchange for a shirt. Clearly he had to get out of the house if he was going to get away from her.

"You hear. You don't listen. There's a difference."

"That's not fair."

"Isn't it? You don't really listen to anyone, Dave. You just pretend."

Dave felt his temper surge like a tidal wave of molten lava. His sister's continually needy and thoroughly selfish spite was beginning to grate on his nerves.

"Then how is it I know every single food you dislike, and let's be clear there's quite a long list of them, and somehow you can't remember the ONE thing I don't eat!?"

Harmony gave him a blank stare as she watched his chest heave.

"Are we back to the black olives?" The look she shot him was one of absolute conviction. "Dave. I know you better than anyone. I am you."

"You are not *me,*" he spoke with such vehemence that Harmony's eyes bulged as if he were an intruder in his own home.

Dave tore from the room before he said anything else he might regret. He hadn't lost his temper with his sister in almost twenty years.

THE ANTAGONIST

2

As he sped through the streets, he absentmindedly noticed that the sun seemed to be shining for the first time all week. It gave Dave little comfort—the rays of light were weak as his constitution. He was jumpy. He hated feeling any sort of negative emotion rise into his personal space. But his sister, she just couldn't let up. Now that he began to pull away just the slightest bit, he realized how much patience and understanding he normally showed. Where had it gone? *But honestly,* he thought to himself, *how much chaos and nagging was a person supposed to take?*

He could deal with Harmony's issues, but for her to come at him like that. Suggest that they were one and the same, when she'd never taken care of a thing for him in his entire life—it was ludicrous, but also extremely painful.

Dave pushed the conversation from his mind. He always believed that the actions of others were not his to control. He could only control how he reacted to those actions. Yet now, in this moment, Dave had the insane sensation that some greater force was pulling at his strings.

∼

The firm was empty when Dave arrived. He made the decision, after driving around for a good half hour, that he should finish the rest of the work he'd not gotten to on Friday—thanks to Desiree's continuous distractions.

And as if the Devil was summoned, there she appeared in the flesh.

Dave had his own set of keys to the office—he was shocked to find Desiree was offered the same convenience. She hadn't spotted him yet, which was fine with Dave. She was on the phone and pacing the floor of her office in her customary designer heels—back and forth. He watched her for a few moments, hoping to catch a glimpse of the woman behind the façade; he was sure there was a heart somewhere deep inside.

He was just slipping into his desk as he caught the tail end of her conversation. "Yeah, Tuesday is perfect. Thanks, you're the best!"

She hung up the phone, a genuine smile lit up her face before her attention was directed towards the small cough Dave tried to hold in. Desiree swung around, her eyes alert and rapid as she scanned for a possible threat. Her gaze quickly found the disturbance—her face flushing with pleasurable surprise.

She dropped her phone onto her desk and made her away across the office towards him. Dave didn't even try to ignore her—seeing as they were the only two souls in the place. He thought back to J's advice and figured a different approach might garner more effective results.

Before she could open her mouth, Dave spoke up, "I didn't mean to interrupt your conversation. Was that your boyfriend?" he asked boldly.

She raised both eyebrows as she reached him, "No boyfriend, free as a bird," she practically purred.

"A date, then?" he pushed—using the same aggressive and intrusive manner she approached him with.

But Desiree was smart. She was already onto his little game. Dave hated that he had to play one at all.

"Why?" she asked as she slid her glorious body slowly around his desk until she was positioned behind him. She bent over slowly. "Are you jealous?" she hissed against his ear.

Dave closed his eyes as he focused his mind. "Just curious how you choose to spend your free time."

She paused. He waited.

"So now you're interested in me? Why is that?" he could hear the disdain seeping into her tone.

Dave shrugged, "Why not?"

She really didn't like the sound of that. She slapped her hand down on the desk directly in front of him. "Why not?" she repeated, clearly incredulous.

"I figured if you were going to make it so easy…"

Dave chanced a glance over his shoulder at her. She looked amused.

"Really, David? Do you honestly expect me to believe that?" she asked as she pulled him back into his chair, her body slinking around him like a boa constrictor. She came around to rest right on the edge of his desk, so that her legs were trapping his between her own. "What is it? Are you afraid of me?" she taunted, reaching her long crimson claws out to pop open the first few buttons on his shirt. "Do you not know how to…handle me? Someone so young and beautiful…"

Dave could feel his heart rate increasing. The anxiety of being trapped and the guilt that would follow raced across his mind—he could not allow this succubus to consume him. He tried to pull away but she increased the pressure of her legs against him.

Dave felt himself wince. Desiree's smile grew once again. "You underestimate me, David. I work out 6 days a week, I have a personal trainer for 3 of those days…my thighs are steel. You can't get away," she leaned closer, pulling herself directly onto his lap as her mouth breathed against his, "And part of me thinks that you really don't want to." She ground her hips against his, her skirt sliding up her thighs, exposing her garters as she traced Dave's hands over her silky skin. Dave resisted the urge to pull away before he had his answer.

"Did you send the olive pizza?" he asked quietly, letting her believe she was about to make a victorious kill.

Desiree continued to rub against him, sensing she was close to breaking him with her sexual power. "Is that some kind of coded message?" she breathed as she grabbed Dave's hand and shoved it between her legs, moaning at the contact.

Dave gasped in shock—her bare and very wet flesh against his fingers jolted him back into reality as he forced her to break her hold on him. He pushed her off his lap as he stumbled back, staggering to his feet and breathing roughly.

He felt numb, incapable of speech. But his body did not react to her—it was, in fact, the opposite. He felt dirty, used—as if he'd never feel aroused again.

She held herself against the desk, watching him with the first sign of vulnerability he'd seen from her usually devious gaze. Dave ran a hand over his face, the one she hadn't assaulted.

"Is this proof enough?" he whispered, gesturing to his lack of erection through his thin pants, feeling sick and incredibly crude in the process. "Do you get it now? I. Don't. Want. You."

She was furious, he saw her switch flip. The confirmation of all her insecurities thrown back in her face—the darkness that entered her eyes foretold of ominous retribution.

"Fuck you, David," she seethed with venom. "Let your wife keep your limp dick anyway."

Dave was finally seeing her truth. It allowed him a small sliver of empathy. "Desiree, I'm sorry—"

This only seemed to enrage her further. "Why is it that every time someone fucks up, they always say I'm sorry? Like it means anything? It means nothing," she spat as she fled on her heels, back into her office with a slam of the door.

Dave dropped his head against his chest, at least he was sure of one thing: Desiree did not have a hand in the recent pranks. How could she? He thought. She knew absolutely nothing about him and probably cared even less. She just wanted her way—she wasn't about to interfere in his personal life just because he turned her down. She'd find a new victim soon anyway, after she stopped pouting like a child.

Dave packed up quickly and left the office, still trying to figure out why he apologized to her—all he'd done was turn her tricks back around, but only because Desiree DeLongo literally backed him into a corner and he refused to feel threatened.

Sunday, October 15th

THE ANTAGONIST

I

All of Robb's messages went unanswered. Dave promised his best friend they would spend Sunday together but he didn't even have the energy to get out of bed and answer his phone. Georgette checked on him around 11 a.m. with a steaming cup of coffee. He gratefully accepted it, assured her he was fine and watched as she left the room, no doubt to return to her office and copious amounts of paperwork. Dave wasn't sure how she managed to get through it all so efficiently and quickly.

After a few sips of the decadently strong brew, he began to feel much more like himself. He sent a quick text to Robb, regrettably informing him he had to cancel. He then turned his phone off and went to look for something to properly preoccupy his mind.

Dave spent the entire afternoon scrubbing away like a madman. He was always thorough but today it felt as if he were possessed. His work was meticulous as he dusted each bannister, made sure to trim every single flowerbed and even waxed all of the floors until they were gleaming with radiance.

The sun was just finishing its descent behind the horizon when Georgette interrupted his agitated stress-cleaning. Dave had retired all the way to the fifth floor to polish his grandmother's silver and was just breaking out the dinner forks when she appeared at the top of the steps.

"Dave?" she asked hesitantly.

His back was to her but he could hear the profound worry in her tone.

"Georgie," he answered quietly, "What is it, love?"

THE ANTAGONIST

"I wanted to make sure you were alright." She paused. "Are you?"

He nodded, getting to his feet and turning to face her. To be honest, Dave wasn't alright—he was filled with shame, horrified by how he handled yesterday's unfortunate run-in with Desiree and the situation that followed.

He was dreading tomorrow morning when he would have to face her wrath once again.

"Everyone is downstairs," Georgie continued, taking a few steps forward. "I know you've been busy so I attempted to cook. On second thought, you might want to skip dinner altogether."

Dave chuckled. Georgie was remarkable at many things, but cooking was not one of them. She appreciated quality food, just lacked the focus and patience to make it.

"I'm sure it will be wonderful, dear," he reassured her as he left the silverware in the box, deciding he could conquer it another time.

∼

They'd just sat down to some unknown concoction of ingredients when the doorbell rang. Dave was beginning to dread that noise—they were not expecting anyone. His mind briefly flashed to Desiree as Sam jumped up from the table without an explanation and headed towards the front of the house.

Georgette looked at him questioningly. Dave shrugged. Samantha never had visitors. Dave could only guess they were about to meet the mystery boyfriend. Judging by the perplexed look on his wife's face, Dave could see that Samantha had still not confided in her.

"This looks…interesting," June commented as she stuck her fork in Georgette's casserole, dissecting it like the fetal pig Dave remembered from middle school science class. His stomach rolled.

August was already eating and Harmony was silent, just staring at Dave with a faraway look in her eyes.

Dave ignored them all, his concentration centered on the footsteps and muted voices that were coming closer by the second.

"Hello," a deep and mellow voice intruded a few moments later.

All heads snapped to the archway of the dining room.

"This is Alex," Sam stated, her eyes on the man beside her as she held his hand, "My boyfriend."

Georgette paused, taking it all in. She blinked a few times as if in a stupor before remembering her manners and jumping to her feet.

"Alex! Hello!" Georgie rushed forward to embrace him as the rest of the family sat in shock. "Welcome," she murmured warmly, gesturing him forward.

Alex took the empty seat next to Sam's and smiled around at everyone in anticipation.

Dave was not impressed. In fact, he was mind blown. Alex had to be in his mid, possibly late 20s. He was absolutely covered in tattoos and his hair was almost as long as Sam's. What the hell was he doing dating a 16-year-old? June and August seemed to be following the same logic as Dave, guessing by their expressions. Harmony, however, looked envious—Dave supposed the man was handsome in his own way.

"Thank you for having me," Alex flashed a set of perfectly white teeth at Georgie, who seemed to be just as taken with the newcomer as her daughter.

"I wish I knew you were coming! I certainly wouldn't have attempted to cook if I'd known that was the case! My husband is the expert chef in this home," she explained, turning a winning smile towards Dave. Her face seemed to fall a little as she realized he was not experiencing the same pleasure as she.

"What do you do for a living, Alex?" Dave asked suddenly, earning him a nasty glare from Samantha. He could not care less. He was experiencing a new sensation. He was feeling…protective. For the first time, he considered his stepdaughter's business to now be his.

"I'm an artist," he replied. Dave stared at him. "I draw."

June let out a snort of derision.

"That's lovely," Georgie replied.

"And if you don't mind me asking," Dave knew this was going to cost him later, but he was too concerned to care. "How old are you?"

June smiled to herself as she watched Georgie's mouth turn slightly downwards. Samantha shook with the beginnings of rage.

"I don't see why that matters," she interjected with a sneer.

"This whole family is going to hell. Didn't I say so?" June casually tossed the comment to her husband who agreed through a mouthful of casserole.

"It's fine, Sam," Alex reassured her as he turned more fully to face Dave. "I'm 26."

"And you realize that Samantha is only 16, right?"

"Dave—" Georgette began, but he held up a hand.

"I do," Alex continued.

"Isn't that illegal?" Harmony chimed in, her food untouched, a look of interest on her face.

"Not if it's consensual," Samantha argued, "And my name is Sam, Dave."

Alex put his hands up in defense. "Look, I don't want you to get the wrong idea. We aren't doing anything illegal."

"Not yet," Sam muttered under her breath.

Dave felt a spike in his blood pressure as the words left her mouth.

"Sam," Alex whispered to her, "You aren't making this any easier."

"God forbid anything is easy in this house!"

Dave couldn't help but let out a sardonic laugh. "*What* are you talking about? How much easier could your life get?" He didn't realize he'd spoken until the words were already out of his mouth, but he was incapable of stopping them. "You have everything you want, you have almost no restrictions and yet you continue to push. What is this really about, Samantha?"

Georgie was staring at him as if she'd never seen him before. Samantha turned to him with a thunderous expression.

"And you know what you would have, you and your whole twisted family? Absolutely *nothing* if it wasn't for my mother!"

"Sam, dear," Georgie began, trying to keep the peace, but she was shut down again.

"I have a responsibility to this family. I care about this family—"

"Yeah, yeah, we all know, you do everything for everyone. Poor, underappreciated Dave."

"Don't speak to me that way," Dave had never uttered these words before in this life. It felt…empowering.

"Then don't say stupid crap! I mean, are you serious? Mom is almost 20 years older than you, hypocrite!" she shrieked with justice.

"Your mother and I are adults. You are not an adult. You are a—"

"I'm NOT a child," she nearly screamed as she shot to her feet, knocking over her chair. "You know *nothing*. Let me fill you in, Dave. When a woman starts bleeding that means she's no longer a child. And I've been bleeding for years," she spat, her double entendre not lost on him. She turned to Alex, chest heaving and her eyes on fire. "Let's go, I want pizza instead. With extra black olives."

She stormed from the room as Alex awkwardly made his exit to follow her. "It was nice to meet you all," his tone suggested the opposite. "I'll take good care of her." He directed this promise towards Georgette who could nothing but nod in mortification.

Then they were gone. Dave felt all eyes on him as he returned to his meal. He noticed his hands were shaking with emotion. Georgette leaned over and softly touched his arm.

"Darling,"

"Later," he corrected, not wanting to have this discussion with his nosey parents in the room. His mother would jump at the opportunity to cause dissension between him and Georgie. It was steadily becoming one of her favorite pastimes.

He was silent for the rest of dinner as June picked up the conversation like she always did. She went on to regale them with every single detail of the new members get-together at church that morning. The focus for most of her story was on the two lost souls she'd personally brought into the welcoming arms of God. The first was an older gentleman—a veteran who'd gave up God after his return from war. The other, and far more tragic tale was that of a young girl named Hope.

"The poor thing," June lamented as August nodded along with a mournful expression, "Absent, addict parents her entire life. No direction or structure…she was raised by her older sister."

Dave was hardly listening, but Georgette's curiosity was piqued. She was always interested in those who needed saving.

"How old is she?" his wife questioned.

"Probably the same age as your daughter's boyfriend," his mother responded with a sad look in her eyes. "You must be so disappointed," she added.

Georgette's expression turned mutinous.

"Anyway," June went on, in a tired voice, "her sister died years ago. She's been on her own ever since, lost and wandering."

Harmony's face was filling with hatred as she listened to their mother speak. Dave could hear exactly what was going on in her head. His sister considered herself more lost than most, yet their parents had no time to 'save' their own daughter.

"It's a good thing she has you," Harmony bit out with as much sarcasm as she could muster.

"She has the Lord. As you would, too, if you let Him into your heart," June preached, nodding her head and not even sparing a glance at her daughter.

"Enough!" Dave barked, dropping his fork down and looking around at all of them. "Can't you just ever stop?"

Emily Dinova

The tightness in his voice alarmed them. In that moment, he wanted to laugh—his family could not compute when he disagreed, or chose not to placate them. It was unbelievable.

Dave got to his feet and, with one last glance of incredulity at their perplexed faces, walked away.

THE ANTAGONIST

2

He was on his fourth beer before he asked the question that had been plaguing him all night.

"Am I weak?"

J looked at him with pity. "You're just not used to standing up for yourself."

His drinking buddy's eyes were glazed tonight. Dave felt a little more relaxed just being here. J exuded a calm steadiness that Dave was craving when he left the house a few hours before. Since he'd been at the bar, it felt as if most of his troubles melted away.

"I can't believe I snapped—at them." His voice held a note of wonder in it.

"I can," J disagreed, with a small smile. "You had enough, like you said. There is only so much battering a person can take before they finally say no. That's what you did, Dave. You said no."

"I did."

"That was brave of you," J went on, "Sometimes we have to face conflict, as opposed to avoiding it. It's difficult, ugly even, but the alternative is much worse." He sent Dave a grim look.

"What alternative?" Dave sat up a little straighter, focusing all his attention on J's next words.

"We let it eat away at us. We ignore our truth, the knowledge of who we are. We let others pile their own stories on top of us until we are buried beneath layers of others opinions and thoughts, *their* wants and needs. We don't attend to our own wishes and fears. The longer these concepts elude us, the more we will decay on the inside, until either there is nothing left, or we go mad."

"I can't help but feel guilty, though," Dave explained as he thought of his behavior over the last few days.

"That is a choice, my friend," J laughed, lighting a cigarette. Since Shawn and Mara were still out of town, Ruth seemed to have relaxed the smoking rules.

"How so?"

"You choose to feel guilty by rerunning events that have already occurred over and over in your mind. They are the past, you cannot change them, you have to let go of them and just keep moving forward. Don't you dare feel guilty about speaking your mind—even if it offends, you must always speak your truth, Dave. Without it, you are nothing."

Dave nodded along, absorbing this information.

"You can't tell me you don't feel better—getting your thoughts out instead of keeping everything bottled up?"

"Yes and no," Dave admitted. "I suppose I'll have to work on it."

J nodded in agreement. As he watched Dave above the rim of his glass, his eyes twinkled with uncertainty. "Do that."

Monday, October 16th

THE ANTAGONIST

I

Georgette's voice broke through his sleep as he listened to her move around the bedroom. Dave chanced a glance at the clock, dreading that he was already late if his wife was up before him.

It was only 7:30. Dave shook away the ache for more sleep and sat up looking for his wife.

"Georg?" he called after her sleepily.

She emerged from the walk-in closet with a brilliant smile, but he could see her gaze was still uneasy about last night's dinner and Dave's disappearing act shortly after. She'd been fast asleep by the time he returned from The Devil's Eye a little before midnight.

"How do I look?" she asked, striking a pose in her tennis outfit.

Dave smiled, running a hand across his scruffy face. "Beautiful, brilliant as always."

She came closer and sat down on the bed next to him, gently running her fingers through his hair.

"I'm sorry about last night," she started, but he cut her off with a kiss.

When he pulled back, he held onto her face and looked deep into her eyes.

"Listen to me, Georgette, you have absolutely nothing to be sorry for."

She smiled, her gaze filled with unshed tears.

"Sam—"

"Will be fine," Dave continued, "She's just in some rebellion against youth."

Georgette sighed wistfully. "I remember those days."

THE ANTAGONIST

Dave could see her beginning to drift into melancholia. He spoke before he lost her to nostalgic thoughts. "What time is your lesson?"

"In about an hour," she still looked distracted. "Guess we'll be playing inside with this awful weather."

Dave turned his head to look out across the balcony—the rain was driving with unforgiving force, the pines swaying with wild seduction.

"Let me know how it goes?" he asked, as she got to her feet to continue her morning routine.

"I will." She began to leave but stopped just at the threshold. "Dave?"

"Yes, my love?" He kept his voice calm—his wife's was filled with concern.

"Is everything going to be alright?"

"Yes," he confirmed immediately. "I promise."

He watched her shoulders relax and felt in that moment he believed his own words as much as she did.

2

Dave entered the kitchen a half hour later to an unexpected surprise. Samantha was nowhere to be seen—Dave's guess was that she hadn't come home at all last night. She was punishing him for his interference in her life. In her place, however, was Robb.

Dave paused in confusion before his brain switched to the inevitable.

"What's wrong?"

Robb looked up at the sound of his voice and laughed, "Hey man! Why's something gotta be wrong?" he was eating a bowl of Cheerios that Georgie must have put out for him—there was a bit of milk dribbling off his clean shaven chin giving him the appearance of an overgrown baby.

Dave took a breath of deep relief—it was rare that his mind swung to the immediate worst, but he had no other explanation for why Robb would be in his kitchen on a Monday morning.

"Then what's up?" Dave hedged, going about making himself a coffee.

Robb paused, a slight frown on his face. "I'm ready for a day of full hangin'," he said, as if that explained it all.

Dave raised an eyebrow. "It's Monday morning. I have work."

"Well yeah, I know that's usually the case, but your message said otherwise."

"What message?"

Robb pointed to a glass Root Beer bottle perched next to him on the counter. Dave stared at it. The bottle was exempt of fluids but the inside contained a rolled up piece of paper.

THE ANTAGONIST

"The one you left on my doorstep?" Robb replied slowly, carefully watching his friend's expression as Dave shook his head in denial. "Remember we used to send notes to each other when we were kids like that? So our parents wouldn't find them? It took me a second when I saw it, to remember," he smiled. "But I'm glad I did. Those were good times."

"What does it say?" Dave asked, feeling an inexplicable chill run down his spine.

Robb popped the letter out of the bottle and handed it to Dave. Dave carefully unrolled it and looked down at the typed words:

```
Let's catch up tomorrow morning.
Just like old times!
```

"I didn't write this." Dave pressed the note back into Robb's hand.

Robb re-read it once more. "Then who did?"

"How should I know?" Dave snapped. Why was Robb bothering him with this crap?

Robb stared at him with the same expression he'd seen on Georgie's face.

"Whoa, man. Are you okay?" His eyebrows lifted at Dave's sudden show of unwarranted hostility.

"I'm fine! But I really wish, more than anything, that everyone would stop asking me that stupid question!" Dave picked up the glass bottle before tossing it into the trash and stalking from the room.

3

He had no time to feel guilty for lambasting his best friend. Dave was going to be late for work—again. How the hours seemed to slip away from him these days was unfathomable.

So what someone left Robb a message—it could have been anyone. Robb hung out with all sorts and there were still a few friends around from their days of childhood. It could have been any of them, so why was Dave being the one harassed? He took a few inhales of air. Robb was his best friend. He hadn't upset him on purpose.

Dave wanted to kick himself by the time he pulled into the firm. In his surprise to see Robb and have new information thrown at him, he'd completely forgotten to ask about their latest pizza delivery. It was another thing he had no answers for. Dave hated when he had no answers.

Dave tried fruitlessly to justify his ill feelings, but the moment he stepped into the office, his attention was focused elsewhere.

He was almost an hour late and Desiree was nowhere to be seen.

Dave dropped down to his desk and carefully looked around—just to make sure she wasn't hiding in plain sight. After another hour passed and he still hadn't caught wind of her, he figured he was in the clear.

Dave got to work, his thoughts avoiding the confrontations of his home life—instead he delved into the lives of others. He attempted to remain focused on work but a small niggling thought kept poking against his psyche—why wasn't

Desiree here? Where was she? In court, or perhaps she was sick…or maybe she was plotting against him.

Dave was attempting to quell these unwelcome thoughts when he was interrupted.

"Hey."

He glanced up.

"What are you doing here?" Dave asked, taking in his thoroughly out of place sister in her baggy sweat pants and converse sneakers.

"I walked. Thought we could grab lunch." Dave was already shaking his head no, but his sister continued, "We need to talk."

Something in her tone made the hairs on the back of his neck stand. As much as his sister was always in crisis mode, he could see that this time was different. She hated crowds of people. Coming to his office was the last thing she would do unless she was desperate.

Dave stared at her for a moment, before nodding and getting to his feet.

They headed to the diner, where Dave knew they wouldn't be likely to be overheard through the din of the usual lunch crowd. As he drove, his sister sat quietly. Dave was just beginning to appreciate the silence when she switched on the radio.

Rape Me!

Dave jumped with a start, the volume had been turned to maximum (he figured Sam must have done this in an attempt to give him a heart attack) and the sound of Nirvana once again came blasting into his eardrums.

Dave slammed it off as he turned to look at his sister. She looked equally startled by the music. He ejected the CD and flung it into the back seat in annoyance.

Even after arriving at the diner, Harmony continued to watch him as they sat down in the window booth and ordered. When they were finally left alone, Dave brought up her apparent urgency.

"What is it, Har?"

"Can you feel it?" she asked quietly, looking around with suspicion.

"Feel what?"

"Someone is watching us."

Dave took a shrewd glance around the joint. There were too many people congregating for him to get a full look, but his instincts told him his sister was just being her overly dramatic self.

"I don't see anyone watching us," Dave commented blandly.

Harmony scratched her eyebrow—a tick she always reverted to when she was nervous. "I was thinking about what you said the other day. About you and I...not being the same. Why do you think we ended up so differently?"

The change in subject matter brought his attention back to his frail and somber looking twin. He felt his cheeks grow red with shame—it had been a low blow for him to distance himself from her in that way, but he was going to follow his truth. He was going to be honest.

"God, I don't know. Genetics?"

She nodded along thoughtfully, "Maybe. Maybe you got all the happy genes, the ones that allow you a bright future and a loving family."

"Loving?"

"Georgie."

"Yeah, she's about the only one who loves me these days."

"Don't say that, Dave. It's not true."

"Feels that way. I'm sick of being taken advantage of, Harmony."

"Who takes advantage of you?"

"To start? Mom."

"Fuck June."

Dave laughed.

"I'm serious. She spends all her time either butting into other people's lives or completely ignoring mine," she frowned. "I mean, I know you've always been the favorite, but it's to the point where I just feel invisible these days, to them at least. Doctor H. sees me, though. She believes in me."

Dave reached across the table and grabbed his sister's hands, feeling a pang of guilt at her attempt to convince herself she was more.

"And she's right to do so, Sis. You're so smart, you have so much to offer."

"Yeah, if only I could get out of my own way."

"Hey, at least you recognize that. That puts you ten steps ahead of most people."

She smiled her small smile, casting her eyes down as she did whenever someone gave her a compliment. It was so rare. Dave was never sure which Harmony he would get—her moods and thoughts shifted so rapidly she was hard to keep up with.

"So, tell me. What's this all about? You walked all the way to my office to talk about our differences?"

Any trace of delight drained from her face immediately.

"Dad wasn't feeling well this morning," she began, lowering her voice even further. So much so that Dave had to lean forward to catch the ends of her wispy sentences. "They didn't go to church. Stayed in and had prayer in the living room instead."

Dave nodded along, knowing it was difficult for his father to get going most days. The stress he continued to put on his body was eventually going to wreak havoc.

"The wind woke me early, I was up late painting again… it really helps the anxiety."

Once Harmony captured his attention, she was known to keep it on her for as long as possible. Dave was the only one who gave her stories the time of day and she savored the ability and privilege to be heard.

"So I couldn't sleep, figured I might as well raid their kitchen for leftovers. I left the guest house, it was terribly foggy, and when I got to the back door of the main house, there was a note taped to it."

"A note?" Dave repeated, as to make sure he'd heard the word correctly.

Harmony nodded, leaning even further into his space, her eyes moving rapidly about for eavesdroppers. For a split second, Dave entertained the thought that his sister was losing her grip on reality.

"Something bad is coming, Dave," she stared directly into his eyes, as if she were seeing through him. "And it's coming for you."

"What did the note say? Harmony?" He grasped her cold hands in his own, squeezing them tightly. She squeezed back.

"Just that. That's what it said."

"Verbatim?"

She nodded again.

"Where is it?" he asked.

"I burned it."

"Why?"

"It scared me," Dave dropped his head into hands with a groan, "And I didn't want June to find it," she said defensively. "You know how she's always snooping about, even going through the damn garbage!"

"Was it written out? Typed?"

Harmony shook her head, "What does that matter?"

"Never mind." Dave sucked down the anger he was experiencing—his sister was scared, that was intolerable. "Listen, I want you to forget you ever saw this message. Alright?"

"Dave, please. Tell me you aren't in any trouble," she begged, her grip on his hand once again becoming vice-like, her nails close to breaking his skin.

"I'm not. You know I'm not." He forced a laugh at the absurdity of the whole thing. "Someone is just messing with me. Probably Robb or Samantha, I'm sure she's still furious with me over the disaster last night."

THE ANTAGONIST

"I thought Alex was handsome," his sister mused, her mind once again darting into another space. "He seemed nice enough."

Dave wasn't in the mood to explain to her why that wasn't the problem. He couldn't. His mind was filled with the newest "prank" from this unknown source. He would confront Samantha about it. This petty behavior had child written all over it.

4

The rest of the afternoon passed in a blur for Dave. After dropping Harmony off at home, he went back to the office, hoping by some miracle that Schworst was gone by now.

He wasn't so lucky. But at least his boss looked busy.

Dave slunk inconspicuously to his desk, not wanting to alert the beast of his return.

As dusk began to fall, Dave's thoughts drifted away from his task at hand and back to his family. More than anything, he just wanted life to go back to the way it had been a few weeks ago. Perhaps Dave was just experiencing the normal doldrums of existence that had been absent from his days for so long. Maybe he was becoming complacent, bored, lazy— was he so pathetic that he was this easily defeated by the outside world? He forced his shoulders back, lifted his chin a notch. He would continue to stand up for himself, but he could not shun his family from his life either. He needed to find a balance in-between, which seemed to be becoming increasingly harder these days. Dave just wished he could put his finger on it. It wasn't any one thing that was rubbing him raw—it was a culmination of something greater that he feared he could not understand.

Dave resolved to pack up a bit early and head straight to the grocery store. He would forgo his drink tonight. He was going to prepare a beautiful meal for the family, and then he was going to apologize to them all. He would right this. But before he could put his plans into action, he was being called back into the firm by Schworst's bellowing voice.

THE ANTAGONIST

His coworkers gave out looks of sympathy as they passed him on his dreaded walk back into the clutches of Kyle Schworst.

"Yes, Mr. Schworst?" His boss turned at the sound of his voice, a belligerent glare swallowing his face. "Is everything alright?" Dave continued when he didn't immediately start screaming.

"I don't know, Dave. Is it?"

Dave hesitated, his mind swinging furiously to pouty red lips and silk garters—it took every ounce of self-restraint for Dave to overcome the monsoon of panic swirling just behind him. Did he think Dave was responsible for Desiree not being at work? Had she disappeared?

"Sir?"

"Were you here, at the firm, on Saturday?" Schworst barked as he stood from the chair behind his desk, offering Dave the other.

Dave slowly sat down on high alert—Schworst never asked him to sit. "I was, I had a bit of extra work to take care of." Schworst's eyes narrowed with blatant dislike. "And the family was driving me nuts," Dave included for further explanation.

"Really? I imagine your family probably gets sick of *you*," Kyle taunted, baring his yellow teeth with a sadistic grin.

"I'm sure they do," Dave agreed.

"And did you happen to have forgotten to lock the door on your way out?" he paced around the office, circling Dave like the bloody-thirsty shark that he was.

"No, Sir. I did not. I never do."

"I see. Were you here alone?"

Dave's thoughts were scrambling due to his inability to predict where this interrogation was heading. Dave was not a liar—but he felt locked in a moral battle. What if Desiree made up horrible things, told Schworst lies about what actually happened on Saturday afternoon? Where was she?

"Dave, why did you wipe the security cameras clean?"

Dave's head snapped up at that, "What?"

"You heard me, you useless shit. What were you doing in here that made you take such measures?" Schworst whispered vindictively.

"Sir, I have no idea what you are talking about. I was here yes, but so was Ms. DeLongo—"

"And why didn't you mention that before?"

"I was about to—"

"And what were you and that tart doing?"

Dave disliked the lascivious greed and imagination he saw come to life on his boss's face.

"Nothing, at all. She was in her office working, I was out there," Dave pointed to his desk, "I left before she did. I locked the door. So maybe you should be asking her."

Schworst gnashed his teeth as if he'd like nothing more than to fire him. "And you expect me to believe that you were alone, here, with *her* and nothing happened?"

"Positive. I have nothing to hide. So if you are finished falsely accusing me of something I did not do, with absolutely no proof, then I'd like to leave."

Schworst was the color of a beet by the time Dave retreated from his office. Dave's feeling of self-worth increased after that. He felt proud—strong at how he handled the arrogant bully. He looked forward to telling J the story next time he saw him. He also felt confident that it was Desiree who'd wiped the tapes, not wanting to risk someone finding evidence of her inability to seduce him. He was in the clear, and still somewhat on schedule. With a little skip in his step, Dave walked out into evening mist, feeling almost at peace.

Almost.

THE ANTAGONIST

5

The house was dark and empty when Dave pulled into the driveway 45 minutes later. He sat there staring at the looming mass of darkness, a slightly crest-fallen expression plastered on his face. He was looking forward to repairing the damage of the week, but it appeared that no one held the same view as his own.

He checked his phone as he went about putting away the groceries. Ironically, it was meatloaf he'd been craving but he knew this wouldn't have gone over well with Sam, so he opted on once again trying to get on the good side of his stepdaughter. He'd make tofu and veggie tacos instead.

But it was all for naught considering he was the only one home.

He changed out of his work clothes quickly as he continued to look over his shoulder. He tried to ignore it, but the silence of the house made him extra jumpy. There were too many rooms, a plethora of dark corners and shadowed walls—it made him uneasy, as it always had—but for different reasons tonight.

Still rattled from his battle with his boss, Dave attempted to bolster his spirits and make dinner regardless of his lack of company. He would be kind to himself, and hopefully by the time he was finished, someone would come home.

He returned to the brightly lit kitchen and sent a family text: *I'm making tofu tacos, should I save some?*

Georgie replied instantly: *Aw! I hate missing taco night! Save me a few, I'll be at the shelter late. xo*

THE ANTAGONIST

A few seconds passed before Georgie texted him on the side: *Sam is sleeping at a friend's...didn't want you to worry. xo*

Dave huffed in exasperation—his wife didn't actually believe that did she?

Dave continued to prep. After another few minutes his phone dinged again. This time it was his sister: *Not hungry. Painting. June and August are at some pastor's house for dinner. GAG.*

Well that was everyone—he felt his heart sink a little. The hours would tick by much slower now.

Dave's task of making tacos only took him another 20 minutes to complete—by then he was positively starving. He reached for a taco just as his phone once again lit up with a message. It was Robb: *Hey man, just checking in on you... sorry for this morning. Hope you're not still mad. Sending you love and good vibes.*

Dave sighed as he felt another pang in his chest. He hit reply: *I should be the one apologizing. I was a total dick. Forgive me? I'll make it up to you next weekend with a bottle of the finest Scotch.*

Robb answered almost instantaneously with a thumbs up Emoji and: *Done!*

Dave considered inviting him over right now, but ultimately decided against it. He didn't need a safety net.

Dave lifted the taco once again to his mouth, his taste buds salivating at the delicious smell.

Dave never took that first bite—someone was knocking, with intent, on the front door.

Dave swung the heavy door open with an air of agitation, looking around.

There was no one.

He stepped out onto the front porch, peering down the misty driveway for signs of life. His gaze narrowed, his eyes coming to rest on the ground in front of his feet.

It was a pizza box.

Dave got down on his haunches and carefully flipped the top open.

Cheese pizza. But the cheese seemed to be moving.

He leaned over further, his eyes adjusting to the dim light.

Cheese pizza covered in maggots.

He pulled his face back—swearing under his breath and jumping to his feet.

From this angle he could see the inside of the top of the box. There was another sharpie drawn face, but this one was angry. The words scrawled beneath it, were written in the same malevolent tone. They read:

I said, HI

Dave used his foot to close the box before picking it up and throwing it into the large fire pit beyond in their backyard. His mind was furious as he went about tossing some logs into the middle of the stacked stones.

Dave lit it up and stood back—watching the maggots crawl their way out of the cheese and melt into the cardboard as it burned in the night.

The flames continued to rise, casting shadows across Dave's stoic face, destroying all evidence of this hostile exchange.

Who could be doing this to him?

Up until now, he'd been sure his family or Robb had been at the root of it. Was there more to it? Had he once again underestimated Desiree's desire to make him pay for his rejection? No. It had to be someone else…Dave racked his brains. He couldn't think of anyone who might want to move against him. Perhaps it was someone from his past, someone he grew up with who now resented him for his wealth and happiness. It could be blackmail; what did they want? Georgette was always going about in her flashy way—

it was unlikely that anyone who lived here for more than five years didn't know her name.

Or could it be an ex-girlfriend? He dated a few girls here and there, nothing serious. It couldn't be that one of them held a grudge? Dave just couldn't wrap his mind around it—any relationship he had in the past always ended on good terms.

He once again brought himself back to the most obvious option. She was the only one cruel enough to keep this up—it had to be Samantha.

Dave returned inside after he was sure the maggots were all singed. He shoved the tacos into the refrigerator—his appetite once again ruined.

He wanted a drink.

6

Dave had one drink. Then two, and another and another, until he lost count—he spilled his guts to J. He was overwhelmed, anxious and afraid…he couldn't help himself as his worries came spilling out as easily as the drinks he continued to order.

Dave would never remember the conversation the two of them had that night.

He would never recall J's words of wisdom.

That evening, Dave was unsure how he even made it home.

Tuesday, October 17th

THE ANTAGONIST

I

No it was definitely morning, well after midnight, to be sure.

THE ANTAGONIST

2

Dave awoke to the sound of hushed voices.

He was not in his bed.

He felt the familiar sag of the couch underneath him as he turned on his side, burying his face into the plush pillow in an attempt to block out all noise and light. His head was absolutely splitting—his mouth like sandpaper. All he wished for in this moment was to return to the still and silent comfort of the unconscious.

"Samantha, please," his wife's urgent whisper inundated his ears from the hallway.

"No, I'm sorry mom, but I'm not going to apologize to your pathetic excuse for a husband!" she bit back, not even attempting to keep her voice down.

Dave winced against the harsh tone.

"He is not pathetic. He's loving and caring. He cares about you, Sam, more than you know." Georgie was pleading for her daughter to understand.

"He doesn't even know me! Or Alex! He only hates him because he's everything Dave isn't—exciting with a spine. Suddenly he decides to grow a backbone and play dad? Who I date is none of his business."

"He will get over it," Georgie spoke on his behalf as Sam scoffed with disbelief. Georgie continued, "He will. He comes from a very different background than ours, he's been very accepting of our lifestyle, but you have to give him a little time."

"Fuck! We've given him five long years. There's no coming back from his type of repression."

Dave opened an eye. His type of repression? He didn't have to wait too long to figure out what that meant as Georgie voiced his thoughts for him.

"What does that even mean, Samantha?" she asked with a hint of impatience to her tone.

"His freak-show parents did a number on him. How could anyone who grows up under religious nuts like that turn out normal?"

"I don't love Dave because he is normal."

"Well that much is obvious, I'm just not sure why you love him at all."

Georgie sucked in a breath as if she'd been slapped.

"Maybe you don't recall what your father was like, Samantha. Maybe you can't remember the black eyes and violent alcohol-soaked fights," her voice was trembling.

"I didn't mean—"

But Georgette was on a roll, "Your father nearly killed me. If I stayed any longer who knows what would have happened…Dave is the opposite of that man. He has never hit me, never spoken down to me, never told me what to do. He eased my pain, helped me put myself back together again… How can you treat someone who means so much to me so poorly? Don't you care about me at all?"

Sam was silent, Georgie near tears. Dave remained tucked into the couch, his heart beating fast as he stayed hidden.

Finally Sam spoke. "Of course I care about you, Mom. I'm sorry."

Dave listened for his wife's small sniffles. They were hugging, he could tell. He heard Georgette kiss her daughter's forehead.

"So," she began, sounding more like her normal self, "What do you have going on today?"

"Driver's Ed after school, but don't worry I've got a ride home."

"Alex?"

Dave listened as their voices moved away from him, down the hall and towards the front of the house. There was no chance of him getting another minute of rest after overhearing that conversation.

Normally Dave felt his mornings were incomplete if he didn't interact with his wife on some level, but right now all he wanted to do was stay completely alone.

He waited until he was positive that he was the only one still in the house before pulling his aching, sweaty body to its feet.

How the hell had he gotten home last night? He was pretty sure J didn't have a car. Perhaps Ruth?

He let the hot steam of the shower roll off his taunt muscles as flashes of the previous evening danced tantalizing around in his mind, just out of reach. He remembered being at The Devil's Eye and unloading his pent-up issues on his new friend. But Dave couldn't pinpoint the actual moments before his memory left him. It was causing him grief. He'd been irresponsible, stupid. And stupid was dangerous. He inadvertently made himself a hostage of the unknown.

THE ANTAGONIST

3

Dave slid into the driver's side of his car and found his keys sitting in the cup hole. His cramped legs loosened out as he adjusted the seat back to its normal position—someone a few inches shorter than him must have driven home. Dave was taller than most people. Perhaps he'd called Georgie. He checked his phone—there were no outgoing or incoming calls and no messages sent after 9 p.m.

Dave knew if he'd been in the car, at least he hadn't been driving—that was a relief. He just hoped to all hell that in some drunken stupor he'd not done anything out of character. He never blacked out. The thought that he was capable of abusing his own body and mind in such a way made him practically quiver with anxiety.

∼

Desiree was once again missing.

He didn't dare ask about her in case he aroused suspicion. Dave spent the whole day in a perpetual state of nerves. Schworst continued to deviously glare at him whenever he passed his desk, but didn't say another word concerning their conversation the day before.

Maybe she got fired. Dave could only hope.

He turned his thoughts away to contemplate another pressing issue—how he would approach Samantha and bridge some sort of truce between them. If she were the one adding extra strife to his world, then he would have to find the middle ground. He was so incredibly disappointed in himself and the thoughts Samantha had voiced about him. Even if Georgie came to his defense, he still felt shameful.

Maybe he didn't deserve them. He'd done everything he could to adapt to their lifestyle, but perhaps it was just not enough. Had his parents screwed him up as much as she seemed to think? Dave always promised himself he would rise above what they'd wanted him to be. He had lived this long into adulthood, thinking he made real progress. It was disheartening to hear he failed, especially behind his back.

Immense relief washed over Dave as the day came to a close. All he wanted to do was go home and sleep. He knew there were plenty of hours before that would happen—still, he couldn't help but wish for it.

He didn't even consider going to the bar. He needed to dry out, take a break. Apparently J's advice came at a steep cost: sobriety. Something Dave had always valued and cherished. But his need to relax his mind, erase his dreaded thoughts, had also become a priority. But no longer—Dave would face the truth.

4

He picked up some sushi before heading home, not in any sort of mood to put together another meal that would go unappreciated.

Georgette wasn't home yet, but as he opened the front door he heard music playing in the living room. The tune was vaguely familiar but Dave was not able to place it until he reached the source.

Samantha and Alex were sitting on the floor together in front of the massive TV. Sam had a controller in her hands and was pressing the buttons furiously.

Dave felt his mouth drop open in awe. He couldn't believe what he was seeing. The words left his mouth before he could help it, "Where did you get that?" he asked with a hint of wonder.

Both Sam and Alex started in surprise, as if they'd been caught red-handed doing something incredibly wrong.

"Jesus, Dave, you scared the shit out of me!" she complained, sounding grumpy but no longer vengeful.

"Sorry," he muttered quickly, "I just haven't seen one of these in years," he trailed off as he stepped closer and bent down to examine the ancient artifact, seemingly lost from the past.

"I thought you'd be too old to appreciate something so cool," his stepdaughter incurred.

"She's a real beaut, huh, Dave?" Alex hedged, feeling out the waters.

Dave turned his head away from the classic Nintendo game system and addressed the other man with a kind and thoughtful tone. "Oh for sure. This was always my favorite game," he added, gesturing to the screen. "What an adventure."

"*Legend of Zelda* is sick. Finally, we agree on something," Sam commented, turning her attention back to the screen.

"Is this yours, Alex?" Dave asked with enthusiasm as he sat down on the couch.

Alex shook his head, "Nope."

Dave fought the urge to again ask Samantha where she found such a relic, but he was disinclined to rock the boat after she'd given him cause to believe the other night was behind them.

He watched for a few minutes, listening as the two teased one another back and forth. Sam seemed happy enough. Apparently Alex was a kid at heart himself—Dave noticed the respectful distance Alex kept from her, and for that Dave was grateful. He only hoped the man continued to be smart until Sam was actually an adult.

"Dave?" Sam asked him suddenly.

"Yeah?"

"Do you remember youth?"

He paused at her question, as Alex turned to stare at him curiously.

"How could I forget it?"

"Was it bad? Growing up?"

Dave laughed, "Bad? Sometimes. But I imagine that's the same for everyone."

She didn't speak to him again and after a few more minutes of noise, the video game no longer amused him. He felt the first signs of a headache coming on which was also probably an indicator that he overstayed his welcome. He got to his feet, informing them that there was sushi if they got hungry. Alex thanked him and Dave left the room feeling as if he finally put out at least one fire of the week.

Wednesday, October 18th

THE ANTAGONIST

I

The following day moved with the pace of a wet sloth.

The only brief glimpse of happiness that Dave found that day was surprisingly from Schworst. He passed Dave's desk around noon talking loudly on his cellphone.

"Yeah, I know. I'm on my way now. Stone is already there with that DeLongo bitch. Yep. I'll see you at the courthouse." He slammed through the doors and out of sight.

Dave felt a tension he was hardly even aware of anymore drop from his chest. At least he now knew he wasn't responsible for Desiree's avoidance of the office. She was probably just ridiculously busy. Dave felt hopeful, bolstered by this news.

He received a text from Georgette shortly before he left the firm, informing him she'd be working late once again—with the charity gala only a few weeks away, she was in crunch mode. Dave briefly considered stopping by the bar but thought better of it. He was still feeling the lingering affects of his two-day hangover. His body just didn't bounce back the way it did when he was a younger man. Apparently neither did his mind.

Dave settled on checking up on Harmony instead. He'd not seen or heard much from her since their impromptu, odd lunch together.

He found her on the front porch of the main house. She was smoking a cigarette as he pulled into the drive. He could tell immediately, before he even got out of the car, that she was in a complex and sullen mood.

"Hey," he started towards her, zipping up his jacket and joining her on the steps. The night air was cool, the last glimmers of light just fading from the sky.

Harmony offered him a drag of the cigarette in response. He declined.

"Good twin, bad twin," she murmured.

"I haven't seen you smoke in years," he commented with a frown.

"Well, desperate times and all that." She took another deep drag. "What brings you by the funny farm this evening?"

"I just wanted to check on you."

"I haven't gotten any more notes," she mentioned with a sideways glance.

"I didn't think you would. Samantha and I have made amends."

Harmony chuckled, "That kid walks all over you."

"She tries."

"No, she does."

Dave remained silent. He was not going to allow her to bait him into an argument he could not win. After a few moments, Harmony mashed her cigarette into the wet ground and got to her feet. Dave followed her, watching the tight muscles of her neck strain as she opened the front door.

"Where are Mom and Dad?" he asked.

The main house was never silent when June and August were home. His mother was either chatting away on the phone or his father was blasting the television—fishing or God was all he ever had patience for.

"Oh, take a wild guess!" Harmony exclaimed with irritation as she flipped on the lights in the kitchen.

"Mass this late?" Dave asked, as he looked around at all the Jesus décor. Each room was bordering on "hoarding" the Lord.

"They are taking this new member shit way seriously. They practically live at the church. Not that I'm complaining. Doctor H. tells me the more I separate myself from them, the better."

Emily Dinova

Dave watched as his sister poured a glass of wine and leaned against the kitchen counter, watching him.

"And what have you told Doctor H. about them?"

"The truth. I talk about you sometimes, too," she added, as if it were an afterthought. Dave knew better.

"Oh yeah?" he encouraged. "What sort of stuff do you say about me?"

"I wonder at what point you decided to be happy and I chose to be sad."

"I don't think those things are completely in our control."

"No? How is it, we came from the same womb at the same time, yet you have always been normal and I'm..." she trailed off. "Doctor H. always says to speak kindly about yourself. It's difficult."

"I understand. But Harmony, we aren't normal. Either of us!" She shot him a skeptical look. "We're both different. We are both not normal."

"Then how come your life is amazing and mine is a pile of shit? I'm stuck here in this house with these lunatics. If not here, I'm residing in a nut house. How is that okay? I have no friends, no social life—a distinct fear of the most irrational things. I've tried for years and years to make myself better. I've done everything in an attempt to mirror you, to be more like you. So that maybe, one day, our parents wouldn't regret the fact that I'm alive."

"Don't say that."

"It's true! I'm sick. I'm less."

"You are not less."

"But I am sick."

Dave remained silent. His sister laughed in his face before she threw back the rest of the wine, "And you know who made me sick Dave? *Them.*"

"I know how much they upset you. You have to learn to ignore it."

"How can I do that when I am practically chained to them!?"

THE ANTAGONIST

If his sister wasn't as fragile as she was, he would have explained how she could become a functioning adult—find work, move out of his parent's house. But as the years went by, Dave saw that chance go from marginal to fleeting to gone. His sister was too deeply rooted in her habits to break them now.

As if she could read his mind she continued on, "Doctor H. says I need to get a job, maybe one I can work remotely, with limited social contact. She says once I do that, I will be free of them. I won't have to rely on anyone for anything anymore. I will be my own person—to a small step towards independence," his sister toasted him with her second glass of wine.

Dave could have kissed Harmony's therapist for saying such a wonderful and helpful thing. Clearly if he couldn't get through to her, at least someone else had.

Their conversation was abruptly halted by the sound of popping gravel as his father's car pulled up into the driveway. Harmony peeked out the kitchen window.

"Ugh, already?" she complained, depositing the now empty wine glass in the sink. "I'm going up to my apartment." She turned to look at him. "Coming?"

Dave was tempted by the offer, but he knew his parents already spotted his car parked outside. His mother had eyes like a hawk and if he chose to purposely avoid them, he would never hear the end of it. He opened his mouth to relay this message to his sister when a sob sounded from the front of the house. He glanced at Harmony who looked towards the noise with confusion.

Dave hurried out the front door and down the stairs to find his mother standing next to the mailbox with a trembling hand covering her mouth. The other hand was holding a large envelope—it was open. June's eyes were scanning several pages. A few of them fell from her hands as August read over her shoulder—all color draining from his normally ruddy complexion.

Dave felt like a deer in headlights. He could not possibly imagine what news they received to make them look so horrified. Harmony stepped out onto the porch just as his mother looked up from whatever it was she finished reading.

"Davey!" she choked out, rushing forward, as she scrambled to pick up the papers she dropped. "Oh, Davey!" She burst into tears as she reached his arms.

Dave helped his mother inside where she collapsed on the nearest chair, tears streaming down her face.

"Tell us it was a joke, son. Please," August pleaded.

Dave was so startled by their behavior he was momentarily struck speechless.

"What is happening?" Harmony's voice was high pitched, racked with terror. Any kind of emotional confrontation immediately attacked her nerves.

June groaned with anguish as she tossed the mail down on the table and covered her face. "It wasn't there this afternoon. I never check the mail at night, but the flag was up," she babbled on as Dave lifted the papers carefully into his hands.

It was a police file.

His police file to be exact.

Dave felt his stomach plummet to the ground as he tried to come up with a rational explanation to subdue his mother's growing wails.

"Mom," he started, looking down at his mug shot. "This was a very long time ago."

"It's true?!" she screeched, jumping to her feet in horror. "You were arrested?"

Harmony sucked in a deep breath of air, regarding Dave as if she never seen him before in her life. "For what?" she asked in a deadpan voice.

"It was a long time ago," Dave repeated, feeling numb as he continued to stare down at the file. Drug possession, driving under the influence—that night came rushing back to him as if it were yesterday. "Robb and I..."

"I should have known!" June railed, as August sat down wearily, rubbing his temples in agitation. "That scoundrel! The drug-fiendish fool!" she howled.

THE ANTAGONIST

"It was his birthday," Dave continued over the racket she was making, "We had a few too many, we were young and stupid. But I swear to you, the drugs were not mine. I've never done drugs a day in my life."

"And we're supposed to believe you?" Harmony chimed in, her eyes narrowing by the second.

"How could you keep this from us?" June sobbed, "How could you let us go on not knowing of your sins? What He must think!?"

"Mom," Dave could feel anger rising in his chest. Who the hell had gotten access to this information? And why, why in the world would they send it to his parents? "Was there anything else in the mailbox?"

She shook her head no. Dave flipped the large manila envelope over—a large smiley face was drawn on the front.

"Bad things coming," Harmony whispered.

"Do you know what will happen if this news gets out?" June gasped suddenly, as she turned to look at her husband, eyes wide with terror. "What will our congregation think of us once they hear about our only son's delinquent behavior? Oh Davey, your soul is in mortal peril! Your actions will be our ruin!"

He could not get another coherent word out of his mother as she once again dissolved into a fit of tears at the prospect of losing her status within the church. August helped her off to bed with a look of disappointment at both of his children.

Dave picked up the files and shoved them carelessly back in the envelope. His sister watched him with rising fury evident in her gaze.

"So," she began, her voice trembling with emotion. "For years you let me go on believing that I'm the only screwed up one. Did you care so much about preserving your own image that you couldn't even be honest with ME!?" she screamed. "Don't you trust me? I tell you everything. How could you keep this from me? What else have you kept from me?"

"Harmony, I swear—"

"You love having me as the scapegoat, don't you? Nothing perfect Davey can do to upset Mommy and Daddy. You disgust me!"

She picked up her wine glass from the sink, grabbed the bottle and stormed from the kitchen without a backward glance.

Thursday, October 19th

THE ANTAGONIST

I

Dave barely slept in his attempt to come up with 101 ways to deal with his parents and sister. The day passed in a blur, he was hardly cognizant of his actions—he was seemingly operating with the mechanics of an automaton. There was no room left in Dave's brain for normal everyday life—his emotions were in an upheaval from the intense rollercoaster ride he was currently experiencing. He still had no inkling as to why he was being punished for something he'd done almost fifteen years ago.

Plenty of people got arrested. It was a stupid mistake and one he hadn't considered in a very long time. He noticed that Robb's information was nowhere to be seen in that nicely put together little packet of information. He hoped his parents would get over it when they realized that it in no way would affect their lives.

Harmony, however, was a different story. His twin felt slighted, lied to—he couldn't blame her. It wasn't as if he purposely kept the information to himself, there just had never seemed like a right time to divulge it. When the incident occurred, Harmony was living outside of Repo in a mental health institution. He could remind her of this, he supposed, but the whole thing seemed pointless. She would forgive him when she wanted to, and not a second sooner, no matter how he tried to make it up to her. If either of them had been born with the predispositions of stubbornness and holding a grudge, it was his sister.

Schworst and Desiree must have spent another long sojourn in court, for Dave saw neither of them that day—which seemed to be the only reprieve. He was distracted, unable to be his normally efficient self with all the wild theories whipping about in his brain. Would someone like Desiree have access to his record after he hired a lawyer to have it sealed? Probably.

He returned home to find Georgette already there. Dave felt such immense gratefulness for her calming presence. If anyone could get him out of this funk, it was his wife. It felt as if it'd been years since he'd seen her and he was desperate for her comfort.

"Your sister called me," she began the second he walked into the kitchen. She was sitting alone at the countertop, her hands folded, her head bent in deep thought.

"How did they find out?" she asked him after a few moments of silence.

Dave shrugged, "Still trying to figure that one out."

He should have been expecting this. Of course the first thing Harmony thought to do was throw him under the bus with the only person who was on his side.

"I'm sorry I didn't tell you," Dave intoned as he sat down across from her, rubbing his face with agitation.

Georgette laughed, "Darling, please. You think I care about a little misdemeanor? You should have seen what I got up to back in the old days."

"I can only imagine."

"Plus Sam thinks it's super cool. She keeps calling you a felon."

"Georgie, please," Dave protested weakly.

"I'm just teasing you! It's nothing to feel bad about."

"I don't feel bad about it. They do."

His wife nodded in understanding, "That's sort of what I wanted to talk to you about…" she hesitated.

"My family?"

She nodded, biting her lip in anticipation.

"What about them?"

"It's becoming a bit much for you. Taking care of them all the time."

Emily Dinova

Dave didn't disagree, which encouraged her to go on. "I was thinking we could go on vacation...but," she paused for a deep breath. "Maybe we should consider moving—away from here. Away from them."

Dave couldn't believe what she was actually suggesting. For a moment, it all sounded so perfect. How wonderful it would be to escape the exhausting reality of his family—quit his job and just go off and start anew. For a moment he craved it, could see it perfectly in his vision.

"I...can't, Georgie. I can't abandon them like that."

"Sort of like how they did to you? Dave, you owe your parents nothing, I'm sorry, if they could even be called parents."

Dave balked at her comment—it felt like an indirect attack on the person he was.

"What about Harmony? What am I suppose to do with her?"

"She will be fine. We can always send her money if she needs it, but what she really needs—don't get upset—but what she really needs is for you to stop babying her. Let her grow up! She could do that without your shadow constantly hanging over her."

"My shadow?"

"You know what I mean."

"So let me get this straight. You want me to uproot my life—leave my family and friends, my home? Just turn my back?"

"It doesn't have to be forever."

"You know Georg, real life doesn't work for you how it does for everyone else."

"I know that. Of course, I'm willing to help them, but darling, it's starting to look like its near killing you."

It is killing me, Dave admitted in his head. "I'm fine."

"Just...think about it. You know I love it here, but a little change never killed anyone."

Dave raised an eyebrow at her, "Knock wood."

THE ANTAGONIST

2

"Is it the weekend already?" was Robb's question when Dave rapped on his door an hour later.

"Can I come in?" he asked hurriedly.

Robb stepped immediately to the side, allowing him entrance.

Dave collapsed on the couch with sigh of resignation. "I have questions."

"Anything," Robb encouraged, sitting down across from him with a perplexed expression.

"Any new customers recently? A woman with long black hair, very attractive?"

"Ah, not that I can recall. I feel like I would remember a smoke show."

Dave frowned, "You're sure? No one has been hanging around or ordering black olives on pizza?"

"I mean, I'm sure someone has ordered black olives on pizza, but not on the regular..." he trailed off, cocking his head to the side in contemplation.

"Do you remember when we got arrested?"

Robb raised an eyebrow, surprised at the conversations change in direction.

"Yeah, I do."

"And you remember I had those records sealed, right?"

"Right. For both of us."

Dave watched his friend carefully. "My record was delivered to my parents last night."

"Ouch!" Robb grimaced, "Who the hell sent your folks that crap? The super attractive woman?"

"Possibly."

"What's her beef with you?"

Dave hesitated, all possible explanations sounded ridiculous in his head, he was sure they would sound no better spilling from his lips. "We work together and don't exactly get along."

"Yeah man, but that seems drastic."

"She's not above it," Dave informed him. "A real snake."

Robb nodded very seriously. "I'll keep a look out."

Dave felt his body finally relax a bit. A very small part of him worried that Robb had something to do with this, especially the police report. But he could see now that his friend was concerned, dumbfounded by the information being thrown at him.

"Is there anything else I can do to help?" Robb asked, lighting a joint and taking a deep breath.

Dave watched the smoke as it sifted and danced through the air like wisps of unreachable thoughts.

"Distract me," Dave encouraged.

Robb's face lit up with his first boyish smile of the night. "That, I can do my man!" He handed the joint to Dave, who wavered, his mind thinking back to Samantha and Georgette's conversation the other morning. His sister's venomous last words, his parent's outrageous selfishness and most of all he thought of Desiree, who he officially believed was his anonymous tormentor. But there was still space in his brain to consider he was wrong. And that was what made Dave accept the joint, and allow his mind the much-needed vacation it longed for.

An hour later, they were both laid out on the futon, a bag of Doritos between them. Dave sent Schworst an email telling him he had food poisoning after Robb begged him to blow off work and stay the night.

"Just like old times!" he reminded Dave with a grin.

Dave sent Georgette a quick text letting her know he would be staying at Robb's. The two listened to some Zen music Robb put on and let their thoughts drift. Hours could have passed—Dave felt a content humming in his brain, the absence of reality was soothing.

"Remember when we were kids?" asked Robb.

Dave opened one eye, feeling the calm induced haze of weed slightly clear from his mind.

"Yeah," he replied offhandedly, sincerely hoping that Robb wasn't about to take a morose trip down memory lane. Dave hadn't smoked in years—he tried to avoid that thought as the concept of drug-induced paranoia trickled across his mind.

"Life was so much easier then, wasn't it?"

"I suppose," he remarked with a slight edge to his tone.

"I mean, not that either of us had it easy when we were real young…but once we got into our teens a lot of that changed, you know?" Dave knew he was referring to his alcoholic stepfather dying. "All those times I thought I was invincible, unafraid of the world." Robb turned and looked at him straight in the eye, "That's what being young is all about. We think it will never catch up to us."

"Has it caught up yet?" Dave murmured, his pulse beginning to quicken.

Robb laughed to lighten the mood. Dave knew he must have sensed his growing discomfort. "Ages ago, brother. I'm starting to look my age for the first time ever."

"I hear you."

They were silent for a few minutes. Dave tried not to think. Instead he attempted to center his mind on one single image, but Robb's voice once against intruded.

"Man I miss the old burger joint sometimes, I really do."

"You've kept it almost exactly the same."

"I know, but still. Maybe I should start serving burgers."

"I take it business has been good?"

"Better than ever. Crazy busy. The kids have been cranky little shits but they listen to the new cook so it's been smooth sailing for this dude."

THE ANTAGONIST

"Can you let me know the next time someone puts a delivery in for my place?" Dave asked suddenly. "Just in case?" He knew it was an absolute long shot, he wasn't even sure if the pizzas were coming from Robb's establishment anymore.

Robb nodded, "I'll tell everyone to keep an eye out."

"Thanks, Robb."

"Hey, what are best friends for?"

Friday, October 20th

THE ANTAGONIST

I

It was the early hours of the morning, the light just peeking through Robb's blinds, when Dave finally drifted off into a dreamless sleep. Dave spent most of the morning unconscious.

They ate lunch together—a cold pizza Robb brought home from work the previous night. Dave forced himself to eat a slice, but the very concept of pizza now made him feel slightly ill.

He'd not heard a peep from anyone. His phone was silent for the remainder of the day and for that Dave was eternally thankful. He had nothing to look forward to but the weekend and hopefully the opportunity to make a few amends.

He was just contemplating his return home as the afternoon came to a close when his cellphone finally dinged. It was Georgette: *Please come home immediately. It's urgent.*

Dave felt his mouth go dry, the color drained from his face—moisture damped his hands in almost an instant.

"I have to go," was the only explanation he provided before rushing out of Robb's, his heart pumping wildly in his chest. He was in sheer terror as he drove furiously through Repo Ridge, begging the Universe that whatever was wrong, let it not be something to do with his wife.

He skidded to a halt as he came flying up the driveway, already half out of the car before it fully stopped. He raced up the stairs, flinging the door wide and called out for Georgette.

"What's going on?" he asked breathlessly when he finally located her.

She was sitting on their bed, a dark scowl marring her normally smooth face. Dave rushed forward, taking her in his arms. She was shaking. "Georg, please speak to me. Are you okay?"

She nodded against him. He pulled back to look into her eyes. There was fire there—fury.

"I had a tennis lesson earlier," she began in a low voice. "When I finished I was going to head straight into the office, but I couldn't find my briefcase…I assumed I forgot it at home." She paused and closed her eyes.

Dave thought his heart was going to explode from the anticipation of her next words. "Yeah?"

"Yeah." She opened her eyes. "But when I got here, the only thing I found was a naked woman in our bed."

Dave felt his brain disconnect. She might as well have told him she found an alien. He laughed in confusion, in disbelief as her eyes shot open piercing him with her stare. He could see instantaneously that this was no joke.

"What? How?"

"She said you two were lovers, having an affair. I obviously didn't believe her."

Dave felt the blood pounding in his brain. "This woman…did she have black hair?"

"Long and dark as night. Very beautiful." He could hear the slightest hint of insecurity in her tone. "She said you work together."

"Desiree," Dave supplied.

"She said you texted her to come over. Told her you finally wanted to give in to her." Her voice was quivering with rage. "I informed her that she was obviously mistaken." Georgie jerked her head to the bedside table. There sat a package of strawberries and a can of whipped cream.

"She brought those with her?" he asked, eyeing the props with distaste.

"She said it was your fantasy…that you wanted to cover her feet with strawberries and cream and then lick them clean." Her voice was a tremor. "She said you told her it was your fetish."

"Georgette, I swear—" he began, needing her to know he would never betray her in such a way.

But she cut him off, "I know, Dave. I didn't believe her for a second," she took a steadying breath. "But I told her, that if she comes near us again I will destroy her. I will use every last bit of my influence to ruin her life. I promised. And you know I never break a promise."

Dave nodded, feeling stunned, furious. How dare she? "How did she get in here in the first place?"

"She said you told her where the spare key was," Georgette informed him. "I already called the locksmith to change the bolts. My God, Dave, I know you said you were having problems with a woman at work, but I wasn't expecting this."

"Neither was I," he agreed, though part of him felt as if he should have seen this coming. "I will handle this, Georg."

She looked at him sharply. "No. It's better that I do. She can very easily twist this whole situation back around on you. I will protect you."

Dave felt his heart swell—he did not deserve this woman. "My job. What am I going to do?"

"Nothing. You are going to do what you do every day and continue to ignore this Desiree. I have a feeling my warning might have caused her to reconsider whatever damage she is wishing to inflict on this family."

Dave's gaze returned to the strawberries and whip cream—where the hell had she gotten an idea like that? The very thought of doing that to Desiree made his stomach twist and revolt with disgust.

"You don't have a fetish, do you?" she asked suddenly, her eyes following his own.

Dave shook his head. "Are you alright?"

His wife nodded. "Are you?"

Saturday, October 21st

THE ANTAGONIST

I

Dave contemplated that question for the entire weekend. His Saturday was spent much the same way as the previous one. He was finally able to polish the rest of the silverware and even got a few good hours out on the grounds raking before the sky decided to unload—as it was doing quite frequently these days.

Dave spent a lot of that time in anticipation of the occasion when he would come face-to-face with Desiree DeLongo. He could not believe her arrogance, the pathological manner with which she lied. How would it be possible to translate any of this to Schworst without becoming further entangled in her web? He still had no idea how she'd known he hated black olives, but this only filled him with a more dreaded questions. Had she broken into his house before? Perhaps left the sticky note he'd blown off as Georgie's? A shiver of dread ran down his spine as he considered the possibility of her lurking around, watching his family while they slept. It didn't help that due to the size of their home—someone could walk around all day and not see another soul. Plus, their hiding place for the spare key wasn't exactly hard to find.

The day seemed to drag on.

Georgette was busy with work, Sam almost never home now between school, Alex and Driver's Ed—normally his parents and sister were crowding him, especially during the weekend, but all remained silent on that front.

Dave continued to stay busy. That was his solution when in doubt.

Sunday, October 22nd

THE ANTAGONIST

I

Georgette informed him that his parents and sister were coming for dinner that evening. It was with a significant amount of dread that Dave dragged himself off to the grocery store.

As he drove through the gathering mist, he made a detour across town, deciding what he really needed was a pick-me-up.

The Devil's Eye was virtually empty. Dave was almost surprised to see J sitting at his table. It had been a week since he visited the bar, and he almost expected the man to disappear after a few days of silence. Dave was thankful this was not the case.

"Rough week?" J began in a slightly slurred tone.

Dave wondered how many the man already had.

"That's putting it lightly," Dave intoned.

"Trouble at home? Trouble at work?"

"Both," Dave conceded as Ruth swung by with his beer and another whiskey for J.

"Enjoy," was all she said.

Dave watched her walk away.

"So what are you gonna do about it?"

"There's not much I can do. My hands are tied."

J shrugged as if this meant nothing to him, "So untie them."

"Easier said than done."

"Why do I get the feeling that you always make things harder for yourself, Dave?"

"Maybe I do. I don't know."

"Have you been truthful with yourself? Is that what's causing your anxiety?"

"My truth isn't the problem. It's other's untruthfulness that I am getting snagged on."

"I see. Well, you know what they say—we can only control our actions. Not anyone else's."

"Hey, do you remember the last time I was in here?"

J didn't hesitate, "Sure, it was Monday. Almost a week ago."

"We drank too much," Dave admitted with a frown.

J scoffed in derision, "Speak for yourself, kiddo."

"Do you happen to recall seeing me with anyone?"

J shook his head, "Just me."

"Well someone drove me home," Dave insisted, hoping to jog the man's memory.

"Guess you got a good friend, then," he cleared his throat and leaned forward, "Why did you get so drunk? If you don't mind me asking…"

Dave sighed to himself. "To forget, I suppose."

"You were going on about all sorts of crazy crap—maggots in pizza, she-devils…to be honest, the more you drank the less sense you actually made."

"Yeah, that's usually the case," Dave replied with a little sarcasm. "Thanks anyway."

J lifted his glass, "Any time."

2

Dave returned home, arms weighed down by plenty of packages—he was going to try a new dish tonight.

He staggered into the kitchen under the weight of the bags, to find his entire family already there. They were gathered around the breakfast table, their heads close together—they were whispering.

As soon as they heard Dave's entrance, they fell silent and turned to look at him.

Dave didn't need to be told something was wrong. He could literally taste the tension radiating off them.

He dropped the bags and moved forward to see what they were looking at.

It was a pizza box.

It was empty.

Written inside, with black sharpie, were two words:

GET READY

"Where did this come from?" he asked quietly.

"It was outside when I got home," Samantha explained, exchanging a glance with Alex who nodded along. "What does it mean?"

"Bad things coming," his sister answered from behind him.

"Nothing bad is coming," Georgie insisted as she breezed into the room, her brow crinkled with thought. She picked up the box to dispose of it. "Just a silly prank that Dave's coworker is playing on him," she replied lightly.

THE ANTAGONIST

Dave was thankful for his wife's discretion—the last thing he needed was for his parents and sister to get even more involved in his personal business.

Dinner that night was more uncomfortable than Dave recalled it ever being before. Harmony was still giving him the cold shoulder. Any question he put to her was met with either icy silence or a muted one-word response. His parents weren't much better. June was completely subdued, avoiding everyone's gaze and speaking only to August about their plans forward with the church. They didn't dare bring up Dave's arrest. He imagined it was causing them significant grief and paranoia. Thankfully Samantha didn't seem to be interested in discussing it either. She and Alex had their own silent conversation throughout the entirety of the meal.

Georgette was not her normal chipper self. Dave could see her mind was distracted, probably attempting to figure out how to solve the Desiree problem. He felt awful about it, completely out of control and now dragging his wife into this mess with him. He should have gone to the police, he should have told someone sooner and maybe this could have all been avoided. But Desiree seemed hell bent on torturing him. Even after Georgette threatened her, she was continuing to persist. He could see this did not sit well with his wife, who was now rethinking her strategy.

Dave could feel his body filling with dread, the anticipation of what that little message might mean for him. It stayed on his mind much longer after his family departed with cool goodbyes. They never even thanked him for the meal they'd gotten so used to having handed to them.

Dave sat up most of the night considering his options. Perhaps they should just leave—pack up and get the hell out of here. Dave hated to consider any sort of rash reaction but he could feel the tightening of a noose around his neck. He had the most horrible sense that if he didn't get out now, he would never be able to leave. He couldn't shake the fear that the latest message he received was not so much of a threat as it was promise.

Monday, October 23rd

THE ANTAGONIST

I

Dave got to the office early, in the hopes of beating Desiree at her own game. He was intent on having a conversation with her, a rational one, where they could come to some sort of agreement. If it was money she wanted, then fine. He would lower himself to be a victim of blackmail if it meant she would leave him and his family alone for good.

Dave started in confusion as he opened the doors of the firm. Schworst, Desiree and Stone were sitting in the main office, seemingly waiting for him.

"You," Kyle Schworst began in a low, deadly snarl. He rose to his feet, his stance aggressive, "Now we know why you stole the tapes, you snake!"

"Kyle. Sit," Stone commanded in his authoritative tone. The man might have been old as hell, but when he spoke, everyone listened.

With a growl of retribution, Schworst sunk back into his chair and leveled a glare at Dave.

"David," Stone intoned, gesturing to the empty chair in front of him.

Dave dropped down into it. His body was numb, his heart racing. He chanced a glance at Desiree—her eyes were red-rimmed. She was sniffling into Stone's initialed handkerchief. Dave also noted several bruises on her arms and neck. His chest tightened with anxiety.

"What's going on?" he hedged, centering his gaze on the older lawyer.

Stone stared at him intently before slowly answering, "We have a problem. Ms. DeLongo told us a very disturbing story. One that involved the two of you, here. At the office, on my property."

Dave had the awful feeling he knew exactly where this was going, "Sir, with all due respect, this woman has been set on destroying my life. I'm not sure exactly what the reason is, other than the fact that I do not want to sleep with her."

Schworst laughed.

Desiree let out a tiny sob, "How can you say that? How can you sit there and look me in the eyes after what you tried to do to me? "

"Because I know, and so do you, that I never touched you."

"Then why is she covered in bruises, you fuck?" Schworst snarled, "Do you realize how much of a liability this is, you selfish prick? You couldn't attempt to rape her somewhere else?"

"Enough," Stone snapped, his patience gone. "Get out of my sight Schworst, you're beginning to make me sick."

The younger man complied, with one last sneer in Dave's direction. "You're done for, Davey."

Dave watched him walk away, wishing he could sink his fist into Schworst's face.

"Now David, Ms. DeLongo has agreed not to press charges."

Desiree interjected violently, "Even after your wife threatened me! She's just like you, stomp on the little people—trying to offer me a bribe to go away. I'm not doing this for myself. I'm doing it so everyone knows what you really are."

"You're insane," Dave blurted out with a laugh, feeling his temper soar. "You are a pathological liar—a manipulative and cruel bitch!"

Dave flushed with fury at the injustice before him as he leapt to his feet. He stared down at his tormentor with absolute loathing.

"David—"

"Sir, I have been with this firm for almost 20 years…how can you take her word over mine?"

"David. Understand we can't risk this type of behavior happening again. I'm going to have to ask you to leave. Take all of your personal belongs with you and get out."

The gloating smile that Desiree threw him over Stone's shoulder as he turned to comfort her, almost made Dave consider attacking her. He pushed down the irrational impulse, telling himself that he was lucky. He was only losing his job, not his freedom. Of course she wouldn't press charges, because she had no proof—but apparently she'd done a number on Stone just fine.

By the time Dave finished packing up his desk, the rest of his coworkers arrived. Rather quickly, Desiree made a show of her distress throughout the office, slandering his good name. By the time he finished gathering his belongings, people were staring at him with open hostility. Talking about him as if they'd never known him. They couldn't believe what a disgusting monster he'd been all along. Dave pushed down the urge to scream at them all. The few sympathetic looks he received meant nothing—even if some people thought he was innocent, they were terrified of being associated with this stigma, and getting fired themselves for even reaching out to him.

Dave was so angry by the time he got to his car he was shaking. He tried to take a few breaths to calm himself, but it was almost impossible. This accusation would be a black stain on him for the rest of his life—as long as he stayed here, in Repo Ridge. Growing up in this valley, Dave knew how small it actually was and how unforgiving its citizens could be. Without a trace of doubt in his mind, he was positive this news would spread far and wide, until it reached the ears of all those who once thought they knew him. He didn't even want to consider what his mother's reaction would be—the thought alone left him feeling faint and weak.

2

Georgette consoled him that night, promising over and over again that they would fight back. Dave was too weary to do anything other than nod along at her suggestions. He didn't want to fight. He wanted to disappear.

Tuesday, October 24th

THE ANTAGONIST

I

Samantha was the only one home when Dave emerged from his room at a quarter past noon.

"Why aren't you at school?" he asked, his voice like gravel as he joined her at the kitchen counter.

"Don't feel like going today," she replied, her eyes glued to her phone as she typed furiously. When Dave didn't argue with her, she looked up, her mouth falling open, "What happened to you?"

Dave turned to inspect his reflection in the metal teapot—his face was unshaven, his eyes rimmed with dark circles, but more than anything it was the defeat in his gaze that caused her startled reaction, he was sure.

"Life," he muttered back, reaching for a beer instead of coffee. Sam's eyes widened with interest.

"Why aren't you at work?" she hovered over him, inspecting his uncharacteristic disarray.

"I got fired."

"Good for you." Samantha never approved of authority or working for anyone other than herself—not that she needed to work at all.

"It's messed up," he said under his breath.

"Feeling angst-y?" she questioned.

Dave didn't even need to contemplate an answer. "A bit, yes."

Samantha grinned evilly. "Wanna punch someone?"

"Actually, I do."

"Then I challenge you to three rounds of *Mortal Kombat*—loser makes dinner."

THE ANTAGONIST

A week ago, Dave would have jumped at this opportunity. Would have smiled so widely on the inside to be included in her life. Instead he felt the heavy weight of the unknown consume him.

"Not today, Sam."

She wasn't deterred, "Let's listen to some music, have a jam sesh or something."

"I really can't—"

"Why not?"

He had no response. The silence apparently convinced his stepdaughter that she was the problem—not him.

Her face went from neutral to annoyed in a matter of seconds. "Fine, but don't ever say I didn't try. I thought you wanted to be a father figure. Mom has done everything to include you in our lives. When I finally give you the chance you don't want it? Ellie was right, you don't care about anyone but yourself!"

She stormed from the room before Dave even had a second to properly digest her words. Who was Ellie? Probably some other miserable teen that thought adults did not understand—like he hadn't been a kid himself.

Dave felt a stab of regret at his dismissal of Samantha, but the last thing he wanted to do was increase his anxiety when it finally subsided—to be replaced with the hollowness of depression. But Dave justified this—he was allowed to sulk, he could give himself a few days to mourn what had been his life.

He lifted the beer to his lips and wandered off in search of a distraction.

2

Although Dave accomplished very little for the remainder of the day, he forced himself to finally get dressed around 5:30. He figured the least he could do was pick up some dinner for his family. And even though the thought of eating pizza distressed him more than anything, he really wanted to see his best friend.

Robb met him at the back door just as he was raising his fist to knock. With a hurried glance over his shoulder, Robb squeezed out the door, shutting it tightly behind him. Dave took a step back and offered him a questioning stare.

"Dave, man," he began in a low voice, "What are you doing here?"

Dave was perplexed by this question. "I wanted to talk to you—"

Robb cut across him, "Yeah, same."

Dave arched an eyebrow as Robb took a deep breath. "Look, I heard about what happened. About…you and that woman."

Dave felt anger once again slice through him. "You mean the woman who falsely accused me of attempted rape?" he snapped.

Robb hesitated, "Yeah, that one."

"Well?" Dave demanded impatiently.

"A few of the waitresses are freaked out about the whole thing."

Dave blinked. "So I'm banned from your pizza place? The one I helped you open?" he added, just to clarify.

"It's not permanent man, relax. It's just until things cool off, go back to normal."

"Don't you get it!?" Dave railed. "This is never going to go away for me. That woman has completely ruined my life."

Dave couldn't believe it when Robb's face split into a sardonic smile and he shrugged. "Nothing could ruin your life. You have a beautiful wife, tons of money…so what you lost some stupid job? It's not like you needed it."

Dave couldn't comprehend what he was hearing. This was the same man who'd been by his side for almost his entire life, like a brother. When Robb went down for his drug use, Dave made the choice to go down with him. He helped pull him back up afterwards, too—and now here he was, showing zero sympathy at his plight.

"Wow," he muttered under his breath, turning away. "Okay. You too, then."

Robb was already opening the back door once again. "It's bad for business, Dave. If there's anything you ever taught me, it's not to mix the personal with the business."

The door slammed shut before Dave could tell him to go to hell.

Wednesday, October 25th

THE ANTAGONIST

I

Dave's disposition did not improve. The rude awakening of a foreign feeling persisted—to think you know someone your whole life, just to be betrayed and turned on when you need them most. Dave wasn't sure if he would ever recover from that blow.

But the blows kept coming. It seemed as if Desiree's actions set off a series of events that bled over into an aftermath much deadlier than the initial accusation itself.

Dave awoke to screaming that morning—sheer-terror, throat-ripping, panic- induced screams.

His sister was unable to catch her breath, causing Georgette to reach for the phone. She was calling for an ambulance. But from the sound of it, there was already one approaching.

"Harmony, breathe," Dave instructed as he kneeled in front of her, rubbing her wrists—it always calmed her down when she was a child. "Tell me what's wrong."

"A-a-a-a-gust," she wheezed, her eyes wide with fear as she clutched at her heart, "H-h-h-ospital."

The sirens stopped. Dave jumped into action, grabbing his keys and throwing on a jacket over his sweat pants and t-shirt. He hauled Harmony to her feet as Georgette protested.

"She's fine. She's coming with me. If something's happened, she needs to face it," he whispered under his breath to his wife, "Trust me I know my sister."

"I'll just get my jacket," Georgette insisted as she turned, but Dave grabbed her arm to halt her progress.

"No," her face fell as he continued, "It will be easier this way, my love, trust me."

The look he gave her, the desperation in his gaze allowed her to comply, even if it was reluctantly.

"I'll be here, if you need anything."

∽

Harmony was whimpering in protest by the time he strapped her into the car. Her face was covered and she was rocking back and forth in a state of complete distress. Dave was briefly reminded of a nature show where he'd seen a snail sneak into survival mode. It crawled far into its shell and played dead—he remembered marveling at such an accomplishment.

Dave was unable to get another word out of his sister other than 'Doctor H.' He knew he should probably contact her therapist, but at the moment it was very possible their father's life was hanging in precarious balance, and therefore Harmony would have to take a back seat to priority.

They made it to the hospital just minutes after the ambulance. June was waiting in the dimly lit hallway with a nurse. Dave was expecting to see tears, grief—but there was nothing, no emotion in her eyes—only a cool calm façade.

"What's happened?" Dave panted, out of breath from their sprint across the parking lot.

"My poor August, God protect him," she murmured, bowing her head in prayer, "My sweet, innocent August."

Harmony was shaking yet silent beside him—her eyes wide and slightly unfocused. He wished, in that moment, that he could read her mind.

The nurse captured his attention instead, "Your father has suffered a massive heart attack," the woman informed him, "We are doing everything we can. I was just telling June here, I thought you'd all be more comfortable in the visitor's room, but she wanted to wait for you."

Dave nodded in compliance as she navigated them into

the waiting room—the sickly yellow of the walls made Dave's stomach twist. It reminded him of the melting-cheese-covered maggots. He clenched his fists and waited in silence, shoved into a lumpy old chair between the two women in his life who would not let go.

Dave easily forgot time as he sat there in a complete stupor. Lost amongst the chaos in a shipwreck of dissonance. He would not surface from this, he did not want to. It was quiet in the in-between, the eye of the storm, the not knowing. Harmony's nails were nothing more than chewed down bloody stubs by the time a doctor finally emerged with a grimly rehearsed look on her face.

"I'm sorry."

Those two words explained it all—his father was dead. He turned to face his mother as the doctor retreated, leaving the three of them alone to process this news. She was livid. Alight with rage. Before Dave could offer any sort of comfort, June was on her feet and glaring down at her children as if they were the cause of her immense pain.

"You," she began, shaking her fist in their direction, "are wicked. You two are the reason August is gone! He had to pay for your sins! I devoted my entire life to God, to save your unfortunate souls!"

"Mom—" Dave tried but he was shut down.

"I will have my say!" she screamed, spit flying from her mouth.

Harmony was cocooning herself into the smallest possible ball she could make.

"Maybe you don't remember, but when you were small, I caught you fondling each other, doing disgusting and shameful things! I thought to blame myself. Maybe I left you alone for too long but the Lord tasked me with a heavy load. No, I see now it was in your souls. And being the good Christian woman I am, I forgave you, you were young, you, David, didn't know what you were doing. But now I see, as I have suspected for very long time—you are bad seeds. The devil cast his shadow over you and I can see it as clearly now as I should have then."

Dave stared at his mother in shock, "That's a ridiculously tall tale, mother. I don't know why you would tell it."

"That one," she hissed, pointing at Harmony, "encouraged you, she was the first one out, the perversion, the one to start it all, wicked girl—rotten to the core," she turned her mad eyes toward Dave. "I thought you were better. But look at the pain your actions have cost us! Your deviant nature!"

"My actions?"

"That woman you work with! The story has spread over town like wildfire. Everyone in the church knows what you have done and they blame us!"

"I didn't do anything," Dave defended. "I didn't touch her," he calmly explained.

"Just like you didn't touch your own flesh and blood? How could I trust you? You've lied to Him over and over again. Nothing will save you now—the pair of you. How I ever created such filth, I will never know,"

Her words were more painful than Dave could stand. His sister would never recover from this slaughter.

"You will no longer blacken my doorstep. I will be right with Him. God, I swear to you, I no longer acknowledge either of these beasts as mine. Spare me."

She fell silent, her head lifted in prayer as if waiting for them to drop on their knees and beg forgiveness—to let her sacrifice them to the church for her own personal gainful pleasure.

The still air was finally broken by the sound of laughter.

It was his sister.

What started as a small chuckle became a raucous hilarity that alarmed him—Harmony laughed until tears were streaming down her face—her shoulders shaking, her chest heaving with humor, she continued to laugh long after June slapped her across the face and stormed from the room. She laughed the whole way home. She laughed herself to sleep in Dave's arms.

～

Dave wanted to believe his mother's reaction was grief, but he knew better.

His sister reemerged around seven that evening. She asked Georgette if she wouldn't mind giving her a ride across town for an emergency therapy session.

Georgette didn't hesitate for a second, leaving Dave once again alone with horrific thoughts. He couldn't imagine the affect his mother's words must have had on Harmony. And what could he do now? It was unlikely that June would concede, or even more miraculously apologize. He hadn't even told Georgette the full extent of what happened yet—he knew she was going to be absolutely livid. Would she cut his mother off? Send her back into poverty or worse, out onto the streets? As much as Dave was disgusted with June, she was still his mother. Harmony, however, would not feel the same. He hoped his sister didn't unload on his wife—it was bound to do more damage than good and Dave had all the damage he could possibly deal with at the moment.

Thursday, October 26th

THE ANTAGONIST

I

He spent almost the entire morning and a good portion of the afternoon helping move his sister out of the guest apartment. She adamantly refused to stay, even after Georgette promised she wasn't going to evict them from the property she technically owned. Whatever happened during her session the previous night lit a fire under Harmony. She was wearing a look of determination that Dave had not seen on her face before.

Almost all of the packing was paintings his sister had done. Harmony kept very few personal items—everything else she owned fit in one knapsack.

Dave attempted to convince her to move into their home for a few months, just until she was able to get on her feet. He was positive she would accept, it's not as if she had anywhere else she could go. When he voiced his opinion he was met with defiance.

"I don't need you," she snapped.

"It's not about needing, I just want to help—"

"You've done enough to help," her tone oozed with sarcasm.

"Look, I know you blame me—"

"I do."

"But what happened to dad is not my fault, Harmony."

She turned to look at him with a false smile. "You think that's why I'm mad at you?"

"Isn't it?"

"No, dear brother, it is not."

He was unable to get another word out of her for the rest of the day. June watched them with beady eyes from the kitchen window as they loaded up the last of Harmony's things. When Dave accidentally caught his mother's glare, she whipped the curtains shut, blocking them out once more.

"Where to?" Dave asked as his sister slid into the backseat of his fully packed car.

"Just drive. I'll tell you when we are there."

Dave sat silently, occasionally glancing in the mirror to check on his sister. She only spoke when telling him to turn. They wove their way toward the outer limits of Repo Ridge. They continued North for another fifteen minutes until Harmony spoke again.

"Here, on the right."

Dave pulled into the small, sad looking strip mall that housed a roller skating rink when they were kids. That was gone—replaced with several small shabby- looking businesses. Only a few of them appeared functional; the rest of the spaces were empty, boarded up and festering with dilapidation. Dave curiously scanned the buildings until he saw a small sign for Psychotherapy—private practice.

"Do you want me to come in with you?"

Harmony shook her head as she moved to exit the car, but Dave reached back and stopped her. She ripped her arm away from his touch.

"Goodbye, Dave."

"Goodbye? Harmony. Please, tell me where you are going. At least so I know you are safe."

"Now you care?"

"I've always cared!"

"If that is true then why did you lie to me?"

"I don't have an excuse. I really don't."

"I've always been a burden to you. I don't want that anymore."

"I've never thought of you in that way."

"Why are you still lying?"

"What is it you want to hear?"

"I want you to admit the truth! I want you to say, Harmony you have wasted your life trying to be like me, someone who is not worthy of mirroring. I want you to say I am better than being your pathetic twin—that I can do more with my life! And now I'm going to."

"I have always believed you were capable of doing anything you set your mind to, you know that. Have I not supported you all these years?"

"Maybe financially. I won't ever forgive you."

"Forgive me for what!?"

"Leaving me with them."

"I could have done a lot worse! I could have left you in poverty. I could have moved away from this shit-hole. I could have let you rot in that mental hospital."

"Well maybe you should have! Maybe I would have had a chance then."

"Your immaturity and selfishness is duly noted."

"Fuck you, Dave. You're just pissed because you finally have to accept that you are no longer perfect."

"I never said I was."

"No, it was just the grandiosity, the emulation of perfection that you have reeked of all these years. Now someone is finally paying you back for all the times you got away. Now you get to suffer like the rest of us!"

Before he could respond she kicked open the door and jumped out. She began to walk away.

"Harmony!"

"Keep the paintings," she tossed over her shoulder.

"Harmony!"

She ignored him.

"Where are you going?"

She paused and turned, "I'm going to start my life."

THE ANTAGONIST

2

There was nothing more he could do—in that moment he felt worse than he could have anticipated. It was as if a part of him just broke off, a piece of his soul was ripped away without a second thought. His sister was leaving him behind, just as he secretly feared she might always do. He loved her dearly, had tried with every ounce of his person to make her happy and give her a shot at a normal life. He failed her—had been unable to protect someone he deeply cared for. He knew Georgette would agree with his sister. She would tell him that it was time to let go. But Harmony walking away from the rest of the family, from him, did not sit right. How would she survive? Surely her therapist wasn't going to be enough. Did she have a plan? He prayed to some unknown force that she would see the error in her ways and return to them once she cooled off. This was worse than when she'd been institutionalized—at least Dave had known where to find her then. Now, he had no clue as to what her next move would be. But once again, he was unable to control the actions of all but himself.

Dave sat in that parking lot for twenty minutes, waiting for her to return. He figured he'd sit there all night if he had to. Just long enough until he knew she was in good hands. But fate had other plans in store. His phone dinged with a message from Georgie: *Come home, please.*

Dave's mind swung to the irrational—his first thought was Desiree. He texted back quickly: *What is it? Are you hurt?*

THE ANTAGONIST

She was already typing again: *I'm fine, but I have news I'd rather tell you in person.*

Dave swallowed the lump that was forming in his throat. Trying to block out the thought of never seeing his sister again, he pulled out of the parking lot and turned his mind back towards home. What news could she possibly have for him?

Hadn't there been enough surprises this week? Dave's stomach rolled—he was so tense. The sensation of knives stabbing into his muscles persisted with no sympathy. His head was aching, his eyes unbelievably exhausted. A quick glance in the mirror confirmed all the dread he was experiencing was real—he looked as if he aged ten years overnight.

∼

Georgette was waiting for him on the front porch, a cigarette dangling between her thin fingers. It forcibly reminded him of his last rational conversation with his sister. Had that really been a little over a week ago? It seemed like centuries to Dave. He approached his wife warily, waiting for the next bomb to drop. She wasn't crying and she didn't look angry—those were good signs. But she was nervous and eyeing him with caution. Dave did not like that.

"Do I look that bad?" he attempted to joke as she shook her head.

"Sit down, darling," she began, patting the smooth wood at her side.

Dave cautiously joined her.

"No more bad news," he whispered with a plea.

She looked at him, "Not bad, no. Just…unexpected."

His mind flew to pregnancy—but that was impossible, Georgette went through menopause a few years back—as if Dave could ever forget the mood swings and night sweats.

"Georg—"

"Sam's left."

"What?"

"Her and Alex…they left."

"Left? Left to where?"

Georgette sighed as she handed him a note, "Now please, don't get upset," she pleaded.

Dave felt his heart skip two beats as he unfolded the letter:

Mom,

I'll FaceTime you tonight, but this letter is just so you don't freak out when you can't get ahold of me. Alex and I are leaving Repo. I fucking hate this place and he got offered a great opportunity up North, in a city with actual people. I can't stay here anymore—after a sparkling conversation with your husband, I realize I've never belonged. I know you are happy, but I'm not. I found my person and we want to be together. I don't want the drama anymore, especially now that Dave has fucked up his own reputation.

I miss you already.

Come visit soon. Alone.

Sam

p.s. passed my license exam this morning with flying colors!

"She can't—" he began, feeling the paper slide from his fingers in a stupor.

"Georgette, we have to find her."

"Darling, please don't panic, I know how this may seem—"

"It is completely inappropriate! She's not even 17!"

"She will be in two months."

"Then she can get her ass back here until then."

"Dave—" she tried to interrupt again.

"How could you let her leave? With that man!" his voice was filled with anger.

"I thought you were warming up to Alex?"

"That doesn't change the fact that what they are doing is completely wrong! Dammit!" he jumped to his feet, smashing his fist into the railing. Georgette started at his outburst.

"I understand this is difficult for you, that you feel responsible…"

"I am responsible!"

"But you're not. Even if you hadn't spoken to Sam, she still would have left. She just wanted to throw a little salt in the wound before she did."

"She tried to engage me the other morning, truly, for the first time ever and I blew her off," his voice broke on the last syllable as he covered his face with his hand and turned away. He was splintering at the seams.

"This is not your fault, Dave. At the end of the day, she's my daughter."

"Exactly! How are you not freaking out!?" he demanded rather roughly.

"Because, I firmly believe in letting things go. A practice I think you should consider implementing."

"Harmony would agree with you. She's gone."

Georgette looked startled for the first time. "Gone? What do you mean, gone?"

He shrugged, "She wants nothing to do with me."

"She will come around. You know how much she loves you."

"I don't think she will, Georg. She blames me for her entire life."

"We both know that's neither true nor fair."

"It really doesn't matter what we know, because at the end of the day the result is still the same—they are gone."

∽

Emily Dinova

Dinner was a quiet affair that night—just him and Georgette…ironically that was what he'd been craving not long ago…and now the reality of the situation was so much worse.

They spoke very little. Georgette kept throwing him sideway glances, hoping that his temper passed. It had. To be replaced with bone weariness that forced Dave to rise from the table after only eating two bites of his roast chicken. He spent most of dinner just moving the food around his plate like his sister would. He briefly wondered where Samantha was, if she was safe. His wife's nonchalance over the situation was making him sick.

He excused himself and retired early, hoping that sleep would bring him a few hours of nothingness. A small sliver of Dave even hoped that morning would not come at all. That he would never wake up again.

Friday, October 27th

THE ANTAGONIST

I

It was dark when Dave left the house. He was restless and barely managed an hour of sleep before his body jerked him awake in alarm. He was sure for about sixty seconds that he stopped breathing. He'd been dreaming. His mind need not attempt to cling to the subconscious thoughts for they were ringing a warning through his brain. He dreamed of his childhood, the nightmarish remembrance of his youth—his parents abandoning him, Dave lying on the floor—dirty, miserable and starving. He could hear his sister crying in the next room, but no matter what he did he was unable to move. He could still feel the pain in his limbs, even now that he was awake. The image from his nightmare that stuck out the most was the cross that hovered above him and the bleeding Jesus nailed to it that kept telling him he was damned, he was unworthy and that he deserved to suffer.

This dream railed against his mind as he drove through the deserted streets of Repo Ridge, hell bent on escaping—he wasn't sure if it was from others, or from his own self.

He reached Parrish Street just as the first muted tones of light began to ascend over the sky. His old neighborhood remained almost identical to how he remembered it: sparse, empty and cold. Small mobile homes lined the block, their bent antennas teetering limply on the dilapidated roofs. The smell of rotting garbage permeated his senses as he parked the car and got out. A sickly looking cat shot out from under a rusted and smashed up truck. Cigarette butts and broken whiskey bottles sat like lawn decorations on each dead patch of ground.

Dave grew up on the very edge of town, all the way East. And although the neighborhood was definitely the worst in the county, it also happened to have the most magnificent sunrises. Dave walked down the middle of the street moving towards the growing light.

He wasn't sure why his impulse led him back here after so many years…what was it that he was missing? Had his attempt to better himself backfired? Did the Universe work in such a cruel way that those who were born in the gutter were destined to return there after they'd gotten away? He fought for everything he acquired, did all in his power to return the good to those who'd been good to him.

He wanted to push on as the sun rose, its magical waves sweeping over him and warming his soul. *But how much more could a person take?* He wondered. What kind of test was he being put to if this was the case?

Dave would have to persevere, if for nothing other than his wife. Though she'd been blessed with wealth, Georgette endured much more abuse than he, both from her father and her ex-husband. He would sacrifice any and everything to keep her safe and happy. The light in the sky was almost fully extended. Dave spread his arms as if hoping he might absorb the healing rays.

He almost felt young again. That could only mean one thing:

He still had hope.

2

The sun was fully up by the time Dave returned home. All was silent.

"Georg?" he called, assuming she'd already left for work. He was therefore surprised to hear slow steps coming down the main staircase. Dave backtracked into the hallway and looked up. His wife halted as their eyes met, her foot dangling carefully above the next step down. Instead of taking it, she moved backwards. Up. Further away from him.

Dave paused at the bottom of the stairs with the slight frown. Georgette was shaking.

"Hey, are you alright—" he started to ask as he moved towards her. She raised her hand as if to halt him.

She shook her head as a few stubborn tears slipped from her eyes, "I don't honestly know what to say," she whispered, her voice raw as if she'd been screaming for hours.

"What is it?" he hedged, once again feeling his anxiety return in full force.

She let out a choked sob. Her knees buckled as she grabbed onto the marble railing for support. "You were the perfect man. You saved my life."

"And I would do it all again," Dave returned with no hesitance. He hated that she no longer deemed him perfect.

"We have been through it, the good, the bad…most assuredly the ugly." Dave nodded along, perplexed as to where she was going with the conversation. "But this. This is too much. I can't do it."

"Can't do what? Georgie, please" he begged, wishing he could get closer to her. He attempted to take a step forward again, but this time she took three steps back. Her feet tripped over each other clumsily as she tried to keep distance between them.

"I can't be with you!" she screamed suddenly, pulling at her hair as if she'd love nothing more than to be able to rip out her own thoughts, "You are *sick*. You are so sick. Oh my God," she turned her face to the side and threw up over the balcony.

Dave closed his eyes as he listened to the sick splatter against the marble floors wishing it were his brains.

"Why? Please—I don't understand!"

Georgie pulled herself together, wiping her mouth with the back of her hand as she turned towards him once again. Her chest was rising and falling with short, uneven breaths.

"I saw the tape."

Dave's mind whirled. Desiree. The video surveillance that had gone missing after their encounter at the law firm—the footage that Schworst accused him of stealing, it was never found. But nothing happened between them, he pushed her away after attempting to figure out if she was the one messing with him. Dave was so relieved he began to laugh. The look Georgette gave him was like a shot of poison through his bones.

"Who are you?" The fury in her gaze was palpable.

"Nothing happened, Georgie, I swear."

She exploded, "How easy it is for you to lie to my face!"

"I didn't—"

"Get the fuck out. Get out and never come back. I don't want to see you ever again you disgusting, vile monster!" her voice broke as she rushed back up the stairs, slamming doors behind her.

Dave felt his own knees give out as he dropped down onto the bottom stair, his brain whirling with possibilities. Was it possible Desiree edited the tape to make it look like he'd done what he was accused of?

Almost instantaneously his mind flashed back to the night he blacked out at The Devil's Eye—when he could not remember getting home. Was it possible that Desiree had been the one to find him staggering drunkenly from the bar? Was it possible that she followed him, or even attempted to rape him? Did they have sex? Did she tape it and make it look like a rape? Dave felt an emptiness fill him.

He could no longer feel rage, or injustice or even the will to fight. He refused to accept that the only woman he ever loved just cast him aside and demanded that he never show his face ever again.

He'd only been away from the house for a few hours. He was sure that'd given Desiree plenty of time to deliver her last blow. She'd taken away everything he was living for. And for what, sick pleasure? The heartbreak began to eat away at his insides as he listened to Georgette's soft sobs echoing back down the staircase.

Dave lifted himself to his feet with barely enough strength left for the task. He would let her grieve. But he would be back, only when he had proof that whatever tape she saw, was false—just another unwarranted attack on his person. He couldn't stay here. But there was no one else he could go to. With that depressing admonition at the forefront of his mind, Dave went to the only place he would be able to forget, and to the only person who was probably still willing to be associated with him.

THE ANTAGONIST

3

He walked to The Devil's Eye. It took him almost two hours, but he managed. It was a little after noon by the time he arrived and the place was packed. Dave was thankful for this—it would be easier for him to blend and disappear into the background. The beautiful thing about the bar was the people who frequented it. They were mostly outcasts and drunks themselves. Even after Dave's horrendously scandalous week, no one in the joint seemed to judge him or care what happened. The regulars nodded the same as they always did, and Dave took his table in the back.

Not only was Ruth absent—J was nowhere to be seen, either. Dave experienced a sinking sensation at the possibility that some horror also consumed his new friend. Not even a week passed since the last time he'd come in—surely J was just drying out before tonight's libations, or maybe Ruth got sick of giving him free drinks.

Dave craned his neck in search of someone to fill his order. But no one came. Maybe that was a sign, that he shouldn't be drinking away his problems. But what other solution did he have? He at least hoped to get some advice from J, but it was clear now—he was going to weather this storm alone. Dave hated that fact. Hated the very idea of being stuck with himself, especially now.

So he sat, not drinking, not speaking, just staring off into space and trying to come up with any solution that might bring a modicum of solace or peace to his mind. The afternoon wore on and Dave lost track of time as the bar emptied, filled up again and emptied once more just before midnight.

THE ANTAGONIST

The sound of two whiskeys hitting the table startled Dave from his stupor. Before he could blink, a woman he'd never seen before slid into the chair opposite him. Dave looked around, the bar was empty—they were alone.

She placed her arms on the table and leaned her face against the palms of her hands. Dave stared at her curiously—she must be the new bartender.

"Your order," she raised her eyebrows and nodded her chin towards the whiskey.

"I don't drink whiskey," he intoned, wishing she would leave him in peace.

"I've been pouring it out for you steadily the last few weeks. I think I would know."

Dave lifted his tired eyes at her somewhat aggressive tone. It was only then that he took a better look at her, "Do I know you?"

She smiled in response. She was attractive—there was no denying that. But there was something about the antagonism in her gaze that made him desirous to get as far away from her as possible.

"You used to drink beer. Then you added whiskey. The last few times you've come in, it's been a lot more of the latter."

"That's for J, not me."

"J?" she wondered, as she sat back in the chair and shot one of the two drinks. "Who is J?"

"If you're so sure about what I drink, I imagine you would also know who I spend my time drinking with."

"How interesting," she mused with a hint of humor.

"Why is that interesting?"

"You drink by yourself."

The conviction with which she spoke those words startled Dave. He paused, "No, I don't. Not anymore."

"I have never seen you here with another soul. You sit in this corner and babble away at the wall. That's what you do."

Dave considered Ruth's behavior towards J, how she never once greeted him or acknowledged his presence…but that wasn't possible. It couldn't be. Dave was immediately consumed by the question of his own sanity.

He stood suddenly, done with this hypnotic witch, who was beginning to grate sorely on his nerves. "Really nice how you treat your customers," he spat.

"You, Dave Collins, are not my customer."

The way she said his name ran a particularly vicious chill down his spine. He felt himself sink back into the chair.

"Georgie left you, didn't she?" she remarked offhandedly.

Dave felt his awareness heighten. "Who are you?" he whispered, tilting his head to better inspect her shadowed face.

The mystery woman leaned forward once more, her vivid green eyes penetrating every pore, every essence of his being—for the first time in his life Dave felt as if he were being stripped bare—it was the inexplicable feeling that this woman knew him better than he knew himself.

"It's been a very long time, so let me refresh your memory. My name is Jane Havens and I am the return of the repressed."

Part II: Jane Unknown

Friday, October 27th

THE ANTAGONIST

I

Tonight was the night.

She could taste victory. Sensed it the moment Dave Collins entered the bar. It was time for the reveal of her true self.

The combination of nerves and anticipation streamed though her veins—she knew she must remain calm, no matter what.

Jane would not be the one to suffer. No, that sentiment was reserved for the man who sat in front of her. Who looked at her like a puzzle, maybe even a figment of his imagination? Perhaps he thought she was like this J he insisted he drank with, but no, Jane was real. And it was finally time to expose the horror she kept locked away in the depths of her soul.

THE ANTAGONIST

2

It was easy enough to deliver the final blow. Jane waited that morning in the dark as she watched her prey depart—she had a feeling where he might be heading, but it didn't matter now. Most of the damage was already done.

She carefully left the wrapped package where she knew Georgette would find it long before her husband returned. Jane specifically addressed it to her, knowing Dave would never do something like open his wife's mail. He was always maintaining that infuriating respect and awe—hiding his true nature and letting the world believe he was one of the good guys. To be sure, he played the role perfectly. *Until me*, she thought with a grim smirk of satisfaction. The tape would condemn him, he'd have nowhere left to turn but the bar, and she would be ready when he finally showed his disgustingly righteous face.

Thursday, October 26th

THE ANTAGONIST

I

"And he just blew me off, like that!" Sam fumed as she pulled the 'student driver' car out of the parking lot.

Jane frowned, "Seriously? After years of him trying to suck up to you? Then you finally reach out and he responds with rejection?"

Samantha's hands clenched the steering wheel tight. "He's a total dick. I've told my mom a hundred times I don't know what she sees in him," she huffed as she drove a few miles over the speed limit. "And now he gets in trouble for fucking his coworker or something? It's disgusting. I don't understand why she puts up with it."

"Why do you?" Jane countered.

"I'm done with it, this whole place."

"I mean from what you've told me about your stepfather, it seems like his whole good guy act is bogus."

"Trust me, it is."

They sat in silence as Jane carefully watched her student. She could tell Samantha was contemplating her future. What life would be like now that Dave was considered a villain—if she'd learned anything about the teen over the last month, it was that she couldn't stand to be associated with injustice. She also knew that Sam hated Repo Ridge and all the suburban bullshit that came along with it.

"Do you ever think about leaving?" Jane finally asked.

Sam's eyes lit up, "It's like you can read my mind. Alex and I have been talking about it, considering it…" she trailed off as she took a right hand turn past Repo Pizza.

"He's an artist, right?"

THE ANTAGONIST

Sam nodded.

"I have a friend in Manhattan I could put him in contact with…he's been looking for new talent. I mean, that's only if you want to live in a city," Jane chanced a glance at Sam—her features lit up with pure excitement. What young woman wouldn't want to move to New York City?

"That would be amazing," her face slightly fell. "but I don't get my inheritance for another year or so…we couldn't afford it right now."

"I have a place there, it's not much at all, really small—in the East Village. It's been in the family for years…I usually rent it out but if you want it, it's yours."

Sam slammed on the brakes, realizing she was about to run a stop sign.

"Eyes on the road!"

Samantha immediately returned her attention to the street, checking both ways before she continued on. "You're not serious," she insisted.

"Dead."

"I will pay you back as soon as I get a job—"

"That's not necessary…the apartment used to belong to my sister. I know she would want you to be there."

A sad look crossed Sam's face as she nodded, "She was so lucky to have a sister like you, Ellie—I wish I did."

Jane smiled. "If I can help a young person out of a bad situation, then I will. I know you have a bright future ahead of you, Sam. But I don't think it's here."

"Neither do I."

Jane directed her attention towards the checklist in front of her, a feeling of hope mounting in her chest. She would save this girl the way someone should have saved her.

"Our two hours are almost up, you just need to drive back to the lot and parallel park."

Samantha did what was required—she hastily killed the engine and turned to look expectantly at her driver instructor. "Did I pass?"

"With flying colors."

"I can't wait to tell Alex the news!" Sam clapped her hands together in glee and then once more focused her attention on Jane quite seriously. "And you're sure? About New York?"

Jane knew it seemed too good to be true—but unlike most people, Jane was selfless when it came to rescuing those who were trapped with imposters like Dave.

"I'll email you all of the information, but only if you promise to keep me posted on your progress," she joked with a slight smile.

Samantha reached across the seat and pulled her in for a huge hug. "You are the greatest human being alive."

Jane felt her throat clog with emotion—she missed her sister Elizabeth so damn much in moments like these. She cleared her throat and squeezed back, "It's nothing. I'm just happy to help you out." *Of here, and away from him*, she finished in her head.

Wednesday, October 25th

THE ANTAGONIST

I

Jane was just closing up when frantic knocking inundated her thoughts. She hurried back across the sparsely furnished office. She peeked carefully through the blinds. With a jolt of recognition, she unlocked the front door and admitted her patient.

"Ms. Collins, are you alright?" Jane asked, guiding the trembling woman forward.

"I'm sorry, I should have called," she whispered hoarsely as she sank down onto the couch.

"It's no problem," Jane soothed as she went about retrieving Harmony a bottle of water.

Jane sat patiently and waited for the woman to calm down and speak. She could not imagine what transpired but it was clearly nothing good; surely if that was the case Dave must be involved.

"August is dead."

Jane was not expecting this, though she could not say she was surprised. The man was an absolute glutton; it was only a matter of time before his heart gave out. "I'm sorry for your loss. You must have a lot of conflicting feelings."

Harmony nodded vigorously. "I hope June burns in hell. Am I a horrible person? For saying that?"

"Not at all. You are human and you will feel what you will. It's not as if you are personally dragging your mother to hell, or hurting her in anyway. It's normal to have these feelings. It's also critical that you voice these feelings and give them representation," Jane explained carefully.

"I can't trust my brother. He's lied to me so much."

THE ANTAGONIST

"I would like to focus on you. What Harmony wants and needs."

"I need to get away from them."

"Do you have anywhere you can go?"

"Back to the hospital."

"Have you thought anymore about looking for a job?" Jane could tell she was quickly regressing—the last thing this woman needed was to be locked away. Just as her family had done to her, just as Dave had done. It was unacceptable. Jane would not allow it.

Harmony let out a growl of frustration, "I just don't know where to start!"

Jane hesitated, but only for a moment. "I can help you."

"You already do!"

Jane leaned forward, looking directly into Harmony's eyes, "I have resources, the ability to find you a low-rent apartment as well as a job." She hadn't planned on getting this invested—it was not protocol, but this was a special circumstance.

"Do you do this for all your patients?"

"No, but not all my patients are you," Jane leaned forward and looked her in the eyes. "Your circumstances are unique. My job is to alleviate your suffering, to help you get to know the real you, the one beneath the layers of doubt and insecurity. If gaining independence from those that have hurt you for so long is the way to progress, then I will do all within my power to help you."

"The day I saw your flyer on that coffee shop wall…it was the luckiest day of my life."

The truth was, that it wasn't luck at all. Jane knew Harmony visited that coffee shop almost every day. It was one of the only places she ever went. She also knew that Harmony's therapist, before her interference, had been a hack. Once Jane was able to observe the woman, it was easy enough to gain her as a client and greatly improve her disposition. Any stress or damage she might have caused this woman, she had not done on purpose—in fact she tried to undo the deeply rooted trauma instead. But if there were causalities along the way, then that would have to be the price paid. An eye for an eye. She hoped it wouldn't come to that. Jane didn't want to hurt them. All her rage and carefully laid plans were for him.

She reached over and gently squeezed Harmony's cold and trembling hand.

"It's going to be okay, Ms. Collins. I believe that and so should you."

Jane would make sure of it.

Tuesday, October 24th

THE ANTAGONIST

I

Jane was thrilled that this would be her final visit—the last time of having to step foot in this Godforsaken place.

Her workload would be light. At least half of the people congregating around the pews already heard the news. Her job would be to whisper the slander to the most vindictive and devout of worshipers: Agatha Grey. She basically ran the church, along with her closest friend June Collins. But it appeared as if the matronly devil herself had already heard of the Collins's latest fall from grace—hearing of their son's police record was bad enough, this was something even worse.

Jane watched as Agatha's beady eyes narrowed—she'd been keeping watch over the front doors for the last 15 minutes as the flock trickled in. Jane smiled; she was the wolf, wearing their clothing. Agatha got to her feet in a huff and cut June and August off before they were able to even dip a pinky in the anointed holy water. Jane wished she could hear the words exchanged, they looked vicious and unforgivable.

June's face lost all blood as she weakly clasped her hands together. She was begging. But Agatha, being the good Christian woman that she always claimed to be, ordered them from the church, loudly informing all who were listening, that the Collins's and their uncouth family were no longer welcome.

June let out a shriek of fury before turning on her heel and storming from the place. Jane watched as August blubbered to himself—clutching at his chest, before following his wife out.

THE ANTAGONIST

Jane turned her attention back toward the alter—over the years, the course of a tumultuous and broken life, she once turned to the concept of God. And he failed her, just like everyone else. Prayers were nothing but unfulfilled dreams and she would not waste another minute on them. She had almost everything that she wanted. She was so close to *true* redemption.

"Hope?" she lifted her head from what she knew looked like deep contemplation to see Agatha squeezing into the pew next to her.

"Yes, Mrs. Grey?" she asked with wide innocent eyes in her softest tone.

"I'm sorry you had to see that, I know you were close to Mrs. Collins…" she trailed off with a frown, clearly rethinking her own association with the fallen woman.

"I was," Jane nodded dutifully, "But I'm much closer to Him."

Agatha patted her hand, clearly mollified. "Good girl."

Woman, Jane corrected in her head, *I haven't been a girl for a very long time.*

"I'll pray for their souls," she added, feeling satisfaction stir in her veins. It would be any day now.

Monday, October 23rd

THE ANTAGONIST

I

She flipped the pizza with ease, twirling it in the air and watching with pleasure. It spun as magically as a flying saucer. She was getting really good at this.

Her 'boss' watched in amazement, his eyes following her movements, his mouth hanging open with awe.

"How do you do that, Chrissy!?"

"I spent a summer making pizzas in New York years ago," Jane lied, thinking of all the YouTube tutorials she subscribed to. Hours of learning how to flip dough. But her favorite channel was Pasta Grannies.

"So cool," he leaned forward and continued to watch as if he had all the time in the world.

Jane suppressed the urge to roll her eyes. Robb wasn't a bad guy, he was lazy and childish sure, but he was a spectacularly good judge of character, unless it came to his *best friend*. Jane couldn't understand it—the man was devoted, blind to the truth. He spent hours singing Dave's praises and it made Jane want to rake her nails down her face. It was infuriating.

She ought to mention 'Chrissy's' concerns.

"Sorry about your best friend," she began with a sympathetic look. "That must be really tough to digest."

As she anticipated, Robb had no clue as to what she was talking about. "Huh?"

She looked around carefully before lowering her voice, leaning in closer to him. "You mean…you didn't hear yet?"

He was quickly becoming hooked on her every word.

"Didn't hear what?"

"He got fired."

"For?"

THE ANTAGONIST

"Attempted rape."

Robb stared at her very seriously. "No," he finally muttered, "that's impossible, Dave would never."

"My sister knows the woman, the one who he did it to." Robb raised an eyebrow, motioning for her to continue. "Covered in bruises, terrified. She has a videotape of the whole thing."

His face became alarmed at that news. "I can't imagine he would do something like that." She could hear the slight doubt creeping into his tone.

"Do we ever really know anyone? Even ourselves?"

"I guess not…"

"She's not going to press charges, too afraid," Jane continued with a slight tremor in her tone.

"I should go see him," Rob said more to himself.

"I heard some of the waitresses talking…they are totally freaked out about that guy coming in here. A few were beginning to wonder what type of person would be best friends with someone like that."

"But I didn't know! I had no clue."

"It doesn't matter—guilt through association. Do you honestly think people are going to want to eat here if they know you have someone like that hanging around?"

She could see the wheels turning in his head. Robb didn't have much, and business was just beginning to really take off—especially with Jane's pizza making skills. She was an asset—making him more money while simultaneously freeing up his time. He was not in a position to ignore her advice.

"Involve yourself if you want," she offered. "I'm just warning you. What's bad for business is bad for us."

He nodded once, turning to contemplation as she shrugged it off and returned her attention to the delicious veggie pizza she was making.

Jane took a little extra care with placing the black olives—after all, they were her favorite.

Sunday, October 22nd

THE ANTAGONIST

I

It was almost too easy. For people with so much money, Jane considered they would at least have an alarm system, but no. The Collins's didn't have security cameras either, which made dropping off her final message quite simple. She considered writing the note out in olives, but she didn't want it to be misconstrued in any way. Black sharpie was effective, that way the words would really stick and no one would be able to wipe them away.

Jane left the empty pizza box on the top step of their mansion. Her only regret was that she would not be present to see the look on Dave's face when he received her final warning.

Saturday, October 21st

THE ANTAGONIST

I

"It was complete and utter humiliation!" Desiree raged as she continued to beat on the punching bag Jane was holding, "There I am, naked and waiting, and in comes his stupid wife! It was like a bad movie."

"I thought you said he told you to come over?"

"He did!" she sneered, taking a high kick at the bag. "He texted me yesterday afternoon, telling me he couldn't fight it anymore, how badly he wanted me….he asked me to bring all these weird props…going on about his fetishes."

"I told you a guy like that would have fetishes!"

"Well you were right!" she snapped.

"So it was a trick then, you think?"

"He wanted to get back at me, embarrass me, shame me."

"Sounds like he did a good job." Jane knew this confirmation would only fuel the other woman's fire.

"I can't let him get away with this. I have to do something." She sent one last upper cut to the bag before reaching for her water.

"Great job. You're getting really good."

Desiree threw her a triumphant smirk, "I know."

Jane dropped down onto the floor next to her to cool off and stretch, "So what are you going to do?" she asked, glancing around the gym to make sure no one was listening. "Make him pay?"

"I know you're a personal trainer, but I swear you should have been an empowerment coach."

Jane smiled, "Oh, maybe in another life."

THE ANTAGONIST

Desiree's thoughts returned to Dave rather quickly. "I want to hurt that righteous little fuck."

"I can't believe his wife took his side." This had been quite the shock. Jane knew Georgette trusted her husband, but still. A naked Desiree could not have been an easy pill to swallow.

"I know! I thought I could destroy him like I do all men, with sex. But apparently he is immune," Desiree frowned, tapping her chin thoughtfully.

"There are other ways to destroy someone."

She really liked the sound of that. "Go on."

Jane chose her next words carefully. "Well, he hurt you, didn't he?"

"He pissed me the fuck off, that's what he did!"

Jane could tell Desiree was revving up—she'd been training her since the paralegal moved to Repo Ridge almost two months ago. Desiree was a great asset to Jane's plans for many reasons…one, she spent a good amount of their sessions lamenting over the guy in the office who wouldn't sleep with her—this allowed Jane a nice perspective into Dave's work life. Two, she was a great cover—her forwardness and cruel nature served well for not only a distraction, but a face to lay temporary blame on as well.

"No, he didn't," Jane stated quite matter-of-factly.

Desiree raised an eyebrow, "He didn't?"

"Of course not." Jane sent her a wink, a devious one. "He didn't make you mad…he *hurt* you."

"He hurt me…" she could see the woman's quick mind working a thousand miles a minute. "Yes…he hurt me."

"You are the victim here, Desi—how does that make you feel?"

Desiree's eyes were alight with malicious enjoyment. "Scared, not safe…who knows? He might try to hurt me again."

Jane nodded along, mirroring the woman's vile smirk. She wouldn't normally consider teaming up with someone like Desiree unless it was absolutely necessary. "Sounds like you're in danger."

The look she sent Jane was lascivious, "Oh, I am. Janell, you're a genius!"

Jane wasn't specifically sure what the devious vixen had hidden up her sleeve, but she knew one thing for sure; whatever diabolical plan was being cooked up—Dave was in for a rude awakening.

And that sat just fine with her.

Friday, October 20th

THE ANTAGONIST

I

Following Dave Collins was easier than Jane thought it would initially be. For someone who seemed to posses a significant amount of awareness, he never once caught her eye. Though she was sure he must, at least at times, feel her glare burning through his well-dressed back.

Last night he never came home. He didn't go to work today either. This morning she learned he'd stayed at Robb's. She figured if she timed the following right, it would be just perfect.

She took out her burner phone and opened a new message chat to Desiree DeLongo. Desiree informed her during a session a few weeks ago that she'd boldly added her number to Dave's phone.

Ms. DeLongo, due to your recent absence from the office, I feel inclined to see you again and soon. I tried to fight it, tried my hardest...but I can't help it anymore. I'm going to lose my mind if I can't have you.

God she was nuts, Jane thought as she saw the woman was already typing back: *David is that you?* Up popped a little devil face. She continued to type: *Right now? I'm already wet for you.*

Jane quickly responded by sharing Dave's address: *Meet me here in an hour. The key is under the potted azalea on the back porch. Bring strawberries and whipped cream, I want to cover your feet with them. Stick the berries between your toes, add the cream and then slowly eat and lick them off of your sexy feet.*

Kinky. I like it.

THE ANTAGONIST

Bedroom is at the top of the stairs, take a left, third door on the right...make yourself comfortable, in case you beat me there.

I knew you couldn't resist. See you soon.

Jane grimaced with disgust as she snapped the phone shut. She wasn't banking on Dave being home—if he was great, if not, that was fine, too. Someone would find her—Desiree, especially naked and covered in whipped cream, would be hard to miss.

2

"You're probably so sick of hearing about my life!" Georgette trilled as the two women made their way across the indoor tennis courts. The sun was shining, but the bitter chill of late October in Repo Ridge was best avoided. *Another reason to dislike this place,* Jane thought.

The older woman had not stopped talking since she surprised Jane in the locker room early and ready to play.

"It's fascinating! I don't mind at all really," she stressed, tossing a look of admiration Georgette's way. It was sad—this innocent woman had not one clue.

Every lesson she spent spilling secrets that Jane greedily coveted.

"I'm just so worried about Dave," she confessed, as she swung the racket back and forth at her side, "His family is an absolute nightmare."

"Your husband, right?"

"The love of my life," she was glowing with pride. Jane resisted the urge to smash her own racket into the ground. Thankfully Georgette's voice continued to distract her. "They drain him. He is always taking on everyone else's problems. I don't know how he finds the time to deal with his own! Not that he has problems, exactly."

Oh yes he does, and he's going to have an even bigger one soon, Jane told herself ferociously.

"But we all have issues, we are only human right?"

Jane smiled in response as they took opposite sides of the court. Jane began to feed her balls and Georgette made a valiant attempt to hit them. It would have been comical if she weren't concerned that the woman might actually knock herself out by accident. She was an absolute hazard.

Georgette wasn't capable of focus, even as her eyes remained glued to each incoming flying object she could not, for the life of her, stop talking. Honestly, Jane didn't mind. She liked Georgette, quite a bit. She was nothing like the woman Jane assumed she would be—that had been one of the few pleasant surprises she'd come across; it made her mission harder on occasion, but that much more worthy of pursuing.

"I just feel like we need to leave this place," Georgette admitted after a few minutes. "Do you like it here?"

"I like it just fine," Jane fibbed. "It's a little boring sometimes, but it's a great place to raise a family, no?"

"Are you married?"

"I'm not, but maybe someday."

"A life partner is the greatest gift."

Jane wanted to disagree, she wanted to say the greatest gift was justice or perhaps knowing yourself, truly, but she nodded along in compliance. "How did you know your husband was the one?"

"Oh that was easy enough—he puts up with all my crap!"

"Noted."

Georgette sighed, once again missing the ball, "I'm just worried—normally Dave can handle anything thrown at him…but lately, he's distracted, on edge…just not himself…"she trailed off, her eyes filled with confusion. "He spent the night at his best friend's. He never does that. I'm hoping Robb will be able to help him."

He won't, Jane whispered in her head.

"Everyone gets in funks, I just wish I could do more."

"You're a good person, Mrs. Collins."

"Please, I've asked you a thousand times to call me Georgie."

"He's very lucky to have someone as caring as you."

"You are too sweet, Heather," she threw Jane a brilliant smile. "Am I getting any better?"

"100 percent." This was of course not true, but she couldn't bear to see the smile wiped off her face, for Jane knew Georgette's joy would be extinguished soon enough. There was no going back.

Their lesson finished a half hour later. Georgette hopped in the gym shower while Jane stole her briefcase from the locker, depositing it instead in the trunk of Georgie's car. She knew the older woman would think she left it at home, and that's exactly where Jane was hoping she'd go next.

Wednesday, October 18th

THE ANTAGONIST

I

The police files were a piece of cake. Robb mentioned the incident casually a few weeks back when they got stoned together in the parking lot after work one night. Jane happened to know her way around a computer. It didn't take long to hack the database of the local police department, seeing as their security system was archaic.

Jane knew this news wouldn't be particularly damaging to Dave's reputation with his wife or stepdaughter, it might even earn him a few points in Samantha's eyes—but that would be remedied before long. She hadn't planned this all out just to fail. The time and energy it took to concoct her path forward was anything but easy. Jane had gotten this far—she would keep going.

She knew however, the files she now held in her hand would cause considerable dissension with June and August, who would be shattered to hear of their perfect son's past discrepancies. It was a nice interlude, a chance for them to get used to the idea of Dave's downfall. It would only get more brutal from here on out.

She popped up the little red flag on the mailbox soon after June and August left for dinner at Pastor Prier's that night. She declined the invitation June personally extended to her. The woman was beginning to look at Hope as a surrogate daughter—Jane felt no sympathy for playing on the woman's weaknesses. In her mind, June Collins was just as guilty as her son.

Tuesday, October 17th

THE ANTAGONIST

I

Driving around with Samantha was always an enjoyable experience for Jane. She found the younger woman to be wise beyond her years, and a little bit snarky—just like her.

She wished these hours they spent together could have been enjoyed at face value. But that was impossible. Not when Dave remained unpunished. Jane forced her stray thoughts back from the dark. She listened to Samantha prattle on about the family drama. Jane had been the one to advise Samantha to tell her parents about Alex. She reminded her that if she wanted to be treated like an adult then she'd have to act like one.

Samantha complied and the result was exactly what Jane was expecting. Dave's inability to accept his stepdaughter's decision would only further the rift between them.

"I have to apologize to him at some point," she huffed under her breath as they took a spin downtown. "But only because it will make my Mom feel better."

"Then you should do it," Jane agreed. "It's not like he's going away anytime soon."

"I wish he would, him and his whole freak show family."

"I don't envy you."

"In this case I should be able to pick my own family."

"You can. "

"How?"

"You stop trying with the ones who are toxic. You ignore them, cut them out of your space. You don't engage, you just move on and surround yourself with those who bring out your best."

"Easier said than done."

"All things are."

"But I do have Alex," she paused, a light blush coming over her cheeks, "and you." Samantha chanced a sideways glance at Jane.

"Of course you do," she promised. "Before we wrap up today remind me to give you something."

Sam's eyes lit up with interest. "More 90's music?"

"Better."

Jane felt genuine pleasure at Samantha's squeal of delight as she lifted the Nintendo into her arms from the back of Jane's car.

"Was this yours?" she asked in awe.

"My sister's," Jane confirmed, feeling a sharp pain momentarily pierce her heart.

"I can't take it."

"No, I want you to have it. Please," Jane insisted, her eyes tight with a smile. It was hard to let go of this piece of history, but she knew it also served as a reminder.

"Alex is gonna freak when he sees this!"

I hope Dave will, too, Jane added in her head.

2

Early morning training sessions were Jane's favorite. The gym was always near empty at this ungodly hour and she relished the silence.

"How are you doing?" she asked Desiree when the paralegal arrived 40 minutes later for her session.

"This week's been fucking brutal already. I hate being stuck in court when it's boring bullshit cases," she complained as she began warming up. "And it looks like that's where I'll be for the remainder of this already fucked week."

"You seem agitated," Jane hedged, knowing Desiree loved to air her grievances.

"Oh I am. If that's not bad enough, Saturday afternoon was a fucking disaster."

"You mentioned you were working over the weekend?"

"Unfortunately, but I presumed the day was shaping up when David showed up."

Jane furrowed her eyebrows with feigned ignorance, "Is this the guy you've been sleeping with or the secretary?"

Desiree's face flamed with color, Jane wasn't sure if it was from embarrassment or rage. Knowing Desiree, it was both.

"That stupid man, I can't understand why he continues to reject me. He should be honored that I even give him any attention at all."

"Is this the married one?"

"They're all married." She rolled her eyes with disgust. "I was so embarrassed I actually wiped the security footage before I left. I even forgot to lock up. I'll blame that on the secretary. Can you imagine what people would think if they knew someone like him turned *me* down?"

Jane hid her smile. Desiree was truly the greatest partner in crime—a partner that had no idea how her own actions would continue to benefit Jane's long term plan.

"It's probably killing him, he's probably torn in morality. You know what good guys are like," Jane encouraged. "How could any man not want you?"

"Thank you for saying that Janell, even if I already knew it."

"Looks like you've found yourself a challenge. You're not giving up, are you?"

Desiree was the kind of woman who didn't understand the meaning of 'back down.'

"Of course not!" she replied flippantly.

"He will come around," Jane assured her.

"They always do."

3

Jane didn't bother to readjust the seat, what difference did it make? Dave would remember nothing. It was almost three in the morning by the time she got home and she was exhausted. But none of that mattered—all of the lost sleep would be worth it when this charade was at its end.

Monday, October 16th

THE ANTAGONIST

I

Jane watched her prey from behind the bar, it was nearing midnight and Dave Collins looked no closer to slowing down on drinking than when he walked into The Devil's Eye several hours before. She continued to remain perplexed over his strange behavior—it'd been subtle at first, but now she realized he was talking to himself, having longer and more elaborate conversations with an empty chair. One day soon she would be the one to fill that chair. Jane wondered briefly if he was losing his mind. She certainly hoped so—the measures she'd taken to infiltrate his psyche were finally coming to fruition. It was a beautiful process—one that Dave still seemed completely flummoxed by.

It was an extraordinary stroke of fate that he became so drunk he could not stand. The rest of the bar emptied, leaving just the two of them alone. Jane roughly dragged him out to his car, the feeling of his arm thrown over her shoulder made her want to die, but she pushed on. Purposely smacking his head against the top of the door as she shoved him in—he couldn't drive like this. If he accidentally got killed, she would never forgive herself. No, Dave was going to stay alive as long as Jane was around. He wasn't getting off that easy.

The conversation was particularly one-sided—Dave at first seemed to think she was his wife, then his sister. That was fine with her; the less he remembered, the better. But she couldn't resist asking a few questions as her heart rate increased with adrenaline and anticipation.

"Do you know who I am?"

His bleary eyes shot to her for the first time. He looked her up and down and then shook his head.

"Is something bothering you?" she asked, watching him carefully. Jane took her time navigating the dark streets of Repo Ridge. "Anything you want to talk about?"

"Someone wants to hurt me," he slurred finally. "I don't know why."

"Who do you think wants to hurt you?"

"Desiree, Samantha maybe…Harmony?"

"Do you think you're a bad person?"

"I try not to be."

"Do you make mistakes?"

"I'm human."

"What do you want most?"

He seemed to think about that for several minutes until he finally settled on an answer: "Peace."

"Tall order," she commented as they pulled into his driveway.

It took him three tries to get out of the car. Jane didn't bother to help him as she took off on foot, searching for a neighborhood kid's bike that might have been left out.

Tonight told her more than she expected. Clearly she wasn't pushing him enough. If she wanted Dave Collins to break, Jane would have to play harder.

2

She left with a cheese pizza around 7:30. This one she was going to deliver herself. Robb had gone fishing over the weekend and already forgotten about the leftover bait sitting in the small personal fridge in the backroom.

The maggots were a little treat, plus Jane was sick of wasting good olives.

This message would increase the threat tenfold.

Robb caught her just as she was getting into her car.

"Chris!" he called out as he jogged across the parking lot from his beat-up truck.

She smiled patiently as she slid the pizza onto the back seat and threw her jacket over it quickly.

"Wanted to catch you before you left!" he approached her with a half-hearted grin. She instantly could tell something was up.

"Are you alright? You look…" she searched for the proper word, "distressed."

He waved it off. "Oh, it's nothing. My friend is just being a dick, which he never is. Decided to take it out on me. That's actually what I wanted to ask you about…I know you two haven't officially met, but have you seen him around at all?" He held up his cellphone to show her a picture of the two of them on a fishing trip.

Jane shook her head. "Nope, sorry."

His face fell. "Man, that's a bummer."

Jane wanted to tell him he was better off without him, but she just patted him on the shoulder and told him to have a good night instead. She had terror to spread.

THE ANTAGONIST

3

"Have I told you the story of how we met? If I have please stop me," Georgette begged as she followed Jane down to the tennis courts.

Jane forced her face into a smile, "I haven't had the pleasure of hearing that one yet."

Georgette smirked, "It's a good one!"

They began to practice. After a few one-on-one lessons, Jane realized that Georgette wasn't so much interested in the sport as she was having another female companion to talk to. One that wasn't related to her, and one that didn't need her help—in Jane's opinion the woman seemed to spend little to no time on herself. Jane admired this trait, once or twice even considered leaving her out of it altogether, but her determination was too strong to take the least resistant path.

"I was in Park City, for Sundance—I used to go every year. I was a mess that particular January, recently divorced," she began, hardly attempting to hit the balls as her face took on a dreamy gaze. "There I was treacherously trying to navigate the narrow and icy streets in 5-inch heels with a martini I stole from a bar, and there was Dave trudging towards me, decked out in ski gear! We locked eyes, I clumsily slipped and he caught me before I could ruin myself completely."

"How romantic."

"Yes, he was on vacation with his family. The first holiday he ever took! Can you imagine such a thing?"

Jane could. She'd never been on a vacation in her entire life—there was no need to respond to Georgette, she would continue talking regardless.

THE ANTAGONIST

"Of course they made it all about religion, wanted to see what the Mormons lived like. Yuck! He's so lucky I found him. Honestly. He might still be living with them now if that wasn't the case. Not that he's unmotivated, just too accommodating to his selfish mother. It drives me insane."

"That sounds really frustrating."

"It is, it's the whole reason I had to leave beautiful sunny California and land here, the middle of Nothingville."

"I imagine that gets tiring for someone as well-traveled and cultured as you."

"The pay-off was worth it. I've done my fair share of grand adventures, what I was really craving when I met Dave was to settle down and find peace."

It's elusive, Jane wanted to say, but instead she said, "Have you found it?"

"Oh, mostly in helping others. Things get strained a little here and there, but after the abuse I've endured, I count myself very fortunate and grateful."

Jane wanted to pry, "Abuse? Sorry, I don't mean to make you uncomfortable—"

"Not at all!" The older woman replied with a gracious smile. "It's my life's work. I was married to a monster once. It inspired me to help others in similar circumstances."

"That's incredible."

"I like to think so. Repo Ridge isn't the most exciting place, but I have Dave and my Sam…and there are plenty of people to help here."

There most certainly are.

"Your family is very lucky to have you."

"What about you? What's your story?"

Jane had been dreading this moment—she'd done her best to keep rapid-fire questions on Georgette and away from herself. But she knew it was only a matter of time before someone as empathetic as Georgette would attempt to assess her emotions and history. There weren't enough minutes left in their lesson for Jane to even begin to answer her question somewhat truthfully. She'd always had trouble with summarizing, but now was her chance to shine.

"I'm pretty boring, honestly."

"That's not true! Did you grow up here?"

"My family moved around a lot. I just ended up in Repo Ridge because of my job."

"Where are you from?"

"A place similar to this one."

Georgette instantly picked up on her discomfort and backed off. Jane was banking on her misinterpreting her short answers.

"I apologize, that was intrusive."

"No it's fine, I just try to stay away from unhappy memories. Moving forward is more my speed."

Georgette nodded sagely, the commiseration prevalent in her eyes.

This irritated Jane. She did not need saving. There was no romantic fairytale love for her to find, no peace of mind, no ability to move forward until this matter was dealt with. The force that she hit the tennis ball with startled Georgette into action as she reached for the swiftly moving object.

She missed. Just like she had when she fell straight into Dave Collin's arms. Jane pitied her for that.

THE ANTAGONIST

4

Jane rolled up the typed notes in her pocket as she finished the last of her root beer. This little bit of mind savagery would continue to grow Dave's suspicions. By now, he was probably thinking that someone in his family was playing a cruel trick. Someone he knew, who knew him. There was no denying that Jane was now an expert on Dave, and to her advantage he seemed to erase any trace of her from his own memory.

The streets were empty, all asleep and hidden away in their homes as Jane prowled Repo Ridge, first visiting Harmony and then Robb. The little messages she left were the perfect beginning to a week that would bring Dave one step closer to his truth, one step closer to her.

Sunday, October 15th

THE ANTAGONIST

I

She'd taken a spare set of keys on her first visit to the mansion. As she popped open the driver's side door of Dave's car, she only turned the key half way. She only needed power. Samantha mentioned that she left one of the burned CD's in her stepfather's car, where else would she be able to listen to them? Jane quickly flipped through the tracks to the one she desired and turned the volume to max. She made sure to shut off the radio and the car just as quickly. Dave would soon remember his long lost favorite song.

THE ANTAGONIST

2

This was a first for Jane—a new members church party. She admitted this was not her scene, but she was determined and therefore played her part to the tee. Everything from the muted and modest pastel dress she wore to her carefully tied back hair…her shoulders slightly slumped, but her gaze was where the true power lay. She emulated the broken doll, the young woman who was childlike almost, afraid of her own shadow and clearly in need of love. She was weak and vulnerable. The type of person the church preyed on. Her misery was an easy target for those who believed anyone could be saved, no matter what. Jane was amused to see them try.

June was lightly guiding her by the arm, promising her introductions with only those closest to Him. It took all of her self-control to bite her tongue against the venomous words she was longing to spew. *That will be unproductive,* she reminded herself.

Agatha and her clan of devoted followers were more than interested in Jane's circumstances. They gathered around her closely as the beast of a woman practically demanded answers to all of her questions. But Jane was ready—she rehearsed several days for this specific trial.

"Dear girl, June mentioned that you are an orphan?" one of the older women asked with sorrow etched on her face.

Jane nodded timidly. "My parents were very sick, the Devil had their souls in his grasp. They abandoned me and my sister for sin and pleasure."

The women around Jane cawed with outrage at such an injustice.

THE ANTAGONIST

"That's horrible, you poor thing."

"It was just me and my older sister until she passed away almost seven years ago."

"So much tragedy for one so young," June commented as she patted Jane's shoulder.

"How did she die?" Agatha asked rather bluntly. Some of the women gave her disapproving looks, but June nodded at Jane, encouraging her to answer.

"She was murdered." Jane knew that wasn't the answer they were expecting.

It gave her pleasure to see the horror slapped across their faces. "I was so lost after that, so alone," she went on, allowing pools of tears to accumulate in her eyes. "Mrs. Collins was the first person to show me kindness in so long."

"We are never alone when we are with Him," Agatha insisted.

"I am so grateful to have found Him. My whole life feels like it's going to change now."

"Oh it will," June replied with reverence. "Now you will know how it feels to be loved. To have a family."

"Yes," Jane agreed, "I believe I will."

Agatha eyed her with growing approval. "June, she would have been a perfect wife for your son."

Jane swallowed the vile laughter that was begging to escape her throat.

"I was thinking the same thing. It's too bad he's married to that pagan."

The women frowned and snorted with disapproval at the mention of Georgette.

"An unfortunate circumstance that I've tolerated with the patience and guidance that He shows me. But yes," June's eyes wandered over Jane with growing interest, "Hope would be the perfect partner, young enough that I might actually get some grandchildren out of such an arrangement."

Agatha watched her like a sly fox. "One can *hope*."

Jane listened in awe as these two old hens went about planning her future for her. She couldn't believe the level of delusional thinking she was hearing—as if she was now their property and could therefore fix her life to their own liking, for their own personal benefit. *Let them try,* she thought. After all, she was here to do the same thing to them.

Saturday, October 14th

THE ANTAGONIST

I

"Do you want to talk about your childhood?" she began, crossing her legs and fixing her pen over the pad. She could see the slight shake of her patient's head over the top of the couch.

"There's nothing there I want to revisit."

"The reason I suggest it is because trauma from the time of adolescence can be carried over into the adult life. In this case, it is more productive to view that trauma by thinking like a child—for that is when the trauma occurred, and it is therefore with that mind-set that we must face it."

Harmony popped her head up to turn and look at Jane. "You want me to think like a child?"

"I want you to consider that the difficulties we carry with us now can only be resolved by focusing on what created them in the past. The adult mind tends to take the position of assertiveness. It says 'let's face this head on' or 'no problem, I can fix it' but in reality that kind of 'doing' isn't the answer. Let me ask you a simple question: what do children do? Don't think too much, just the first answer that comes to your mind."

"They play."

"Exactly."

"I don't understand."

"When you are playing, you are just being. You aren't trying to focus on fixing whatever is wrong or worrying about how you can change this thing before it changes you. No, you just exist. You just be."

"So by being, I will heal?"

THE ANTAGONIST

"By facing your past, knowing that you cannot change it, only accept it."

Harmony was silent for several minutes. Jane was used to this. Over the last couple of months she'd gotten to understand Dave's sister on quite the personal level. These sessions were the reason she was beginning to despise June, almost as much as she did Dave.

In the beginning Harmony barely spoke at all—Jane was comforted by the idea that she was actually helping this woman out of her shell, out of the constant despair she lived with. Harmony wanted to be better, so Jane knew she would open up once she trusted her.

"Dave's always been the favorite," the resentment was heavy in her tone, "and that has only grown over the years."

"Were you two close as children?"

"Very. Almost inseparable—we spent all of our time together, with our parents always at that fucking church."

"Did you not attend with them?"

Harmony let out a small laugh, "When we were very little, I assume they didn't take us because who wants two crying babies instead of one? To be fair, June loves telling us how Dave never cried and how I was the screaming shrew."

"And when you were older?"

Jane could hear the hesitation in her voice, "I was already damned by then."

"What about Dave?"

"Oh, he could go with them if he wanted, sometimes he did when I needed to be alone. But if I asked him to stay with me he would never leave."

"How did your parents' rejection make you feel?"

"Awful, at first I blamed myself. But as I got older, I blamed them."

"Why did your parents think you were damned?"

A timid sound escaped Harmony's throat. "Having a twin is not like anything else."

Jane leaned forward and scribbled down a few notes. "Tell me about it?"

"You understand things about one another that no one else can get. You have full conversations without saying a word, just by looking into each other's eyes. You know when something is wrong with the other, and also when something great is happening. It's just this wild connection of feelings."

"Would you say your brother was the first man in your life to show you love?"

"One hundred percent, he's the only man who has ever loved me. He knows me better than I know myself. And vice versa."

"Well that is something we are going to work on."

"What do you mean?"

"Therapy is about finding your truth, Ms. Collins. That means knowing *yourself* truly."

"We used to…touch, when we were kids," she admitted softly.

"Each other?"

Harmony nodded. "Is that sick? I mean, we were so young, I don't think it was meant to be sexual, just exploratory."

She was desperate for reassurance. Jane could tell this was the first time the other woman had ever spoken these words out loud. Before Jane could respond, Harmony continued, her voice becoming slightly hysterical, "I mean, how could we not? We were always left alone with no guidance, no one to care for us except one another. Even as we were growing up, we never had a sex talk with our parents, it was a taboo subject, apparently something we had to learn on our own."

"Does this make you feel guilty?"

"Yes! Yes. It's been eating away at me for years. But now…I think I might be gay, you know? I've never told anyone but my sister-in-law. She's the only one who truly listens anyway."

"And you feel like these experiences somehow defined your sexuality?"

"Maybe. Maybe not, I just know I never want another man to touch me again in my life."

"Did your brother ever hurt you?"

Harmony's face filled with defensive shock, "Never! He's my greatest protector."

"Have you maintained any sort of physical relationship over the years with your brother?"

"Gross," Harmony grimaced, "No, like I said, it was just when we were kids."

Jane glanced at the clock, their fifty minutes was almost up.

"Can I ask you to do something for me before our next session?"

"What?"

"I want you to play. Search for the happy memories and allow yourself to just be. All judgments aside, alright?"

"I can do that," Harmony promised as she sat up and turned to face her therapist.

Jane smiled, "I know you can."

"Thank you for believing in me. It's nice to finally add someone to that very short list."

"I know you are capable of anything you set your mind to. Don't let anyone tell you different."

"I think I'll go see Dave. If anyone needs advice on how to play, it's him."

Jane smiled, "That sounds like an excellent idea."

Friday, October 13th

THE ANTAGONIST

I

Jane only caught a glimpse of him as she tended the bar that evening. She was sure when Dave entered he spotted her, but his gaze only held for a half a breath before he turned to search out his table. Jane let out a sigh of relief. She hoped he would come here after the day of hell he experienced, but it was still not time for him to truly see her.

She wished she could get close enough to hear whatever he was saying. It was so dark and smoky in the joint tonight. She couldn't tell if he might be wearing headphones; he was clearly talking to someone.

THE ANTAGONIST

2

Jane took most of the day for herself. It was a rarity in the past few months seeing as how most of her attention was focused on Dave and his inevitable downfall. Today would be traumatizing for him, she knew. And that thought made her relax even more.

The only place she had to be was Repo Pizza and then her shift at The Devil's Eye. On her way into work she picked up a few extra cans of black olives.

Repo Pizza wasn't too busy tonight. She assumed there was some stupid high school football game or what not. There were only two waiters working when Jane arrived, and a sullen delivery girl who was slouched against the front counter, tapping her foot impatiently for the next order. Being Friday, Jane knew it was only a matter of time before Dave called in for his pizza. She settled comfortably into kneading dough as she waited for the hours to pass.

When the order finally came in, Jane made sure to personalize it. This was probably the last time she would be able to get away with someone else delivering her dirty work. She was sure after tonight Dave would make certain to mention the incident to Robb, who was lounging in the backroom on his old desktop computer playing Solitaire.

Jane made sure to turn off his cellphone which he'd left lying on the counter unprotected. If it affected Dave the way she was sure it would, he'd call to clarify the confusion he would undoubtedly feel at this reoccurring and strange 'prank.' She hoped she was making him sicker than hell.

It was nearing 10:30 when Robb finally emerged from the back to tell her she could wrap things up.

"It's a miracle, finding someone as capable as you in a place like this."

"Happy to help," she offered as she went about cleaning up.

"Seriously, you're a blessing, kiddo."

Jane fought the urge to scowl against the irritating presumption of her youth. "I've been called a lot of things but a blessing is not one of them."

"Well there's a first time for everything!"

"Yeah, I guess there is." She wondered if Dave's day had gone as spectacularly awful as she planned. She still had a long way to go; she could not let her impatience rule the situation. Slow and torturous was the only way.

She just wanted to remind Dave how much he truly loved black olives.

Thursday, October 12th

THE ANTAGONIST

I

"Maybe you're looking at this all wrong," Jane informed Desiree as she added weight to the machine and indicated for her client to continue the reps.

"He's literally the only man in the office who isn't interested in me," Desiree snapped as she dropped back down onto the bench.

"So that makes him the one you want most?"

"Exactly."

"You know, some men don't like forward women. Why don't you try a different approach?"

Desiree paused mid-lift and looked at Jane as if she'd gone insane, "That's the only approach I do, Janell."

"Well it seemed to work out fine with your boss," Jane reminded her.

Desiree made a face of pure disgust, "Sleeping with that wrinkly old toad has been one of the great challenges of my life."

"Why do you do it, then?"

Desiree smiled her sneaky smile. "It has its perks. You always want to get on the good side of whoever is going to benefit you most in the long run. Especially a lawyer."

"Is it worth it though? You said he's old enough to be your grandfather."

"It's not ideal, but you never know…I might need him at some point down the road, and the safest way to make sure you have a man's loyalty is to keep him so satisfied and feeling powerful that you become indispensable to him."

"Sounds like you have it all figured out."

"Yeah. With apparently every man except David," she snarled.

"Maybe he has a fetish. Seems like the type," Jane offered, a twinkle in her eye.

Desiree shook her head, "I can't see it."

"Okay, how about this…you said he was married, right?"

"Yeah."

"Well there's the possibility that he's terrified his wife might find out. Why don't you reassure him that you are discreet?"

"That's an idea. I mean most men jump at the chance to sleep with me regardless of their marital status. He's one of the good ones." She made a face as if this disgusted her to no end.

"So let him know you aren't like the rest, either. Show him what kind of pleasure he is missing."

"I will, " Desiree smirked at her newfound friend. "We should totally get drunk together sometime."

"I would love to, but I don't drink."

Desiree's eyebrows lifted in shock, "Why the hell not?!"

"I like to keep my mind clear." Jane could tell this was not a sufficient answer. Desiree liked everything given to her straight. "And my parents were ugly drunks."

"Gotcha," she said dismissively. "Okay, you know this shit-hole town better than me; where can I get this good guy nice and drunk in a romantic setting?"

Jane was happy to once again have Desiree's attention back on her own dilemma. "Why don't you ask him? You're new to town, surely he'd do the honorable thing and help out a nice woman like you?"

Desiree almost shrieked with laughter, "You're good, you know that?"

Jane smiled in response—if she only knew.

2

Jane wasn't sure what she was saving this money for. It seemed as if now was as good a time as any to make a contribution. As much as she was able to justify the dark path she was steadily trekking down, she couldn't help but feel that balancing the karmic scale might give her some extra cushion for her raging revenge. The donation would be anonymous, but hopefully appreciated and put to good use. Jane couldn't help but see the irony in the whole thing. Georgette was a good person and after doing a substantial amount of research on her foundation and philanthropic work, Jane grudgingly admitted how impressed she was by the woman's commitment to helping others. Jane was doing the same thing, wasn't she? Even if she was taking a much more twisted and dangerous route…their end goals were still the same, were they not? Helping those who could not help or see themselves. The small bubble of guilt that worked its way up her throat dissipated as she dropped the check off at the shelter. It slipped from her hand as easily as Dave had gotten away without punishment.

Wednesday, October 11th

THE ANTAGONIST

I

Church was an exhausting experience. Jane was not raised religious, she knew very little about the subject matter as a whole, which worked perfectly fine in the case of Hope. June loved the fact that the young woman she was attempting to guide was seemingly clueless about most things. This made her an excellent candidate for conversion. June spent the last few weeks educating Jane on all the church meant and all the good it was able to do. The power she was giving June seemed to intoxicate the older woman—Jane assumed this was because June never successfully convinced anyone to join her on her quest into the arms of the almighty. Her ridiculous calling and shouting to anyone who passed by her regular set-up near the bus stop was futile. Busy people had no time to stop and hear about how God would change their lives. But not Hope. Hope was most interested. So much so that she tried to stop by and see June at least once a week. She didn't want to seem too willing—instead she was determined to make the older woman think she'd been the one to finally convince Hope to make it official.

The smug smile that now sat on her face as the two of them entered the church was enough for Jane to know the other parishioners were shocked that June Collins actually found a new follower. And follow, Jane would. The trust she gained here would be invaluable for the near future. Knowing June, she would tell Dave all about the lost and helpless woman whom she saved.

THE ANTAGONIST

2

The clips will be a nice little trigger, Jane hoped as she boxed them up. She'd taken these with her when she came to Repo Ridge five years ago. Jane wasn't sure exactly how they would fit into her plan, but she knew she could not leave them behind. She was momentarily distracted by the sound of wailing coming from the other side of her thin apartment wall. At first, she mistook it for a child crying, but the more she listened, she realized it was actually a woman having an orgasm. She shoved a pair of headphones into her ears with a grimace and turned back to her task.

The butterflies on each individual clip were beautiful, covered in glitter and fake gold. She loved holding one on the palm of her hand and watching the light sparkle across it as the wings flapped on their own accord against the springs that held them. Her sister handed these down to her for her 12th birthday—Elizabeth was the only one who ever remembered the date. It was hard to let go, but it was necessary. With one last loving glance at the dancing insect, Jane gently lowered it into the box. She felt stubborn tears forming behind her eyes as she recalled her sister lovingly doing her hair. That would never happen again. Ellie was gone, dead, never allowed to shine and sparkle much like the clips themselves—no, she was buried, forgotten by all but Jane—but not for long.

For a brief and excruciating moment, Jane recalled Ellie's coffin being lowered into the ground—she blocked out the glittering of the clips as she shut the cardboard box and taped it shut. She scribbled Dave's name across the top with

THE ANTAGONIST

the address of his office. She wanted to keep him on his toes and would continue to switch it up. There wasn't a chance he was going to find her until she was damn well ready.

Tuesday, October 10th

THE ANTAGONIST

I

"Do you prefer Samantha or Sam?" Jane asked, looking up from her clipboard to the teen with bright purple hair standing in front of her.

"Sam," she replied, with a slight smile, clearly pleased that she'd been asked as opposed to assigned.

"Nice to meet you, Sam. I'm your driving instructor, Ellie."

Sam looked approvingly at her—Jane knew her young and calm demeanor would be considered cool, especially the lip ring that sat in her lower lip.

"Sweet."

The first hour was basic. Jane kept everything professional, the last thing she wanted to do was push. As a teen herself she'd been much like Sam—sick of people telling her what to do, against conforming to any sort of authority just because it was expected of her.

"Do you mind if I put some music on?" she asked as Sam carefully concentrated on her driving.

"Please do. Music totally relaxes me."

Jane grinned, "Me, too."

She flipped the radio on. Judging by the young woman's style, Jane had a hunch of what kind of music she enjoyed. Jane was here to add some age to her lyrical palate.

Nirvana was a win/win. She watched from her peripheral, realizing Sam definitely knew the band, but only the songs that were played on the oldie stations. She could tell she never heard some of their greatest and unknown hits. Sam began to drum her fingers against the steering wheel in time.

"Do you play an instrument?" Jane asked.

"Only every one I've ever picked up," she was smirking. "I would recognize Cobain's voice anywhere, but I've never heard this song."

"This album is classic."

"Is it on a CD?"

Jane nodded with a small smile, damn that made her feel old.

Sam continued to listen, her body becoming more relaxed. Jane could see the tightness in her shoulders loosening. Jane resisted asking her any more questions. She would let Samantha come to her. After another 20 minutes, the teen asked the question Jane was hoping she would.

"Do you mind if I borrow this?" she asked, indicating the music.

"Not at all, I've got a whole stack of burned CDs like this in my car."

Sam's eyes lit up with interest. "Really?"

"Yeah, I was actually trying to get rid of them. I moved all my music onto a laptop, so if you want them, they're yours."

"No fucking way!" she yelled, realizing almost instantly that she might have overstepped herself.

"Fucking way," Jane responded.

Sam laughed, tossing her long tresses back as she pulled past Stone & Schworst Law Firm.

"Do you smoke weed?"

"Sometimes, but lately I've been really busy with a new project so there hasn't been a lot of time for recreation."

Sam nodded in understanding. "Still, it's really cool that you do."

"I used to be a lot cooler."

"No way."

"Yeah, back when it was my sister and I, hell we got in so much trouble together."

"What was the craziest thing you ever did?"

Jane gave Sam a sneaky sideways glance, "When I was seventeen, there was one summer she stole a car. We drove around drinking whiskey sours until she crashed the thing into a motel swimming pool."

"That's insane! Did you get in trouble?"

"We ran. The car wasn't ours, so they never found us. We laughed about it for weeks."

"That is so badass. You're so lucky to have a sibling like that."

Jane felt the warm memory fade, the small smile playing about her lips gasped on its last breath. "I did. Unfortunately I don't anymore."

"I'm sorry." Sam couldn't seem to help herself, "Did she die?" The voice in which she asked somehow lessened the pain of the answer Jane hated to relive.

"Yeah. Seven years ago."

"That fucking sucks."

"It does."

Sam fell silent, and Jane didn't comment again. The lack of words unspoken was comfortable. Samantha seemed to recognize a kindred spirit—after all, they both came from broken homes.

"Being an only child sucks, too," she finally said. "Being a stepdaughter is even worse."

Jane's heart lifted at these words. It felt as if someone else in the Universe was seeing with the same eyes as herself.

"Is he an asshole?"

"Worse," Sam spat viciously. "He's perfect."

Jane contemplated those words—perhaps Samantha might not even realize why Dave bothered her so much. It could be she was picking up on unconscious feelings that the man evoked.

"Well, we all know that's worse than being an asshole."

"Exactly."

They fell into small talk for the remainder of the lesson. Jane hadn't thought it possible, but she gained this woman's trust in just under three hours. That was a new record.

THE ANTAGONIST

"Great job," Jane encouraged as Samantha pulled into the parking spot and tossed the car out of drive.

"Thanks, same time tomorrow?" Her face lit up, hopeful that this arrangement would be permanent.

"That's right."

"Cool." She looked genuinely pleased with this information. Jane knew the look—she had been banking on it. Sam admired her.

She'd make sure to spend the next few weeks becoming the older sister Sam never even knew she needed.

Monday, October 9th

THE ANTAGONIST

I

"I can't believe I let you talk me into this!" Georgette was a basket of nerves this morning. Jane was just thrilled she hadn't backed out.

"No judgment here, " she told her enemy's wife. "I could barely hit when I was a kid. I never played sports. But look at me now! Anything is possible."

Jane knew that Georgette realized she found someone she could talk to, someone who made her feel listened to and valued, instead of the other way around.

"This is something you should do for yourself. It seems to me like you're the type of woman who is always taking care of everyone else." That final sentence from Jane was the winning hit.

"Oh, alright! I trust you!"

"You're going to be fine, Mrs. Collins," she assured the frazzled woman.

"Please call me Georgie. And Heather? Whatever I do, don't let me embarrass myself!"

"Consider it taken care of, Georgie," she promised with a smile.

To be completely honest, Jane hated the wretched sport, but it was a guaranteed way of gaining entry to the expensive Repo Country Club. There was no way she was going to spend her hard-earned money on a membership when she could just become an instructor. Jane was in great shape and her charisma made her an ideal candidate for such a position. Padding her resume and creating another new identity had been easy enough; years of research and experience was serving her well. It was a beautiful miracle that Georgette showed interest in the sport, even if it wasn't completely active—tennis was a rich person's game after all, exactly what Jane was banking on.

She listened that morning as Georgette told her all about herself and her family. Jane absorbed everything she said, every small detail that would help her move forward with her plans.

Georgette was so consumed with her stories that she continued to tell them all the way into the women's locker room. She went on about her days in France over the noise of the falling water. While Georgette showered, Jane pretended to look for something in her locker.

She grabbed a stack of sticky notes. Jane had taken pains to copy Dave's handwriting exactly. That information was easy enough to acquire on her last trip to their mansion.

Jane carefully placed each loving note with messages like 'I love you' and 'You're special' in different parts of Georgette's bag—in between a book, tucked into her inside jacket pocket, rolled up in her makeup case, stuffed into her cigarettes and so on. Georgette would assume the obvious, and being the adoring wife that she was, she would most definitely thank Dave for his sweet gesture.

The more confused he was, the better.

Sunday, October 8th

THE ANTAGONIST

I

She honestly couldn't believe how much time June spent here—after church, before church, every damn day. Jane wondered if she actually ever gained a follower from this? Over the last few weeks, the only people Jane saw approach June and her little pop-up pamphlet corner were the homeless looking for spare change. Jane's eyes narrowed as she watched the older woman shoo every single one of them away empty-handed.

Jane's assessment had been correct. Parents were the ones responsible for their children, and this woman's delusional and festering soul was almost enough for her to dig up a small sliver of sympathy for Dave. Almost.

She spent quite a lot of time, during her sessions with Harmony, hearing about June and August Collins. From what she gathered, August was interested in three things: food, attractive women and obeying his wife's every command. June, on the other hand, seemed to delight in control and maintaining power over the rest of her family. They were the type of people who came from nothing at all, only to be handed everything by their much too generous daughter-in-law. Jane knew June could afford to feed every single homeless person who approached her, yet she did not. Because people like June Collins only cared about those in a privileged enough position to do for her. Even then, her kindness was false. Jane could spot a liar and a hypocrite from miles away. She'd grown up with parents like that herself.

Today was the day Jane finally approached the booth. She shuffled her feet, and feigned indecision—as if she was so

THE ANTAGONIST

close to stepping into the welcoming arms of the church. June spotted her with her beady hawk eyes and pounced at the opportunity, practically forcing a pamphlet into Jane's hand.

"I see the Lord in you, dear girl."

"You do?" she asked hopefully.

"Oh yes." June grasped Jane's hands. "The faith is strong within you, you believe."

"I want to so very badly," Jane whispered shyly. "Are you sure?"

"He has chosen me as His shepherd, it is my duty to find those who He deems worthy and to bring them into the folds of his gracious embrace."

"Oh, but I'm not worthy, I know nothing of your teachings or practices."

"Don't you see? You were sent here by Him, to me. This is your calling, your destiny, child."

"You think so?" With a tiny step forward she opened the pamphlet and began to browse.

"My dear, I'm more sure of it than I have been of anything ever in my entire life." Still Jane showed a bit of hesitance. This only seemed to encourage June's intense ranting. "Join us at the new members gathering next week and I will show you His light. It will be all the proof you need of your own worthiness."

Jane nodded, "Okay…I'll—I'll try."

"That's all God will ever ask of you. You don't have to be perfect…" she trailed off, extending her hand towards Jane.

"Hope. My name is Hope."

"How lovely. You don't have to be perfect, Hope, you just have to believe that everything will work out in the end. He always has a plan for each and every one of us."

So do I, Jane agreed, as she let the older woman latch onto her arm and turn her attention to the teachings of God.

Saturday, October 7th

THE ANTAGONIST

I

The day was a busy one—there was no denying that. Everything was set in place. All of her hard work finally would pay off.

Jane was nervous tonight, a bit on edge as she wiped down the bar and chatted with a few of the locals who moved in and out like ships passing through the eye of a storm.

She was surprised when the doors opened to reveal the man it had taken her years and great pains to find. Jane was not expecting this deviation from his normal routine, but seeing as he'd not come in last night, she supposed he was just making up for lost time. He seemed like that sort.

They locked eyes.

Dave Collins stopped half away from crossing the bar. Jane held his stare, begging the Universe to spare her from any interrogation—she was not ready for the final confrontation. Yet.

He looked as if he might say something, but his attention was suddenly pulled from her and directed to one of the chairs at his usual table. She followed his sightline as he frowned at thin air—there was no one there.

The bar was too empty for Jane to feel comfortable and invisible—she made a quick exit through the back, leaving a note for Ruth about an emergency—it was only her second shift, she couldn't lose this newly coveted position but she also couldn't risk blowing her cover.

Jane's heart was pounding by the time she got into her car. She sped down the slick streets. The rain was driving hard and it was darker than usual. The dimly lit lamps that ghosted

THE ANTAGONIST

the road were bathed in fog. Jane focused her mind on Dave's expression—how he stared like he'd seen a ghost. She didn't want to chance the idea of his mind catching up to him. Perhaps he wouldn't recognize her face, but the rage in her eyes would raise questions. Ones she was not ready to answer.

Emily Dinova

2

The Country Club of Repo Ridge was probably Jane's least favorite spot she was now inclined to frequent—it was almost as intolerable as her soon being forced to attend church.

She learned quickly from her interview that club managers only wanted two things: money and no problems. Her chipper attitude and well-researched history of tennis fell on deaf ears, though; the manager, Mr. P, was much more interested in ogling her fit body and attractive face. That was fine with Jane. All she had to do was channel Desiree—anytime the two of them were working out and either man or woman looked her way, Desiree immediately turned up her sex drive—she was all seduction, dark promise and sultry eyes. Jane was a great student if nothing else.

Mr. P hired her on the spot.

The first few weeks were rough, as Jane did not actually enjoy having to entertain the elite. Anyone who was taking lessons was either drunk or abysmal.

This worked in her favor as she was now regularly overdosing on gossip. It amused and annoyed her how privileged and silly most of them were. They had no real problems—it was laughable that some of them even attempted to relate to her! She smiled through it and took their money, all the while listening for any mention of The Georgette Collins. This was the hot topic per usual—they either loved her or hated her, there was no in-between. Jane deduced the latter was out of jealousy when she bumped into Dave's wife that very afternoon, seeing as the woman was nothing if not completely lovely.

THE ANTAGONIST

Bumping into Georgette meant Jane finally spotted her alone, for the first time ever. She was sitting by the tennis courts, sipping on a cocktail as she gazed with longing at the players in front of her. Georgette was always swarmed with bloodsuckers—ones that were itching to have a bite of her outrageous wealth and social status. But she couldn't care less about what people thought of her.

Jane liked that.

"Do you play?" she asked quietly as she sidled up next to Georgette.

The woman turned to look at her, a large beautiful smile on her delicate face. Jane felt ridiculous in her club uniform, like an annoying little gnat that had come to bask in this creature's glory.

"God no! I'm absolutely atrocious!"

"Have you ever tried?"

"Well, no," she frowned, turning back to look at the players across the court, "Actually, I haven't."

"Then you might be a pro! Waiting to claim your super power!"

Georgette threw back her glorious head and laughed with delight. "It's more likely that I can fly," she continued to giggle as she took a large sip of a Bloody Mary. "What's your name, dear?"

"Heather. Nice to meet you, Mrs...." she hesitated as if grasping for the word.

"No, Missus, please! Georgette Collins, lovely to meet you, Heather," she reached out her jewel-covered fingers for Jane's bare ones, "This sounds completely ridiculous, trust me I'm aware, but it's so nice for someone not to know me for once!"

Jane smiled at the irony, but it was also true what Georgette said, Jane didn't know her at all. She only assumed that if the woman had fallen in love and married Dave Collins, then she was going to be as horrid and awful as Jane hoped.

"I find it equally refreshing to meet someone who actually cares what my name is," Jane countered with a little laugh of her own. She almost wished she hadn't voiced those thoughts out loud as pity instantly consumed Georgette's features.

"Join me, won't you?" she asked quite unexpectedly.

Jane was thrilled, nervous—this was what she wanted, wasn't it? The perfect opportunity to get close? She hesitated and looked around the nearly empty courts.

"If you're worried about Peter throwing a fit, don't be. He's my biggest fan," she rolled out her arm to indicate Jane should take the seat next to her.

"I can't afford to lose this job." Jane once again struck gold. Georgie was no longer looking sympathetic. Her eyes filled up with determination.

"I won't take no for an answer. Trust me, I pay these bastards a fuck ton of money to do what I want. No one will question it," she winked and turned to reach down at her side. When she reemerged, it was with a giant pitcher of Bloody Mary's and a devious smile. Jane slowly slid into the chair, hating how much she already liked this woman.

"Alright." Jane felt like pushing her luck. "But only if you try tennis. One lesson in exchange for one cocktail." She knew this would be her in—she had to concentrate, not get wrapped into emotion.

Georgie let out a little yelp of victory and busied herself pouring the drink. "You can never just have one, darling."

That's what Jane was hoping for. She never drank, but this specific invitation made it unavoidable—Jane was going to do anything to continue growing her relationship with Georgette Collins.

THE ANTAGONIST

3

Jane always enjoyed driving—the freedom of flying down a deserted road, the wind whipping across her face, the sun drying her tears. It was a place she could escape to, one with no destination in mind. Jane spent quite a lot of her teen years exploring the roads. She would get lost only to prove to herself that she could find her own way. Ellie had been the one who taught her how to drive before Jane even turned thirteen.

So signing up for a certification in driver's education was a cinch. The woman behind the counter smiled pleasantly as she took Jane's credentials and looked them over.

"Everything seems to be in order here," she said. "Can you start this coming week?"

"I'd love to," Jane replied honestly.

It had taken her months of planning to come up with the perfect way to get close to Samantha. Like all the others, Jane studied her in order to acquire information with which she could then make plans. Samantha was a loner, someone who didn't quite fit in, that maybe felt the need to escape. Driving was a step closer to independence, one Jane could relate to. Someone as rebellious as Samantha wasn't going to stay put for long. This accelerated course that the teen signed up for would give Jane a good amount of hours to dive into Samantha's mind. It would aid her in her quest to turn Dave Collin's life completely inside out.

"Great, just sign here, Elizabeth, and you're all set."

Jane smiled, "You can call me Ellie."

THE ANTAGONIST

4

"I never noticed before, but have you?"

"What's that?"

"You can't spell painting without pain."

"What made you think of that?"

"I'm staring at this painting instead of you. Why is that?" Harmony asked as she lifted herself off the couch and turned to look at Jane.

"Well, by not concentrating on me and allowing yourself to relax, your mind is more apt to respond instinctually."

"Is that true?"

"I believe it is. Try closing your eyes. Whatever comes to your mind, say it. That's what I'm here for, to help you interpret these thoughts. This is a safe space. I am not judging you, I am not going to be upset with you, no matter what."

"Is there pain in painting?"

"Are you asking my personal opinion?"

Harmony nodded.

"There is pain in all art. Great art makes us feel deeply, and sometimes that can be very painful. The process of creation is filled with doubt and edits and thousands of hours of work and hard time…but the change, the beauty that's created is certainly worth it. That's what I think of when I look at that painting." Jane gestured towards the wall. It was the last one her sister ever made.

Harmony turned her attention back to the piece of art. "I see a lot of pain. And sex."

"Do you associate those two things?"

"Not really...I guess."

"You sound unsure, think...try to make a connection."

"I've never had sex. But I imagine it's painful."

"Good, that's really well done," Jane complimented. Harmony was still new to this sort of treatment, so taking things slow was essential.

"Does sex hurt?"

"Sometimes, if it is forced, or not consensual."

"I don't want to have sex," she burst out like pouting child.

"You don't have to do anything you don't want to. That is your decision and your decision alone."

"Do you think it's because of my parents? That I'm all fucked up?"

"I want you to try to not use negative speech when referring to your mental health. You must learn to be kind to yourself, Ms. Collins. "

"Dave's kind to me—my brother, I mean."

Jane felt her heart jump into her throat. This was the first time Harmony mentioned him by name.

"I will say it again, you need to be kind to yourself," Jane insisted, feeling in that moment as if she were speaking more to herself than the patient who lay on her couch.

The first few weeks of therapy, Harmony spent every moment talking about the various stays she had at mental institutions. Jane didn't push her. She knew it would only be a matter of time before they arrived at 'family.'

To Jane it was inescapably clear that Harmony very much enjoyed being a semi-permanent resident. She treated each visit to the hospital as if they were vacations, small reprieves from what her life normally consisted of. It was incredible to think that one would rather be locked in, their free will taken away, just to avoid their family—Jane couldn't say she didn't understand it.

But it was time for Harmony to let go of hiding, cowering and running away. It was necessary for her to take a stand,

and that began with finding the truth of the trauma, the reason that her escape was formulated in the first place. This relationship would be symbiotic, just as Jane planned. Harmony was easy to feel sorry for, her life was epically sad. But Jane felt injustice in her heart—this woman didn't deserve to suffer like the rest. She was a casualty of the Collins's as well. Jane would help pull her out of their toxic grip.

"Do you think I would like painting?" Harmony's voice pulled Jane from her straying thoughts.

"I've always heard it's very relaxing. An excellent task to stave off anxiety."

"I think I'll try."

"My sister was a painter. I have some of her old things in storage. I'd be more than happy to have them put to use."

"You mean, give them to me?"

"Yes, if you'd like."

"Yes. Please! I never got anything good growing up, no presents, Dave would try to scrape something together for me…I miss those days."

"Let's talk about them," Jane began, "Tell me what you miss most."

I know what I do.

First Friday of October, 6th

THE ANTAGONIST

I

"Hey, you must be the pizza maker!" The man came bounding towards her with a rush of friendly energy. Jane took her cue, a large smile sweeping across her face as as she stuck out her hand.

"I'm Chrissy. You're Robb, the owner?" This was the easiest identity to fake seeing as Repo Pizza paid their employees in cash.

"That's right!" he confirmed as he shook her hand and gestured her towards the kitchen.

"You received my resume and everything alright?" she asked.

"Yup! Gotta love email, I'm all about saving the trees."

"Oh, definitely," she agreed.

"So I'm guessing you know your way around a kitchen?" He hadn't bothered to call any of the elaborate references she made up, but just in case, Jane made sure to have a direct number and email for each. She was also really good at accents.

"Absolutely, I've been making pizza for years." This was not a lie. Jane lost count of how many failed pizzas she attempted in her cramped kitchen before finally getting it right.

"Sick! I can't wait to taste what you're cooking!"

"I'm excited to get started!" she returned with equal enthusiasm.

"Alright, so I'll just go over our system with you, show you where everything is—if you're comfortable being on your own, I'll get out of here a little early and the kitchen is yours for the rest of the night. We will go from there and see how things work out if that's rad with you?"

"That's rad with me, Sir."

THE ANTAGONIST

"No sirs! You'll make me feel like an old man."

"No problem."

"Great, well, let's get started then."

"Yes, let's," Jane agreed as she felt excitement creep into her veins. Not only was she going to have the place to herself for the evening, she was going to make Dave a pizza that would trigger memories and bring a taste of misery into his life. "Thanks so much for the opportunity, Robb, you have no idea what this means to me." And he really didn't, not at all.

He turned to look at her with a hint of surprise, "Hey, you seem like good people. Good people, good pizza, that's what we do here." That was what she'd been banking on.

Jane spent the rest of the evening feeding the good people of Repo Ridge, all except one. She wondered if Dave's family knew how much he loved black olive pizza. Jane continually observed that she never saw him eat it. Now was time to delve into the past and see if his palate really changed, or if he was lying—maybe to all of them, or perhaps just to himself.

2

"You should go for it," Jane insisted as Desiree ran on the treadmill beside her. "What do you have to lose?"

They were the only two in the gym at this outrageously early hour, as Desiree's schedule permitted 'before dawn' sessions occasionally. It was on a morning like this when they first met—Jane's physique inspired Desiree's envy. She insisted that Jane train her without a second thought.

Jane spent months keeping track of Dave's coworkers. But she knew from the second Desiree flounced into the firm that she would be the one to cause the most damage.

"Well normally, I wait for them to come to me. I don't see why I have to do all the work," she complained.

"But you said every time one of them attempts to try, you shoot them down."

"Yeah, it's boring otherwise, but if they are persistent, I do reconsider."

"Sounds easy. "

"It is. I want a challenge."

"Well, then suck up your pride and ask him out," Jane insisted.

She still couldn't understand what the younger woman saw in Dave, other than a conquest she could not master.

"Ugh, I think he's just shy. Maybe I should give him a couple more days to adjust to me."

This was not good enough. Jane needed Desiree to begin her destruction now, today. She already wasted time and resources on other employees who were not nearly as capable of twisting this plot into her favor. "I don't see how that's going to make a difference. You've been there for two weeks already and you told me he hasn't even asked you your name. He must be insane."

"I'm beginning to think so. I mean, look at me," she gestured to her outrageously perfect form. Jane's training sessions sent Desiree from 'hot 'to 'smoke-show'—didn't she realize Jane gave great advice?

"I bet he's intimidated. It's a good sign that he hasn't crowded you, though. I can't stand pushy men."

"But now I want what I don't have!" Desiree whined. She was pouting like a petulant child.

"Desiree, there's only one way to get what you want. You aren't normally this indecisive about anything. Just talk to him."

Desiree huffed with annoyance but conceded. "Alright. Fine! I'll do it today. As soon as I get in."

"Good, you never know what could be if you don't try."

"That's true. And it's always the quiet ones that are the best in bed."

"Are you speaking from experience?"

"Is there anything else I speak from?"

"Touché."

"Mr. Secretary is going to be my personal slave once I get done with him."

Jane sincerely hoped if that came to pass, that Desiree tortured Dave within an inch of his life. She needed him alive for her plans, but she did not need him well.

Secretary! Jane scoffed to herself. It was the perfect job for someone like Dave, who pretended to be as unassuming as he looked. But wasn't that just it? People never took secretaries to be any sort of serious threat—their job was always to assist and help. But to Jane, if given the opportunity, she believed that the position of secretary held a lot more power than others realized. For one, they had access to all sorts of personal information and data that could easily be used against other employees. No one would expect this from Dave's kind smile and willingness to do other's bidding. Secretaries observed as well—their desk was usually situated in the most convenient spot for anyone to reach them if needed. Jane could see it in her mind's eye now—Dave just watching and studying all that went on. Someone continually underestimated by those around him. Of course he would want to blend in, be a nobody…Jane knew it was a front. It might not even be on his conscious mind, but he was most certainly hiding, right in plain sight. He was as clever as she always knew him to be. The difference now was that Jane was the watcher, the invisible woman who would slowly but surely force him to remember. Until then, she would let Dave go on, believing that he was the one in power.

"Keep me posted," Jane encouraged as they slowed their pace to a walk.

"You'll be the first to know of any developments," Desiree promised with a wink and a cunning smirk. Jane was beginning to appreciate having someone as devious as Desiree DeLongo on her side.

"Good luck."

THE ANTAGONIST

3

The moonlight gleamed eerily through the high glass windows as Jane crept through the seemingly empty mansion. It was 30 minutes after midnight when she saw the last light turned dark from her hiding place in the backyard. She made sure to stay close to the trees, hidden in shadows of the dense forest beyond, just in case someone decided to look outside and discover a creeping anomaly. She couldn't risk it. Yet here she was, now tip-toeing silently through Dave Collins's enormous home. She spent months watching and learning the routines of the family, countless hours mapping out the blueprints and discovering the easiest way inside.

This was her first visit to the mansion, but it would surely not be her last. Jane kept to the bottom floor, not wanting to chance waking one of the slumbering occupants. It didn't take long for her eyes to adjust due to the amount of moonlight streaming in and across the high ceilings. The wind was wild tonight, and every little creak and groan set her teeth on edge. If she were caught now, all of her work would be for nothing.

She found what she was looking for in a study off the living room—a bunch of personal receipts and jotted-down notes that she instantly recognized to be in Dave's handwriting. The way he dotted his I's and crossed his T's was forever embedded in her memory, but it was still good to have a reference for her future plans. A set of keys were shoved in the back of one of the desk drawers—Jane lifted them up to the light to discover they were the spares for Dave's car. She pocketed them, assuming they might come in handy in the upcoming weeks.

THE ANTAGONIST

Jane knew for years that this was the kind of extraordinary wealth Dave accumulated, but seeing it all now, actually being inside of his comfortable and beautiful home, made the blood pound in her brain like an untapped volcano. She wanted to slash curtains and tear down walls, she wanted to take a sledgehammer to their fine marble and burn every lush piece of furniture she passed. But Jane resisted. All of the physical destruction she could cause to their property wasn't enough, for it could easily be replaced. The devastation she had in mind was much more psychological. And once the damage was done, there was no way of ever fixing what she was going to break.

Jane left the note on the refrigerator door, knowing Dave was always the first one up in the morning. A pattern he was unwilling to break, just like the rest of his perfectly organized and wonderful life.

"You're special!"

...gleamed back at her from where she placed the sticky message.

Jane wondered if he would remember that saying, the one he'd told her over and over again. It seemed now as if that had been a completely other life—especially for Dave. Jane was curious how long it would be before he began to accept the truth. She took a deep breath and turned to sneak back out the way she'd come. There was no going back now. This was the first piece of the puzzle, the one that would begin to unravel her foe until he was left as exactly as Jane had been—terrified and alone.

Early Autumn 2017

THE ANTAGONIST

I

Her plans were finally in motion after five long years of study and hard work.

The planning and organizing of this venture consumed Jane until she figured out exactly how she would approach the end of Dave Collins's perfect life. Jane was an observer—she followed him everywhere and took note on his interpersonal relationships and his meticulous schedule. She learned all she could about those who surrounded him—whether it was his family, coworkers or friends, Jane was on top of each and every connection.

She wanted revenge for so many things that she was sometimes unable to put them all into words. The feelings were there, though, heavy with resentment, pain and undiluted rage.

Over the last few months, there were moments when she wavered. After all of her accomplishments to get to this point, Jane considered maybe her plans were impossible to execute after all. She wasn't naturally the type of person to be able to stomach such vile manipulation and falsities—she fought with her conscience on more than one occasion, but at the end of the day it all came down to the future. Jane was stuck, unable to move forward, unable to let go until Dave paid for the horror and destruction that he so carelessly heaped onto her life. Seeing his smiling face and the love and devotion of his family surrounding him was by no means the catalyst, but it still fueled her beyond what she thought were her normal capabilities. There would be no more hesitation, no more nights of uncontrollable sobbing and self-sacrifice. No, the

THE ANTAGONIST

reckoning would begin soon. She hadn't come this far just to turn away now and let it all go. Jane's freedom would remain unattainable until the monster that took it from her suffered as she did, as her sister did.

2017-2012

THE ANTAGONIST

I

It was curious that the thing Jane chose to study and excel in, before this deviation of revenge, was mental health. Becoming a therapist was one of the more challenging things she'd done in her life. She obtained a Bachelors and Masters in Psychology before making the decision to move back to Repo Ridge. She attended a community college and won a scholarship for Grad school. Not that there was anyone to share her amazing news with—Jane had no one left by then. If Dave was never in her life, she wondered if she still would have chosen this same route? Fate seemed to be working in her favor.

Jane always remembered her dreams. She studied them and used them to better understand her past. It was how she'd been able to conquer her unreachable reasons for anxiety—it was the only way for her to name her demons out loud as they appeared to her. The context was always different, but the players were usually the same. There was one dream that reoccurred to her over the years. It involved a black raven in the night that stared down into a pool of water, where a white raven stared back, surrounded by sun. Jane was never sure if they were separate entities, or one bird seeing its own reflection—it represented balance, the two sides of the coin, good and evil, the dark and the light. Ravens were known to appear after wars on bloody battlefields. They were often associated with death because of this and the fact that they were scavengers. For years, Jane assumed that this was an ill omen, a representation of a punishment that she deserved. It was only after years of study and training her mind that she realized what the dream actually meant. Jane was blaming herself, taking the appearance of this creature in her mind too literally. She was not cursed. She was not a bringer of death. The black raven was waiting for her to make a move, to reach out and grasp the light that for as long as she could remember, seemed unattainable. She could no longer wage war on herself. The raven was truth, intuition and wisdom—the tools she would use to guide her future.

Psychology was the study that grounded her and allowed her to search for answers over the years. She found plenty, but none that excused or took away the pain Jane experienced in her relatively short life. She spent hours studying in her dreary, cheap apartment on the outer skirts of Repo, completing her final qualifications for private practice online. It was a small blessing, but she couldn't give up. Not when this skill would allow her to confront the minds of those she needed to infiltrate.

Jane went to the gym on a regular basis. It was another thing that helped quell her depression and anxiety—the two feelings that continually kept her moving up and down on a seesaw of despair. She was now in the best shape of her life. She wanted to feel strong and capable, safe on her own. Jane learned to defend herself, while protecting those who couldn't. She wasn't sure how this skill would come into play as she moved forward, but she liked how it made her feel—impenetrable and tough.

She ate a lot of homemade pizza over the years. Sometimes it was good, most of the time it was crap. But she didn't give up. If she were going to slide into Repo Pizza and snag a job, she would have to know her way around the kitchen. As of now, she knew they weren't hiring, but that would not deter her.

She watched countless tutorials, and eventually, much like she did with anything she put her mind to, Jane was able to conquer and accomplish the task. No matter how many times she failed, she refused to stop pushing. She read somewhere that if a person performed a task for 10,000 hours, they became a professional at whatever it was they were doing. Jane wondered briefly how much time she spent stalking Dave Collins's life…she was getting pretty good at it, in her opinion.

The rest of her time was spent planning, creating all of the personalities to go along with her alter egos. She began to weave a web as seamlessly as possible, one that would trap Dave in the center. And then she would devour him.

Learning about the people who were closest to him allowed Jane to develop these individual personalities—having a background in psychology helped her navigate the best ways to go about inserting herself into their separate lives. The process was painstaking and had to be planned just right. If one person caught on to what she was doing, the whole thing would fall apart—she would be recognized, or worse, accused of stalking and harassing an 'innocent' man. Then the truth would be buried along with her dead sister and that simply wasn't an option for Jane.

⁓

Jane was born and raised in Repo Ridge but she never once planned on moving back until it became unavoidable. She hated the quiet streets and nosey neighbors—the best part about Repo was its lush surrounding forests and magnificent sunrises. A good number of years passed since Jane set foot in the small and inconsequential town. The day she left, Jane assumed she would never return, back then there had been no reason for her to do so—not one her young mind would be able to understand let alone uncover. So she attempted to let go of the place. There was very little over the years that she was able to recall. All of her memories of the past faded as she grew up and moved on, all but one…the one that resurfaced, the one of Dave Collins.

Jane's mother and father died in a car accident a few years after they left Repo and moved north to a smaller and more miserable town—being addicts and unreliable sources of in-

THE ANTAGONIST

come, Jane's parents could no longer afford to keep her and Ellie fed and dressed down in the fancy valley. Instead, they moved into an even shittier home than the previous ramshackle mobile home they occupied on Parrish Street. She never truly considered them family. They were always gone, always out for their own needs. If they came home it was with strangers who partied and fought all through the night.

Jane learned to take care of herself, especially after Ellie moved to New York with some guy she met at a bar two years earlier. The large age difference between them always made Jane look to her sister as a mother figure. The distance only made things more difficult and Jane wished every night for her to return.

Her parents deaths had been a blessing in Jane's eyes, seeing as this tragedy prompted Ellie to move back from New York and legally become Jane's guardian—they were once again a family. Those years were the happiest of Jane's life. There were no rules, just fun and love—they were occasionally reckless, but Jane trusted her big sister with her life. It was Ellie and Jane against the world, nothing and no one would be able to change that.

Yet now she was alone once again and back in the place where all the horror began. She wasn't leaving until she found justice.

It was the summer of 2012 when Jane landed in Repo, just days before she finally made the concrete decision to return. It was as if the town lay untouched, a magic spell encasing it for all these lost years. Jane imagined it frozen in time and waiting for her inevitable return.

A storm rolled in along with her, the dark grey skies contrasting in a deliciously foreboding way against the vibrant greens of trees reaching up around it.

Thunder shook the sky, sounding like the unavoidable drums of war. Jane loved that sound.

Life would never be the same again—it was her time to fight, and win.

2011

THE ANTAGONIST

I

It was a beautiful wedding.

The most elaborate and decadent Jane could ever remember experiencing in her life—not that she'd been to many weddings. But over the years she picked up shifts with a catering company here or there for a little extra cash while still in school. Thankfully she kept her formal uniform—it allowed her to blend in at this specific occasion without anyone giving her a second glance. Except, of course, to grab a champagne flute off the silver tray she carried throughout the throngs of the wealthy, smiling guests.

Today's spectacle was nothing like she'd ever seen before. Thankfully, Jane prepared herself to endure the inevitability of seeing Dave Collins in person for the first time in 10 years. But even the mental pep talk Jane had given herself was not enough. He entered the reception, glowing with pride, his eyes dancing with merriment, his lips turned up in a beautiful and victorious smile.

Jane thought it might kill her—the second he appeared she thought her heart was going to explode with fear and rage. But it didn't. She was unable to tear her gaze away throughout the night—she fantasized about plunging a knife through his chest as she watched him feed his beautiful wife a piece of decadent cake. She imagined him slipping on the polished marble floors as they danced to their first song and breaking his neck. The feelings that coursed through her were unstoppable, uncontrollable. She knew her sister would have told her that she was torturing herself, that no good could come from this masochistic act, but Jane couldn't help it. She couldn't believe that this imposter was living such a magnificent life, seemingly perfect—and somehow the Universe decided to forego punishment. If there were true balance in life, then Dave Collins should be suffering, he should be alone with only his self-loathing for comfort—but clearly this was not the case. Jane would not tolerate the injustice, the unfairness of the situation that she was witnessing. Dave got to have it all while she lost everything? If karma were not real, then Jane would make it so. She would take this man's fate into her own hands, just as he'd done hers.

2

Jane was numb, unsure if she would ever be able to feel again as she watched her sister's casket lowered into the frozen ground.

They'd been together only six weeks earlier, when Jane finally confided in her sister the secret she kept buried for the last decade.

"Do you remember Dave Collins?" she asked Ellie, who had sat across from her at the diner, sipping on a black coffee. She'd looked thinner than normal. Jane wondered if she was even eating.

Her eyes perked up at the name, "What made you think of him? God, talk about a blast from the past."

"Do you ever hear from him?"

"No! Why would I? We dated like 20 years ago when we were still kids."

"You weren't a kid."

"Thanks, Sissy, way to make me feel young," Ellie rolled her eyes with a little smile. "Anyway, why do you ask?"

"I have to tell you something…"

Ellie had been shocked, beside herself with personal blame, even after Jane promised her that all that transpired was not her fault in any way. Jane was concerned with her sister's mental health at the time, could see that she was not her usual extroverted self. She wondered briefly if Ellie had taken to their parent's habits of late. She was always dating one kind of scumbag or the other, and Jane knew addiction ran in their veins. Her sister's drawn features and shaking hands were a blaring alarm. But Ellie brushed off her questioning and promised that she was just overworked and underpaid, like most New Yorkers. Jane was unwilling to let up on it. She beat herself up afterwards for even mentioning her own problems to Ellie, who'd been the one to care for her all these years. She didn't want to distress her sister, cause her more grief than they already experienced, but she couldn't keep it to herself, not any longer, not after Mike and certainly not after all the memories that came along with her most recent discovery—she was broken, and if anyone would be able to put her back together, it was her sister.

How wrong she had been. Jane's actions had the exact opposite effect of what she was hoping. She thought the reveal of her past would bring her and Ellie closer together, that perhaps her sister would give up the city life and return once again to Jane. Her plan, her hopes, backfired and now she lost more than she was ever willing to gamble. She wanted to scream at the sky, she wanted to jump into the ground beside the only person who ever loved her. She wanted to die in that moment, but she couldn't, she wouldn't give up.

Jane's confession was the final push, the one that allowed Ellie to drown in guilt and take her own life, rather than continue on with the knowledge of what happened to her little sister. Jane would never forgive herself for piling more pain onto her already fragile mental state. She would see that Ellie did not die in vain—Jane could no longer remain broken, she would put herself back together, if only to destroy the man who'd taken everything from her. She vowed in that moment she would never stop or rest—Jane would ruin him. Not until Dave Collins was at her mercy and begging to be saved would she finally be able to breathe without pain. That was her promise to Ellie, to herself.

2010

THE ANTAGONIST

I

She lay naked and sobbing as Mike attempted to comfort her.

"What is it, did I hurt you?" his soothing tone only made her cry harder, "Jane, please. Tell me what to do."

"Go," she choked out as she buried her head in her shaking hands. "Just leave."

He hesitated, unsure if that was what she really wanted. He placed a hand on her back as she jerked away with a small scream, "Fucking leave!" she railed, turning to face him with tears running down her eyes and blurring her vision.

They hadn't been dating very long, but apparently he knew not to question her in this state. He began gathering his clothes.

"If you need me, just call. Please let me know you're alright. I'm sorry."

She knew he had no idea what he was apologizing for—this wasn't his fault. Jane was the one to suggest they have sex—she never considered herself overtly sexual or desirous, but now that she was eighteen, she wanted to feel normal. And normal 18 year olds had sex. Forcing herself into this was a huge mistake. She was now severely regretting it. As soon as he put himself inside of her, something even deeper inside of her snapped.

Jane ignored him as she continued to whimper, her knees pulled up to her chest as she tried to form herself into the smallest ball imaginable. She wanted to disappear. She wanted to cease existing. She couldn't stop the images that were flooding her mind. Her psyche could not process it all at once. For a few brief moments she convinced herself that she was actually losing her mind.

"Get it together," she whispered vehemently. "You can do this, make it stop, make it stop." Her insides were burning with disgust.

She heard the door to her apartment shut quietly as she let out a shudder of relief—all she wanted in this moment was to be alone. But that was impossible because Dave was right there with her. He was latched on and rotting her brains from the inside out. She felt like tearing at her skin, ripping out her hair—anything to make the memories stop.

Jane showered until the scalding water burned her flesh raw, she shrieked until she lost her voice. The tears continued to fall until there was nothing left. Eventually, it could have been hours, perhaps days, the feeling of fear and horror began to ebb, just enough for another emotion to enter and slide up alongside them—rage.

2001

THE ANTAGONIST

I

"One last time before you go!"

Jane watched, her teddy bear latched safely in her arms, as her sister jumped into Dave Collin's arms. Ellie laid a huge kiss on his lips. He spun her around in his arms like she was a princess before her sister turned away with a wistful sigh and back towards their packed car. Jane's family would be leaving Repo Ridge today and Ellie's boyfriend had come over to give her one last goodbye. Ellie told Jane that she didn't see the long distance thing working out. This made Jane sad. Dave was always so fun to be around. He made her sister laugh and always wrote such sweet letters to Ellie that Jane secretly read. He always penned them in black sharpie. Jane once asked him about it and he told her he loved the smell. He delivered the letters to Ellie rolled up in a glass root beer bottle on their doorstep.

Dave loved them both—he told her a million times over the last few years. And just when Jane was beginning to feel cared for by someone other than her sister, they would have to leave. It was upsetting, but Jane hoped Dave would come visit. He promised that he would.

But he never did.

For a few months she held that against him. She continually asked her sister when he would come to see them. Ellie finally told her they decided it was best to part ways. They were both young and Ellie didn't want to return to the past, she wanted to move forward. Shortly after that, memories of

THE ANTAGONIST

Dave began to fade, and eventually Jane stopped asking about him. Life became different—any joy of childhood was extinguished and even at a very young age, Jane began to grow up quite quickly due to unfortunate circumstances and death. Her teen years were a blur of chaos and survival. And for a long time, the name Dave Collins lay waiting in her subconscious, resting until the day the first trigger would be pulled.

2000

THE ANTAGONIST

I

Jane felt warm. She couldn't identify the source immediately. Was it the tears leaking from her wide, innocent eyes? Was it the feeling of being pressed against a hard mattress? She wasn't sure. All she knew was that the man above her continued saying everything was okay. And she believed him. Why wouldn't she? He constantly told her she was safe with him, protected, that he would never let anything happen to her. So what was happening now?

"Oh Janey, I love you so much. You're so beautiful," he murmured as his lips ran over her bare skin.

Jane shivered, despite the hotness that began to consume her. She felt every touch, every caress as his hands continued to touch her in places she only just recently became aware of. She was panting now, this seemed to make him happy—encouraged him to reach lower and lower. Jane bit her lips as he let out a groan, rubbing his fingers against her.

"I'm going to protect you, I promise. I will never let anyone hurt you," he cooed as he pulled back to look into her gaze. "Don't cry. You aren't scared, are you?"

She shook her head no. Jane wasn't even sure why she was crying, other than the fact that she somehow knew that whatever they were doing would definitely displease her sister. He told her before that no one could know. That horrible things would happen to the both of them if that was the case. He made her promise that whatever they shared together was a secret—their secret. It made Jane feel special to have a secret with someone—it gave him her trust, even though her eight-year-old self was unaware of this.

"You don't want me to stop, right?" he begged, fondling her small frame as he continued to drag his lips from her neck,

THE ANTAGONIST

down her flat chest and towards the center of his sick desire. "Don't I make you feel as good as you make me feel, Janey?"

She couldn't disagree with him—her lips would not let her. All she knew was that what they were doing pleased him so immensely—the last thing she wanted to do was make him mad, or worse, make him leave. He was the only person besides her sister who ever told her he loved her.

He took her silence as confirmation. She watched helplessly as he pulled away from her, only to start untying the string on his faded pajama pants. He was back on her in what seemed like a matter of seconds. Jane felt as if she'd been lying there for hours. She had no idea what was coming, only that it must be something monumental. All of the times before, he'd never taken his clothes off, only hers. The feeling of his manly body was foreign. She was highly aware of his chest hair scratching against her softness, the feel of something hard and hot pushing insistently between her legs. He flattened her out as his flesh moved over her, slowly. Jane felt a twinge of panic, the inability to get free as he held her in place.

She would have screamed but at the last second, he muffled her voice with his tongue, like a frog trapping a fly in its mouth. She tried to pull away but he wouldn't let her. She could feel her tears now steadily falling down her cheeks and landing against the wrinkled sheets beneath her. The pain inside of her was unbearable.

His large hand replaced his mouth as he pulled back to hush her in the softest voice she ever heard, "It's okay sweetheart, don't worry, it will stop soon. I promise you after that you're going to feel so good. I promise, Janey. You're my special girl. Who is my special girl?"

He moved again and she whimpered against his hot palm. Whatever was inside her was much too big, it wasn't right. She didn't want this. But she couldn't tell him. She watched him instead—his face in rapture, his eyes closed as he moved in and out of her. After a few minutes the feeling became different, numb. This didn't feel good like all the times before. It was nothing like the soft touching and teasing. This was too much. But Jane loved him. So she continued to lie there and pretend she was having fun.

"Move with me," his ragged voice encouraged.

It seemed to last for hours. She concentrated on the shadows dancing across the walls, the elegant flow of the movement she could not recognize as her own.

Finally he stopped, once again removing his hand from her face to replace it with his lips. His tongue in her mouth felt soothing now that he was no longer hurting her and Jane grasped onto that. She would show him the affection that he needed just as much as she.

"Did you like that? I did. It made me very happy."

"Yes," she lied as she smiled up at him through her red-rimmed eyes.

"We can do it again, Janey. As many times as you want."

She rolled over onto her side as he began to dress. She pulled the covers over her body and attempted to fall asleep. He'd slipped in from Ellie's room sometime around midnight. Jane turned her head to look at the clock—it was now almost four. A small red blinking dot caught her attention from the dark corner of the room.

He was back now and dressed, his breath ghosting against her brow as he leaned down one more time to kiss her, "Who is my special girl?" he asked in a low tone.

"Me."

"That's right. And this is our special secret, right?"

She nodded her head in agreement.

"I love you, Janey."

Those words made any pain worth it. Her eyes were beginning to fall shut, her young body exhausted from their 'playtime.'

The last thing she saw was Dave Collins move into the blackness beyond and disappear along with the red blinking light.

1999-1997

THE ANTAGONIST

I

Jane was in love. She knew it.

Dave was the perfect man. Her sister was so lucky. He brought them pizza every Friday. He'd have to drive all the way out of town seeing as Repo Ridge had zero Italian food. The order was always the same: cheese with black olives. That was Dave's favorite, so it became Jane's favorite too. They would spend most of the weekend together, Dave, Ellie and Jane—sometimes Robb would join them—Dave's best friend. He was always 'high on drugs' as her sister put it, and never spoke to Jane.

They would play Nintendo for hours or listen to Nirvana CDs on repeat—seeing as Ellie and Dave were both 21, Jane was getting quite the education from them—not that her parents cared or even bothered to come home unless they needed money. On nights that Ellie worked, Dave offered to babysit Jane. The neighborhood wasn't the greatest and he told her sister he thought she'd feel more comfortable not having to leave 'the baby' alone. In Ellie's opinion, this made Dave one of the good guys, the best. And anyone who her sister thought was worthy, Jane also worshiped.

Ellie worked most of the evening shifts at the local bar, so sometimes Dave would sleep over. Jane always liked that best. She preferred it when it was just the two of them, when she didn't have to share his affection with her sister. She was jealous sometimes when she watched them kiss—she wanted to be kissed, too. When she mentioned this to Dave, he took her request to heart and taught her how, just like he did to Ellie.

They also played strange games where Jane would lay down on the couch in just her underwear and Dave would stick strawberries in between each of her toes. He would cover them with whip cream and eat them off, extending his mouth to fit around her toes, one at a time. He would maintain eye contact with her throughout as she giggled at the feeling of his warm wet tongue tickling her feet.

He would bathe her too and afterwards wrap her in a soft towel, put her on his lap and braid her hair before bed. Jane loved this, the feeling of his fingers combing her long tresses—it made her sleepy and relaxed. He would always kiss her goodnight, but never stayed when she asked him to lay down with her until she could fall asleep. She never complained. The last thing she wanted him to do was leave—to reject her.

Dave always encouraged Jane to take off her clothes and dance around naked when they were alone. He would sit, with his legs spread wide, on the dilapidated couch and watch her. After a while he would pat his lap and she would fall on top of him with hugs and kisses. He would wrap his arms around her—his hands sliding over her skin making her feel a tingly sort of pleasure. He never hurt her when he touched her. Jane never felt any pain. Instead when he teased her most sensitive parts it awoke feelings in her for someone much too young to comprehend.

One time, he caught her stealing Ellie's coveted butterfly clips—she knew she was going to be in trouble with her sister if she found out. She begged Dave not to tell her. He promised her he wouldn't, as long as she did something for him in return.

He wanted to play a game.

Jane stripped bare, jumped on his lap and began to ride him like a cowgirl. That was what he wanted. She could feel his large rough hands lightly slapping against her bottom, encouraging her to go faster. He was telling her the bad guys were going to get away if she didn't pick up the pace. She was a cowgirl, she had to catch them and Dave would help her get there, as her trusty steed. The friction of her naked skin against his sweatpants made Jane squeal with delight. She never played a game like this…she could feel the butterfly wings clapping in succession against one another—the sparkling light from the glitter kept catching her eyes as an explosive feeling took over her. She gasped at the new sensation, not sure if something was wrong, but how could it be when this felt so good? Dave squeezed her against them, the wings of the butterflies slowly coming to a stop as she rested on his chest, panting. When he pulled back from her, he was smiling with the most satisfied look on his face.

"You got them, Janey, you got the bad guys," he whispered, his hands tangling in her hair as he pulled out the clips one by one, "Now go put these back before your sister gets home and we might have time for one more game."

THE ANTAGONIST

2

"Sissy, I want you to meet my boyfriend, Dave."

Jane looked up from the picture she was drawing, sprawled amongst crayons and broken colored pencils on the messy living room floor. Her eyes were wide as she took in the smiling, very handsome man. His blondish hair was wavy, his deep blue eyes inviting. She knew immediately that she liked him.

"Hi Dave, I'm Jane."

Part III:

The Return of the Repressed

Friday, October 27th 2017

THE ANTAGONIST

I

Dave continued to stare at her. Silently allowing his brain to catch up to all the information she'd just thrown at him. He was reeling—unable to comprehend.

Jane stared right back, her eyes blazing with fury, her fists clenched in rage.

"Fun little trip down memory lane," she hissed, watching him carefully for signs of breaking.

"Why," he began in his soft tone, "Why would you do this to me?" he couldn't believe it. Dave wasn't sure if he was hallucinating in this moment or if she were entirely real.

"To you?" Jane could barely control the tremor in her voice, "To you?"

"Janey," he tried, reaching for her hands—this was a misunderstanding, he could fix this.

She wrenched them back in horror with a startled gasp.

"That's not my name," she spat, "Don't fucking touch me."

Dave felt his heart ache at the absolute loathing in her eyes. "I loved you," he said. "I did."

"You took advantage of me. You used me, manipulated me, you destroyed my life!" she snapped, slamming her hands against the table in order to keep herself from flipping it over. "But you did not love me."

"I took care of you. I was there for you when your parents and your sister weren't," he reminded her.

"My sister was always there for me, you fuck," she burst out with brutal vengeance.

He looked her dead in the eyes, "And so was I."

"You actually believe your own lies, don't you?"

THE ANTAGONIST

"There is no lie," he returned heatedly, his gaze boring into her with an intensity that set her nerves even further on edge. "You were perfect, our *relationship* was perfect," he insisted, as memories began to replay over and over in his head of their times together. He almost smiled at the way she adored him back then.

Jane gazed at him with incredulity, "It wasn't a relationship. I was eight years old and you were my sister's twenty-one-year-old boyfriend!"

Dave shook his head in denial, "I never saw you as a child."

"It doesn't matter what you think you saw."

"I never hurt you," he promised with sincerity in his gaze.

Jane let out a loud bark of painful laughter. "You raped me."

"I made love to you. We shared something sacred. We loved each other," he clarified, thinking of all the times she would run into his arms and kiss him—practically begging him to play with her.

"Then let me ask you something—why did every reminder of our time together make you sick?" Jane questioned, infuriated that his brain warped everything she threw at him.

"What do you mean?"

"Black olives. You hate them now even though we ate olive pizza every weekend. I sent you memory after memory—the hair clips, the smell of sharpies, the root beer bottle, strawberries and whip cream, Nirvana CDs—all of it, Dave. I gave it all away to you, and every time I saw you interact with one of those lost pieces of the past, you deteriorated. I watched you get drunker and drunker—I witnessed your life fall apart around you. Now, if what we had was so beautiful, do you honestly think you would be where you are now?"

He could not ignore her logic. Jane hoped her question would finally dig out one truthful piece of his mind.

He evaded her as he shook his head, his voice filled with sadness, "Why was betrayal the only option?"

"Betrayal? What was I supposed to do? Stroll up to your house, knock on the door and say hello? Include your family in a chat about our relationship? Do you think they would see it the same way as you?"

He was silent, but the look in his eyes told her she finally cracked through some level of this delusional farce he was currently playing out.

"I want you to admit it. What you did to me, how wrong it was. How much you hurt me and Ellie."

"Ellie? How did I hurt Ellie?"

"I told you, she killed herself—overdosed. After I told her what you did to me."

"Jane—"

"It's your fault she's dead," she bit out, fighting back the tears that were threatening to fall. She would show him no weakness.

"She was always troubled," he tossed out with patronizingly false remorse.

Jane leapt to her feet, seething with rage. She hurled the glass she was holding with all her might. It shattered into pieces. What was left of the sticky liquid slowly dripped down the dark wall. How dare he talk about Ellie in that way—Jane was seeing red, but she needed to remain in control.

She took several calming breaths. She knew this was what he wanted—to make her seem unstable, possibly insane. She forced herself to sit back down and lower her voice.

"You have no idea how many years I've spent trying to understand you. To cognize why you did to me what you did. Your parents are no better than mine were, but I never raped anyone, especially not a kid. Not only did you rape me, you groomed me, normalized what we did. You normalized it because it was truly that horrific. You locked it away and thought about it as often as you'd think about any other ordinary or inconsequential act from your past…but not me, Dave."

He watched her with calculating eyes. If she was capable of devastating his life in this manner, what was stopping her from taking it altogether? Dave needed clarification.

"So you came back here, for me."
"To destroy you."
"And ruin my life."
She nodded, "I was only returning the favor."
"I didn't realize it meant, I meant, so much to you," he commented with a look close to reverence cresting his eyes. "I am honored."
"You are nothing. You are pathetic and weak. You are a coward and a liar and more than anything I wish I could feel sorry for you. But I can't. I'm no longer that girl, the one who would do anything to make you happy. Your time is up, Dave. Apologize to me."
He let out a morose sigh, "I wish I could Jane, truly, but I can't."
"Why not?"
"Because I'm not sorry. I don't regret it. And I don't think you do, either."
How had she come this far without considering that Dave's reaction would be anything but this? He was a narcissist, a pathological liar…it was how had he hidden so well for so long. It was only now that she was calling him to the carpet that he was forced to show his true colors. The reflection was broken, his bubble close to bursting.
"Your choice to do what you did to me, in your head, comes from a place of care. I know your story, it's similar to mine…the difference I'm not entirely sure of. Maybe it's epigenetic, the affect that your environment had on your genetic make-up, or perhaps your prefrontal cortex doesn't properly regulate impulse control, or maybe you were born with a predisposition, a sickness that was allowed to fester because you never received any sort of nurture in your childhood."
"I understand your need to justify what we did, but I think you're making it a lot more complicated than it needs to be. I wanted you, you wanted me."
"I didn't know any better! My brain wasn't even nearing full development. Don't attempt to put any of this on me. I

was the child and you were the adult. You were the one who should have been teaching me the difference between right and wrong."

"And what is the difference between right and wrong?"

"You say you loved me, wanted to protect me…but how is having a sexual relationship with a child in anyway helping them?"

"Throughout history there have been many cultures that follow similar practices."

Jane let out a laugh of disbelief, "Textbook. You're unreal. It doesn't matter what I say, does it? You will find a way to protect yourself from accepting the truth. That's all I have been trying to do this entire time, Dave, is make you accept your truth."

"The truth is, you've spent your entire adult life focusing on me. Are you going to deny it?"

"Of course not! I can't move on. I'm not able to have a normal sex life, or a healthy relationship because of you. The first time I tried to, all I could see was you on top of me, holding my mouth shut, forcing yourself inside of me. I have had to live with the shame of what we did for years. Feeling dirty and disgusting, like there was something wrong with me, but there's not. It's you that's corrupt and twisted, not me."

For the first time, Jane saw true anger in his gaze.

"And now? Now that you've upended my life, you think you'll find happiness? You think you'll be able to let go of me?"

Jane could tell he was beginning to wear down—there was only so much truth a person could take before they reacted. If he made a move to harm her in any way, she was ready. Her body was strong and relishing the possibility of a fight. She would be more than willing to return her pain to its original source.

"Do you remember the first time you saw me here, in this bar? We locked eyes and I thought for a second you recognized me, and I think a part of you did. It was after that, that you began ordering whiskey for your invisible friend. But you know who I think J is? Your conscience, even if you won't admit it. I think you saw me and even if you didn't know it at the time, something was triggered. You created a personality to have conversations with. A split. A fragmentation to protect yourself and dissociate from what was right in front of you all this time. What did you talk about? Morality? Did you convince yourself that everything you've done in your life was true and right? Are you the victim here? Do you understand how repression works? And how it returns? You've been suffering, not because of the outside actions around you, but because of the internal thoughts and feelings you have ignored and discarded for years."

"I never forgot about you," Dave accused.

"But you tried, you never thought for a second that I was the one torturing you. You knew something was off, wrong, but you pushed me so far to the back of your mind you completely eliminated the possibility of me coming back for you someday. I bet you never thought that would happen, huh? You thought you'd get to screw with my mind, rape and use me and then move on and live your wonderful life with no consequences."

"I didn't!" he yelled, slamming his fist onto the tabletop as his body leaned into her personal space. Being this close to his mouth made Jane's stomach roll. She couldn't stand the rise and fall of his chest, the passionate energy he was exuding as his breath fell across her face. But she didn't flinch, she didn't back down, she stared directly into his eyes.

"Yes, you did."

Whatever he saw in her eyes, terrified him—that much was clear. He slowly retreated back to his side of the table, as if he only just realized he'd moved. His fist was making repetitive squeezing motions around thin air.

They sat in silence, just watching one another.

"You took quite the gamble," he finally spoke.

"There's a difference between counting cards and bluffing."

Dave felt a rush of exhaustion sweep over him. He was beyond weary but still stood by his statement. What they'd shared together all those years ago was not wrong. It was consensual.

He was delusional. It was infuriating. Jane took a deep breath as she hammered in the final nail of his coffin.

"I have proof," she whispered. "And so does Georgette."

That got his attention.

She watched his eyes widen, his hands once again jerking forward as if he meant to reach for her. She slid her chair back in anticipation of his next move.

"Proof?"

If Jane thought he looked terrified just moments ago—it was nothing compared to the fear he was experiencing now.

Jane liked that—she liked it a lot.

"She saw the tape, Dave."

He frowned in confusion, his brain working on overdrive, "I never touched Desiree. I never raped her, what did you do? Doctor up the video surveillance from my office to make it look that way?"

"This has nothing to do with Desiree."

"Then what are you saying?"

"Don't you remember? How deeply buried is that recollection?" she taunted, feeling control return to her side of the table. "The first night you raped me, you recorded it. For years I wondered about that red blinking light in the corner of my room," she watched what little color was left in his face drain away. "I can see I'm jogging your memory."

"No," he whispered, horror prevalent in his eyes.

"You gave me that tape the day before my family and I left Repo Ridge. You hid it in one of my stuffed animals and told me, with astounding arrogance and grandiosity, that it was a little something for me to always remember you by. *Your special girl,*" she sneered with contempt. Jane spat the words as if they were poisonous and burning her insides.

THE ANTAGONIST

Dave's head fell into his hands, his shoulders slumping in defeat. He began to shake as agonizing sounds erupted from his throat, much like a dying animal.

Jane felt her fury soar at his unfair display of emotion.

"Oh Jane," he sobbed over and over again.

Jane was waiting for the rush of satisfaction that would accompany this final blow.

But it did not come.

His tears were not enough.

"Apologize to me, Dave. Admit it. Admit what you did and how it was wrong."

"What difference does it make now? My wife, my Georgie…she will never forgive me."

"No, she won't."

"You kept it all these years," he moaned with anguish.

"I didn't even know what it was until after Ellie died. I found it when I was cleaning out our old things. Do you know how it felt, to have to relive that again? To watch you hold me down and fuck me like some object, even as I cried and struggled to get away."

She could see she was breaking through his defenses—he was finally remembering, finally accepting.

"No," he begged, "No, you wanted me. You loved me, Jane."

"An eight-year-old girl with a broken family looking for affection trusted you. You took advantage of that trust. Look at me," she snapped as he lifted his gaze of sorrow to hers. "You are a monster and now the love of your life knows it. She knows it and so will everyone else. You cannot hide any longer. Accept the truth, your truth Dave Collins. You are a child rapist and pedophile. Soon that is what everyone will associate you with when they hear your name. Now you can see how it feels to be powerless, broken and alone."

He let out a choked scream as he grabbed at his head. His hands repeatedly smacked against the sides of his face as if he were trying to dislodge some parasitic creature eating away at his brains. She'd gotten through. The tape was the hard, factual evidence that he could not ignore.

"Fuck!" he screamed, "Fuck, fuck, fuck!"

He stumbled from the chair and looked around wildly for a means of escape. But there was none. No matter where he turned he couldn't get away.

The tape.

He could remember it all so clearly—the images of Jane and him together. He could see his hand slapping over her mouth, her small cries and the fear in her beautiful green eyes.

He was shaking uncontrollably. His mind was breaking at the thought of exposure, of feeling bare and naked for the world to inspect. To see all his wrongs thrown into light—the rape of a defenseless child, was that really what it had been?

Jane watched him, wondering what his next move would be. In her experience with unearthing repressed thoughts, whenever a patient was confronted with a truth that was unacceptable to them, one of two things happened. The first being that they accept the truth, no matter how hard—they move forward while living in continued misery until they are able to work through the issue and change. If this were impossible, the patient would likely create another reality, an irrational one based in fantasy that would allow the mind to protect itself from the actual truth of the situation.

Dave looked on the verge of a psychotic break.

"Where are you going?" she asked as he staggered towards the front door.

"Away from you, away from this," he slurred. His eyes were twitching, his mouth slightly foaming.

"You have no one to help you," she reminded him, "By morning everyone in Repo will know what you are." She couldn't confirm this, but she knew how fiercely Georgette fought to protect the abused—this news would not go unshared. Even at the cost of her own reputation, Georgette would do the right thing and help put her husband behind bars.

THE ANTAGONIST

Dave turned. His hand was wrapped tightly around the knob of the door when he looked back at her one last time, "You win, Janey. You win."

And he was gone.

Jane took a deep steadying breath—her heart was pounding like chaotic drums on the eve of an ancient battle. The emotions racing through her were fluid, there were too many feelings to place all at once—she conquered the monster, faced him, called him by his name and returned his memories with true context.

Her job was done.

But her story wasn't over.

She got up slowly, her knees buckling slightly beneath her—a side effect, the release her body gained from this confrontation. The come down of adrenaline.

Jane carefully followed after him, out into the night, curious as to what his next move would be.

She wondered if he'd run for it—attempt to get as far away as possible. It didn't matter if he did—she would find him and drag him back here to face the consequences of his actions.

Jane stepped out of the bar just as a wild screeching inundated her ears. Her head snapped towards the sound. Jane watched with wide eyes—everything appearing in slow motion.

Dave was tossed into the air as the car smashed into his body with a deafening crack. He flew gracefully through the night sky before landing on the wet pavement with a sickening crunch. Jane grasped onto the side of the door, her mind reeling.

The driver was already getting out of his car. Jane stood frozen as an old man rushed toward her, begging her to help him. She numbly pointed towards the inside of The Devil's Eye where he would find a phone.

She was in shock.

She hadn't considered the third option: when someone is presented with a truth they are refusing to accept—instead of facing it, they take their own life.

Emily Dinova

That thought propelled her forward as she jumped into action, approaching Dave's bloody and battered body.

He looked like a twisted marionette, legs and arms all bent—a piece of metal from the bumper was lodged in his throat. Jane reached forward, ignoring the sickly feeling of having to once again bear touching him.

There was a pulse. It was faint, but it was there.

Sirens wailed in the background as Jane smiled to herself.

It wasn't Dave's time to die—it was his turn to suffer.

6 Months Later

THE ANTAGONIST

I

Ellie,

Thank you so much for your letter! Totally old school but I love it so I decided to send one back. New York is amazing, we are absolutely in love with the East Village and Alex has been networking like crazy—your connection at the gallery really helped him find his way, I can't thank you enough for that. Enclosed you'll find all the cash I owe you for the last six months of rent. I know you said not to worry about it, but a promise is a promise. I'm glad to hear you are leaving Repo as well, someone as awesome as you doesn't belong in that shitty little town either. I'm hoping my mom will come to visit soon, or even better: take the same advice I'm sending you. There is nothing left for her there now but I feel like she stays to punish herself...I'm sure you heard all about the horrific shit that went down after I left. I can't even bring myself to write about it without feeling sick to my stomach. Anyway, whenever you want your apartment back, just say and we will find another spot. I would love if you decided to move here...hint, hint! Let me know all is good with you and keep me posted on your travels.

The little sister you never had but always needed ☺

—Sam

THE ANTAGONIST

Dear Sam,

I'm thrilled to hear you and Alex are doing so well! Enjoy the apartment, I'm not sure where I'm headed yet, but if I make it up to New York you will be the first to know! The money was unnecessary but I thank you regardless. I'm sorry to hear about your mom, hopefully she's able to find the courage to put what has happened behind her and move on. Repo has been relatively quiet since, well, you know. To be honest, it's just not the same and I'm anxious to get on my way. Don't forget to contact me if you need anything at all. I promise, I will be there.

Your surrogate sis,

—Ellie

Jane smiled as she tipped the envelope into the mailbox at the corner of her street. It was a beautiful sunny morning. She was the only one out and about. A smooth breeze was blowing over the budding trees and the balm of humidity felt comforting against her skin. New life was all around. She took a deep breath as she surveyed the early birds going about their normal Saturday routine.

Normal.

That wasn't a word the residents of Repo Ridge used lightly these days. After the scandal that rocked their town, an air of suspicion and doubt settled over them like lightly fallen dust that you can't see until you run your fingers across it, leaving patterns, marks and scars. Jane assumed it would take years before the people of this place stopped talking about what happened. It was probably the most dramatic occurrence to ever wreck their monotony.

Emily Dinova

That Friday night replayed over and over in her head. She dreamt about it often, but there was no horror, no pain associated with it. Just relief.

Jane quit bartending at The Devil's Eye the day after the explosive confrontation and all that followed. Thankfully, there was no alcohol in Dave's system that night, allowing the bar to go unpunished for such a horrible accident. Jane cited PTSD from the experience. She recalled to the cops that although Mr. Collins was in the bar, she had not served him, or noticed anything suspicious. They went easy on her, especially once they saw how 'upset' and 'traumatized' she was by the whole debacle. Maybe she'd become a professional actress next—the world was her oyster and Jane was ready to begin anew.

She would be leaving tonight. Where she was headed was still unclear, but that didn't matter. Jane wasn't concerned with a destination—she already spent years of her existence driving on a one-way road, to the pinnacle of her purpose. Now that she achieved her goal, life seemed to open up before her. It spanned out like some great wave of possibility. There was nothing she couldn't do, nowhere she was unable to explore. For the first time in her life, she felt peace and genuine excitement for living. She was leaving her past, the person she'd been here, and taking her new self to greater heights than anyone could imagine, most of all herself.

But before she could embark on this journey, it was essential she tie up all her loose ends, for it would be the last time she left this place. And Jane knew deep in her bones that there would be no coming back.

THE ANTAGONIST

2

Jane was just exiting the gym when Desiree came flying into the parking lot in her red sports car. She hopped out, looking disappointed to see Jane already finished for the day. Jane figured now was as good a time as ever. She'd only come to close her account and clean out her locker. This meeting was their first by chance.

"What do you mean you're leaving!?" Desiree screeched at her as Jane finished telling her the news. "First my sessions and now this!"

Jane avoided the gym lately, instead taking herself on long solitary runs—Desiree was furious when Jane told her she would no longer be able to train her. Jane insisted her 'other work' schedule was just too much. She blamed a bunch of other projects that she couldn't put off any longer. Desiree accepted begrudgingly. Now, ironically, she kept track of Jane so they would end up working out at the same time anyway.

Jane didn't want the emotional drain of spending time with someone like Desiree, but it was the price she paid for bringing her into her plans to begin with.

"I've been given a job opportunity," she fibbed, trying to look as disappointed as possible, "I didn't want to take it, but I really need the money."

"I have money," Desiree snapped impatiently, "Why didn't you just say?"

Jane forced herself not to roll her eyes, "That's really nice of you, but I couldn't possibly."

"But what am I supposed to do? I'm going to get ugly without you here!"

THE ANTAGONIST

Jane didn't bother to remind her that she was already a pretty ugly person. Over the last few months, Jane tried to improve the other woman's disposition. She even attempted to move her away from psychological manipulation and meaningless sex, for the wrong reasons—but she was not Desiree's therapist. And it was clear that Desiree had absolutely no desire to work on herself. She already thought she was perfect the way she was.

"You won't get ugly," Jane insisted, "Stop being dramatic."

"Who is going to give me advice all the time?"

Jane did roll her eyes then. Desiree could be so incredibly needy and selfish—it made her wonder what trauma she experienced in her life that made her so angry and vicious. Possibly the same as Jane's—and that's what allowed Jane to endure her negative attitude and energy—but no more.

"You're going to have to figure it out yourself, Des, you're a smart woman."

"Where are you going?"

"Europe."

"What? I'm never going to see you again!"

Probably not, Jane wanted to say, but instead she squeezed the other woman's hand in comfort. "If our paths are meant to cross again they will."

Desiree eyed her skeptically, "It was sort of fate like, wasn't it?" Jane lifted a curious brow as she pushed on, "Meeting you at the time I did, right before all of the craziness started happening."

Desiree spent a ridiculous amount of time exhausting the story of Dave Collins. She told everyone she spoke to how she was the one to discover that something was off about him before anyone else. She prided herself on being the catalyst that set off the final week of events that shocked and astounded all of Repo Ridge. Jane was pretty sure that at this point, Desiree believed her own lie about Dave attempting to rape her. She ran with the false accusation and justified it based on what happened to actually be the truth. Jane was happy to let her take the spotlight and the credit—to the rest of them she was just a ghost, an unidentified face that moved amongst them, not subtle enough to be suspicious, not outlandish enough to recognize.

"I guess, yeah, it's a little weird," Jane acknowledged.

Desiree looked around carefully before lowering her voice so only Jane could hear, "Can you imagine if he and I had actually...you know, done it? I don't think I would have been able to live with myself if I had."

Jane nodded in agreement, "You dodged a bullet."

"You know sometimes I think, 'Hey Des, you're a shit person!' But that thought sits a lot better with me now, after seeing what a true monster looks like."

"That's the thing about monsters—you might never even know you're with one, until it's already too late."

Desiree continued to watch her—the woman was shrewd and Jane knew if she stayed around, this one would not stop digging. Jane no longer wanted to be her partner in crime. The true difference between them was that Desiree enjoyed destroying others' lives. Jane only wanted to destroy one, and as much as it had been necessary in her mind, it was still a painful process with very little pleasure involved.

"Take care of yourself, Desi."

Desiree scoffed with disbelief before pulling Jane to her in a tight hug.

"You better keep in contact, bitch," Jane could hear the emotion in her voice. "Thanks for being my friend."

Jane hugged her back, unable to speak. No one had ever called her a friend before. In all her years of solitude, of avoiding relationships, Jane was left with no one but her demons. Now that she accomplished the seemingly impossible, there was room for others—that was a good feeling to recognize. And even if she couldn't stay, it was elevating to believe that moving on would come with things as simple as friends.

3

Jane knocked softly on the edge of the office door.

"Boss?"

Robb didn't bother to look up. He was staring listlessly at the blank computer screen in front of him. She called him again, this time by name and he seemed to snap out of it—but only a little.

"Hey Chrissy, sorry I didn't hear you," he murmured, rubbing his blood shot eyes. "What's up?"

"I just swung by to grab my last check," she started carefully.

He nodded to himself as he opened the top drawer of his desk and handed her a wad of cash. He didn't even bother to count it.

"This is way more than I'm owed," she began, but he cut her off.

"Just take it."

Jane hesitated—her feelings were conflicted when it came to Robb. He'd been Dave's best friend, a man she assumed could be no better than the one he claimed was like a brother...but Robb was good to her. He was generous and kind. She felt a pang of guilt at the sadness he was experiencing.

"Do you want to talk about it?" she asked.

He turned to stare at her with deadpan eyes. He aged quite a bit over the last few months. "I just keep asking myself the same question over and over again: How did I not know?"

Jane nodded in understanding as she took a few steps closer, "It wasn't your fault, what happened."

"I knew that girl," he choked out suddenly as his eyes glazed over with unshed tears, "The one that he...."

THE ANTAGONIST

Jane held her breath. Her feet were stuck to the floor.

"I mean, I didn't know her personally, how could I? I was such a mess back then and she was only a kid…just a kid." He buried his hands in his face in an attempt to block out a black hole of bad memories.

His anguish was heartfelt and it made Jane's compassion towards the man increase exponentially. She pressed her cold hand against his back and rubbed gently as he broke down.

"I could have helped her, if I had known. I would have—"

"It's the past. You can't hold onto that," she whispered. "Justice was served."

"But not soon enough."

She agreed with him there. "All you can do now is move on. Let go of him and stop blaming yourself—I'm sure she doesn't," Jane insisted.

Robb raised his gaze to hers once more. He looked into her eyes with thousands of questions bleeding through his own. "You know you're wise for someone so young."

"Sometimes we don't get a choice. Sometimes we have to be."

He nodded in understanding as he pulled himself together. "I'm gonna miss your pizza."

She laughed, anything to fight away the emotion clawing to get out of her, "I'll send you a pie from New York," she joked, knowing she would never see him again. "Promise me something?"

He looked at her curiously but nodded in consent.

"Don't let someone else's actions define you. You know your truth, you've fought hard to get where you are. Don't let the mistakes of those you trusted fall on your shoulders. You're a good man and he didn't deserve you."

He was crying again then claiming they were tears of gratitude. Jane always thought that was a funny expression. People didn't cry for any other reason than sadness—even if they didn't realize it at the time.

Emily Dinova

She sighed as she wrapped her arms around Robb, who sobbed onto her shoulder. She was all too familiar with the sound of those grief-ridden tears—they were a childhood being put to death.

THE ANTAGONIST

4

The afternoon sun was just finding its peak in the sky when Jane turned onto Parrish Street. No one heard a peep out of June Collins since news broke and chaos reigned. The God-fearing woman promptly moved out of the house Georgette had given them and back into the poverty she was previously comfortable with. Jane knew that June's decision hadn't been made lightly. It was one thing to be poor your whole life, it was quite another to be given a rich taste of wealth before once again returning to hunger and discomfort—the constant of living in survival mode.

Perhaps she was punishing herself as well. With her family gone and the church turned against her, June was left with just God. It's not as if she should be bothered by that—but isolation, especially after stressful events, could attempt wicked tricks on even the most sane person. And June wasn't anywhere near sane to begin with.

Jane wasn't sure why she felt the need to say goodbye to the woman. Perhaps a small part of her wanted to make sure she was suffering for all she'd done.

June, much like her son, was unable to face the hard truth of reality. She refused to let her in, and when Jane reminded her of who she was the woman went berserk.

"You! I brought you in to Him and I was forsaken! Devil in disguise! Be gone demon!" she screamed through the broken screen door.

"You are sick, Mrs. Collins. I hope you get help."

"Away! Get away from me!" she threatened, raising the wooden statue of Jesus in her shaking hand.

THE ANTAGONIST

Jane thought it would be ironic for her to use such an icon of peace as an instrument of death. She backed away slowly, but not before she took one last shot at the woman. "It's no mystery your son went the way he did. You only have to look at his family to see where all the poison came from."

The shriek of outrage that tore from June's throat was filled with denial and fury, "To hell, to hell with you!" she ordered Jane.

"But I've just gotten back!" Jane replied as she turned to survey the neighborhood one last time.

If she were a wicked woman, she would have set the whole of it on fire. She would have stood back and watched the past burn. But life would go on. The people here were not responsible.

As she got in her car Jane tossed one final glance back to where it all began.

She expected to feel sickness and anger. But it was gone. Her chest was light. Empty from the remorse and guilt she carried like shackles all these years. Now June Collins and her damned son would be the ones to take up those reins.

And that was more than Jane could have ever hoped for.

5

In contrast to her mother, Harmony was absolutely thriving. The last six months were a new start for her, a release from the things that kept her bound to the past. Jane worried that the combination of her own actions, Dave's accident and all that followed would significantly affect the self-chained woman. But she was thrilled that it, in fact, had done the opposite.

With Jane's gentle guidance and logistical help, Harmony secured herself a job at the Repo library. She moved into a tiny apartment a few blocks from Jane.

From here she could walk to work every morning and absorb the vitamin D she lacked for so long. The library was a perfect place for someone like Harmony who enjoyed spending most of her time alone, though she was getting better with social interactions each and every time Jane saw her.

There were still years of underlying issues and trauma for her to get through, but she was committed to making the change, to becoming a new person. And now, without the shadow of her family cast over her, that's exactly what she was doing—slowly but surely growing.

Jane would not miss the reminder that Harmony was. But she did feel guilty about leaving her during such a crucial time in her healing process. So Jane went above and beyond and took extra measures. She called around to a few of her contacts in the mental health world and subsequently learned that a renowned psychotherapist she once sat next to in Psych 101 was practicing just forty minutes from Repo Ridge.

At first, Harmony was against the whole thing, but Jane promised her that she would continue their appointments virtually if Harmony disliked her new doctor. Thankfully, the trial session was a success and a nice adventure for Harmony—Jane taught her how to use the bus and now she was looking forward to getting out of Repo on a weekly basis.

Jane also felt freed by this. The responsibility for another person's mental health was not to be taken lightly. And although her intentions had originally been to manipulate and use Dave's entire family with cool detachment, she still found herself personally involved in the welfare of those who were nothing like Dave. A part of her wanted to protect Harmony. But now that was over.

Jane just finished packing when the other woman knocked on her door.

"Can I come in?" she called from behind the wood. Now that Harmony was no longer her patient, she'd taken to the habit of stopping by on her way home from work almost every day.

"It's open."

The transformation was unreal—she hardly resembled the same meek and drawn woman who entered Jane's office all those long months ago. She was filled with confidence. There was a skip in her step and lightness to her shoulders. Her face was glowing with a hint of color from the warm sun and Jane felt a moment of pride as she took her in.

"Hi, Harmony," she said with a genuine smile. Jane noticed lately that her own features seemed lighter in wake of all that transpired. "What's up?"

Harmony's face fell slightly as she looked around the empty apartment, "I forgot you were leaving tonight. It's tonight, right?" she questioned with dismay.

Jane pulled the zipper shut on her last duffel bag and turned to comfort her former patient. She smiled sadly, "That's right."

Harmony huffed as she dropped down onto the bed, "I'm going to miss you. How am I supposed to keep myself sane?"

"We've talked about this. You are sane."

"I know and I love Rick, that's what he tells me to call him," she cooed, her eyes becoming a bit lovesick.

Jane knew that patients often romanticized or fell in love with their therapists. Jane couldn't blame Harmony. Rick was a handsome man, but he was also extremely professional and one hell of a counselor.

"I'm glad you are finding his guidance helpful."

"It's all thanks to you. I owe everything to you."

Jane shook her head, "I only helped you find your way. You did all the ground work, the hard work."

"I feel different now. I mean I feel like I was already healing after seeing you for only a month…but now? With all of them gone—it's like I can finally see me, for the first time."

"That's wonderful, Harmony, really."

"I still get sad sometimes when I think about Dave. But that might just be our 'genes' talking to one another. I used to be so jealous of him…how the tables have turned. I bet you he wishes he had my life now," she bragged, a vengeful look cresting her eyes.

Harmony had taken Dave's actions personally, almost to the extreme. Along with blaming her parents for the disaster that was their lives, she also felt justified that she hadn't been the crazy one all along. Her family's downfall was the rise of her own. This didn't surprise Jane seeing as June, August and Dave had beaten Harmony into a shell with their individual forms of repression.

"He was always the righteous one, telling me how I should live my life. Pretending to help and care for all of us, when in reality he was only doing it to keep the attention off his own sickness. I would have tried to kill myself, too. I wonder if he thinks about me?" she trailed off as her eyes flashed back to the past for a swift moment.

"Only he knows what he's thinking. We can't assume to understand," Jane muttered as she grabbed the few items that were left out—a black sharpie and a small pad of sticky notes. She tossed them in the trash.

THE ANTAGONIST

"I hope he's suffering," Harmony whispered viciously, "Like I did for all those years."

"Like I said, we'll never know." Jane was done with the conversation. Done with this life. She didn't care what happened to Dave now. It was out of her control and she liked it that way. She spent enough time bringing him to his truth, and now she was ready to find her own.

"Can someone like him be cured?" As much as Harmony spent the last months blaming, renouncing and debasing her brother, Jane could still hear the soft hint of hope in her voice.

Jane paused at the question—the truth was always the hardest to tell, "No. It's already too late for him."

6

The last stop on her tour of farewells was going to be the hardest. The sun was just falling behind the horizon as Jane turned onto the dark and private drive up to the Collins's mansion.

She passed the FOR SALE sign that'd been sitting there for six months now. It looked as if someone tried to run over it several times. The faded black graffiti across the top blared at her like an alarm, it read: DIE RAPIST.

Jane kept in contact with Georgette through texts—they'd grown quite close over the last few months—which began after Jane sent her a beautiful fruit basket. It was one of the very few gestures of good health Georgette received. Sometimes they chatted briefly on the phone, though Jane never attempted to disturb her solitude and peace. But today was the last chance she would have to see her in person before Jane turned her back on this place and broke all the relationships she'd so painstakingly formed.

⁓

"Heather?" Georgette Collins opened the door just a crack. Her narrowed eyes relaxed in relief at the young woman. Jane imagined she was expecting a reporter or worse, someone reminding her she married the devil.

Georgette looked tired, worn, but entirely alert as she opened the door further, welcoming Jane into her house. Jane knew no person in their right mind could still consider it a home.

THE ANTAGONIST

"Hi," Jane began, looking around the marvelous foyer as if it were her first time viewing it. "I'm sorry to intrude," she began but Georgette waved her worries away with the flick of a wrist and motioned for her to follow.

"It's no intrusion, honestly. I'm thrilled to see a familiar, and not snarling face!" she joked, but Jane could hear the obvious strain behind her vocal chords.

"You have a beautiful house," she remarked as they walked down a long marble corridor, past columns and out onto a sprawling terrace.

"Thank you, dear," she intoned, offering Jane a seat as she joined her at the wrought iron table. Georgette fixed her elegant robe and sat back in her chair. She lit a cigarette with a slightly shaking hand before sliding the pack towards Jane, who declined.

"Smart girl—it's a filthy habit," she admitted. Jane watched the smoke circle above her head like little clouds weighed down with resentment, "One I've been unable to break." The far off look in her eyes spoke of immense grief.

"Have you been to the club at all?" Jane broke the silence—it was tearing at her heart to see this woman so distraught. Lost. It was reminiscent of Jane's own torturous years of living with the truth.

"Oh, I gave up on that. Though maybe I'll give tennis another shot. But it seems silly to enjoy such leisure when others are suffering."

"Have you been working much?"

Georgette's eyes lit with an insane gleam. Jane thought she resembled her former self much more in that moment. "I haven't stopped. Practically living at the shelter. It's been a lot more comfortable than this place."

"Any potential buyers?" Jane asked, "I saw the 'For Sale' sign."

Georgette let out a sardonic laugh, "Yeah, plenty. They come here pretending to be interested in buying, but what they really want is to gossip, harass me, you name it."

"That's disgusting," She bit out. "Atrocious."

Georgette's eyes filled with tears, "Thank you for saying that," she whispered softly.

"You don't have to stay here, though, do you?" Jane was thinking of Sam's latest letter in her back pocket.

"I don't," Georgette sighed wistfully, "I just have no idea where I'm supposed to go. Now. At this age, at this point in my life, after everything that's happened." Her eyes once again glossed over with potent sadness.

They sat quietly listening to the soft rustle of leaves drifting from the forest as the cool night air was cast upon them. An owl hooted in the distance and the soft lull of the cicadas was beginning to grow as the sky darkened with velvety illumination.

"I've been looking for her," Georgette said after a several minutes, "The child that my ex-husband raped."

She said this so calmly that if Jane hadn't been listening, she would've confused the cadence with that of a lullaby.

"Did you find her?" Jane asked, as she wiped the emotion from her shadowed face.

Georgette shook her head, "She's a ghost."

It was common knowledge throughout Repo Ridge that Dave Collins was what Jane had known him to be all along. Georgette went to the police before she even knew that Dave tried to kill himself. The evidence was hard proof and so the tape was mentioned in the news. But the information regarding the victim of the crime was privy to only a few.

"Perhaps she doesn't want to be found."

But Georgette was not listening, "That's the real reason I haven't left. My whole life's work has been to protect the helpless, the abused, and all along I was in love with…with…" she stopped. Taking a deep drag of her smoke, she turned her face into the night.

"It's not your fault," Jane insisted. "People like that, they can trick even the smartest—"

"I am not smart. I'm a stupid, foolish woman who traded one kind of monster for another," her voice was filled with self-inflicted scorn.

THE ANTAGONIST

"This wasn't about you, Georgette," Jane tried.

"No, of course," she said, "but I feel responsible. I have to try—at least apologize to her and tell her I had no clue, if I had—"

"I'm sure she knows that. Why else would she send you proof?"

"You think it was her?"

"Who else could it be? Have you ever considered that maybe she was trying to protect you?"

Georgette's face turned thoughtful. Jane could tell that in the haze of her misery and guilt, she'd not considered this option. "I hope you're right. I hope she's happy and safe now, wherever she is."

"Me, too."

The small fairy lights adorning the pillars around them automatically turned on just as the last bit of natural light left the evening sky. This time it was Jane who broke the silence.

"I actually came by to tell you that I'm leaving."

Georgette turned slowly to look at her, "Why?"

"I got a job offer," she shrugged.

"Congratulations, dear. I'm happy for you."

"Thanks."

"I will miss your friendship. You're a real one. I might be shit at picking out men, but I'd like to think my female intuition is stronger."

Jane smiled, "I appreciate that. I'm going to miss you, too." Jane hadn't expected to actually mean it. The genuine emotion brought tears spilling from Georgette's eyes as she reached over and pulled Jane into a hug.

They stayed like that as the night came alive around them. There were no words, but they clung to one another like two broken pieces—giving and receiving energy that was positive and strong. They'd been hurt, deceived by the same man, and yet here they were, together. Jane knew she would remember this feeling for the rest of her life. She hoped Georgette would too.

When they finally broke apart, it was with a few sniffles and some awkwardness on Jane's part.

"The power of women," Georgette said quietly. "It can be stomped on, torn to pieces, thrown into the hottest flames of hell, yet it perseveres. We persevere," she emphasized, a small knowing look in her eyes.

Jane felt in that moment that there was nothing between them but an unspoken truth that neither felt necessary admitting.

"We rise," Jane went on, "Not because we can, but because we must."

THE ANTAGONIST

7

Jane Havens left Repo Ridge under the cover of darkness, unlike the way she returned. Her heart was less raw than she expected it to be as she drove through the dark streets, once again recalling that final night with Dave.

The statute of limitations made it impossible for him to be convicted of her rape. Even with evidence and hard proof of the crime, Jane was unable to drag him to court to face the music. But that had never been her intention. She knew when she began this journey that time had already run out. The law failed to handle the situation with its own dirty hands—so Jane became the higher power. This journey was personal. And that was how it would end. Even if he wasn't prosecuted, she didn't care—it would not change what happened. All that mattered was that Dave was broken—he would never be able to hurt another again.

Jane's work was done. She was finally able to leave this all behind, to move on and grow without the shadow of her past continuing to plague and torment her mind. The night air whipping against her face through the open window was a soothing balm, a representation of the freedom she could now taste. The aroma became stronger and stronger as she flew past the welcome sign to Repo Ridge. The dusty road behind her billowed up with particles that swam through the air, and settled once again as if she'd never been there at all.

Jane was free.

Epilogue

THE ANTAGONIST

Dave was unable to scream but the pain went on. There was no end to it, no stopping the consuming sear of heat that rocked his broken body every second of every day.

He lost track of how long he'd been in this institution—after Georgette left him, he was designated as a dependent of the state and deemed unable to care for himself. Any assets of his that remained were being used to pay for this 'treatment.' And what treatment it was.

Dave lost almost all ability to move his arms and legs. His voice box was shattered by the metal that ripped through his throat. And his mind tortured him, replaying that night over and over again in his head. He remembered how he wished desperately that death would get to him before Jane.

He thought of her constantly, wondering where she was, what she was doing. How she so carelessly threw his life away all because of a small incident that took place over 25 years ago. He could not reach her now, there was no one left. His family, what was left of them, did not visit once. He wasn't sure they were even aware of where he was, but it didn't matter. Dave knew deep in his brain that he was already dead to them. His heart broke every time he thought of Georgette, and the divorce papers a lawyer had shown up with only a week after his suicide attempt.

There was nothing left for him now, nothing but pain and emptiness and chaos. The constant reliving of all the moments he could no longer grasp, the ones that no longer belonged to him. When existing in reality became too much, he would slide into psychosis. That was when his brain played tricks on him. It allowed him to imagine his life once again whole, sur-

THE ANTAGONIST

rounded by all those who he loved. These visions never lasted long. Instead they were replaced by demons of Jane who danced around him, taunting him while she ripped away layers of his skin and wore his flesh as her own. Coming out of these delusions was actually more painful than the experience itself. Even in his dreams, Dave could not escape.

He would never rest again.

He was able to wheel himself around his small room while he waited each morning for someone to check on him—to make sure he was still breathing. He watched every sunrise, remembering the glow of Parrish Street and the hell he once thought he escaped from. This morning however, he was distracted by the sound of small feet tapping away outside the door and up the corridor.

Dave moved the automated switch on the chair's console to investigate the disturbance. He'd long given up on the idea of someone coming to rescue him, to save him from this neverending night. But still, his curiosity had not been taken away with everything else he'd lost.

The sight that met him, as he peered out the glass door, was one he would not forget anytime soon. She looked just like Jane had at that age—curly brown hair, the greenest eyes and beautiful pouty lips. Dave blinked hard. Part of him knew this could not be the same girl, yet the fantasy world in which he also dwelled was strongly suggesting that it was.

She was carrying a bouquet of flowers. The small sparkling butterfly clips danced in her hair as she passed by the door to his room, much like a friendly little wave. The girl slowed down as she caught his eye—she had noticed him watching her.

Dave held his breath.

The girl gave him a small smile. Then she turned the corner and was gone.

But Dave knew the truth—he saw the way she looked at him. The twinkle of desire in her eyes was all the confirmation Dave needed to know that he was wanted.

Emily Dinova

No one loves you! Jane's voice screamed with laughter on the inside of his head.

Dave Collins was once again begging for death.

If you or someone you know has been sexually assaulted, help is available.

RAINN (Rape, Abuse & Incest National Network) is the nation's largest anti-sexual violence organization. RAINN created and operates the National Sexual Assault Hotline.

The National Sexual Hotline is free, confidential, and available 24/7.

Call 800-656-HOPE
(800-656-4673)

RAINN also has live chat available on their website.

For more information, visit:

https://www.rainn.org

Thank you for reading
THE ANTAGONIST.

Please leave a review on your favorite
online bookseller's website.

For the latest updates on new books
from Henry Gray Publishing,
join our membership list at

www.HenryGrayPublishing.com

about the author
Emily Dinova

Emily Dinova is an artist who lives in Hoboken, NJ with her sociopathic pet eel, Ivan the Terrible. She enjoys the beach, cooking, practicing martial arts, and is currently working towards a license in psychoanalysis. Emily's debut novel, *Veil of Seduction,* was published in 2022. She is also the co-founder of G&E Productions, a cinematic and theatrical production company.

www.gandeproductions.com/emily-dinova

CHECK OUT OTHER GREAT READS FROM HENRY GRAY PUBLISHING

THE LAST STAGE by Bruce Scivally

Dying in his small Los Angeles bungalow, with his Jewish wife, Josephine, whom he calls Sadie, at his side, famed lawman Wyatt Earp imagines an ending more befitting a man of his reputation: returning to his mining claims in a small desert town, tying up loose ends with Sadie, and – after he strikes gold – confronting a quartet of robbers in a showdown.

VEIL OF SEDUCTION by Emily Dinova

1922. Lorelei Alba, a fiercely independent and ambitious woman, is determined to break into the male-dominated world of investigative journalism by doing the unimaginable – infiltrating Morning Falls Asylum, the gothic hospital to which "troublesome" women are dispatched, never to be seen again. Once there, she meets the darkly handsome and enigmatic Doctor Roman Dreugue, who claims to have found the cure for insanity. But Lorelei's instincts tell her something is terribly wrong, even as her curiosity pulls her deeper into Roman's intimate and isolated world of intrigue.

THE UNDERSTUDY by Charlie Peters

"Tell your boss that I have one of his employees." With those words a kidnapping plot begins in the middle of a high-stakes corporate merger. But the kidnappers' plans don't unfold—they unravel.

"If you're thinking of committing the perfect crime, read Charlie Peters' elegant new thriller first. Find out just how many ways perfection can go wrong." – Dan Hearn, author of *Bad August*

THE DEVIL IN THE DIAMOND by Gregory Cioffi

World War II is coming to a violent close. As the Battle of Okinawa rages on, American soldiers seize Shuri Castle and find a single survivor: Yuujin Miyano. The U.S. private put in charge of watching the prisoner is Eugene Durante. Although enemies, the two men find they have a common multi-generational bond: baseball. Their grandfathers – one in Japan, one in America – bore witness to the magical birth of the game and helped shape it in the 1800s. When the war ends, the two men return to their homes to face a postwar world neither expected. Then both receive messages that change their lives forever: once more, the veterans will face off in a final dramatic clash.

For more info visit HenryGrayPublishing.com

...AND HERE'S MORE PAGE-TURNERS FOR YOUR READING PLEASURE!

THE MAN FROM BELIZE by Steven Kobrin

Life-saving heart surgeon Dr. Kent Stirling lives in paradise, dividing his time between two medical practices in the exotic Yucatan. Deeply in love with the woman of his dreams, he has everything a man could desire... until enemies from his secret past as a government hitman convene to eliminate him, including a death-dealing assassin known as the Viper.

SHELBY'S VACATION by Nancy Beverly

Fantasy. Sex. Despair. (Hey, what are vacations for?)

Shelby sets out from L.A. on a much-needed vacation to mend her heart from her latest unrequited crush. By happenstance, she ends up at a rustic mountain resort where she meets the manager, Carol, who has her own memories of the past inhibiting her ability to create a real relationship in the present. Their casual vacation encounter turns into something more profound than either of them bargained for, as each learns what holds them back from living and loving.

TOO MUCH IN THE SON by Charlie Peters

In Martinique, Leo Malone meets Taylor Hoffman, a young man who could be his identical twin. Whey they run afoul of a local gangster, Taylor is murdered and Leo assumes his identity to sneak safely out of the country and back to Los Angeles. But when Taylor's estranged parents meet Leo at the airport, mistaking him for their son, Leo's best-laid plans spiral out of control. Part Agatha Christie, part Elmore Leonard, with a dash of David Mamet and served with a Larry David chaser, *Too Much in the Son* examines the lies, intrigue and violence that make an unexpected family.

I CONFESS: DIARY OF AN AUSTRALIAN POPE by Melvyn Morrow

"When I became pope, almost the first word the Curia taught me was 'ricatto'—blackmail."

- *Pope John XXIV*

From acclaimed playwright Melvyn Morrow comes this engrossing tale of an Australian cardinal who has, through extraordinary circumstances, become pope. His personal diary reveals the inner workings of the Vatican and—when he realizes his tenure may be short and begins enacting sweeping reforms—the centuries-old system in place to make sure that the status quo is maintained—at any cost.

For more info visit HenryGrayPublishing.com

Printed in Great Britain
by Amazon